THE GREEN TICKET

A Novel

Marching Ink LLC

This is a work of fiction. Names, characters, places and incidents are either the product of the author's imagination or are used fictitiously, and any resemblance to actual persons, living or dead, events, or locales is entirely coincidental.

Cover Design by Scarlett Rugers
Copy Edit by Sara Palacios/Marching Ink LLC
Copy Proof by Kira Matthias

THE GREEN TICKET

ISBN: 978-0-9855914-4-1

THE GREEN TICKET

A Novel

Samantha March

To the Honor Girls

CHAPTER 1

Bustling salon and spa seeking a full time manager to oversee daily operations. Job duties will include but will not be limited to: hiring and scheduling staff, assisting with appointment management, scheduling training opportunities, dealing with cash flow, marketing and advertising of the business, and ensuring salon and spa is run with class and enthusiasm. No experience in salon and spa business is required, but a business degree is preferred. Serious, enthusiastic, and hard-working individuals please email résumé and cover letter to danidohlman@blissfulsalonandspa.com. Hours will vary, pay is negotiable and based on experience.

I cracked my knuckles against my palm, tiny pops of the bad habit music to my ears. A manager at a salon and spa? This job listing was practically screaming my name. I didn't have any experience with managing a salon—or anywhere for that matter—but I loved getting my hair done. And mani/pedis. And my bushy eyebrows needed a good hot wax job at least once every thirty days.

I bookmarked the job listing, making a note on my daily to-do list sitting next to my laptop. *Polish résumé*, I scribbled, right after *60 minutes Pilates/yoga workout* and *finish cleaning kitchen*.

Lila burst through the door at that moment, her long blonde hair flying behind her. "We must work out tonight. Please come and motivate me. I'm getting my pictures taken in two weeks and I really need to drop some weight. And tone up. Look firm. Look good. The TV adds ten pounds, you know. Did you get your assignment done yet for Bater's class? I need to work on that too." Even though Lila Medlin had been my best friend for years, the speed at which she did everything still amazed me. I watched her beautiful virgin hair (she's a natural blonde—the bitch) barely make it past the doorframe before getting caught.

"You're in luck. I was going to do some Pilates and yoga tonight anyway. Just do it with me. That will help firm and tighten. Even though you know I don't think you need it."

"When I fit into your size two jeans, I'll finally start listening." Lila walked into the kitchen, opening cabinets, then the refrigerator. "We have no food! Want to order a pizza or something? Ooh, maybe some wings? I'm craving hot sauce."

I walked into the kitchen behind her, peering into the depths of our pathetic excuse for a dorm fridge. "We have food. Here's a bag of lettuce, some carrot sticks back here and croutons in the cabinet. I snagged some packets of ranch from the lounge yesterday. Voila—let's make a salad!"

Lila pulled a face, reacting like I asked her to go on Survivor and eat cockroaches. "Uh, yeah. Salad sounds great if I was trying to starve myself, Alex. I'm craving real food, not rabbit food."

I held my hands up in surrender. "You're the one talking about toning and firming. I'm just saying a salad will give you better odds than buffalo wings." I wasn't going to mention the calorie count I had just estimated in my head.

Lila dreamt of one day becoming an entertainment reporter and was itching for the chance to get out of Dodge—or rather, Iowa. Lila and I had been best friends since we came to Kaufman College in Des Moines three years ago, and had been living together for two. We wanted to move out on our own and get a house, but neither of us had the financials to support that yet. Lila was saving every penny to put towards photography sessions, voice lessons and even acting classes. Her big goal was to head out to Los Angeles and somehow land an audition for Buzzworthy, the hottest celebrity news show at the moment. I supported her goal of being a reporter, though I had no idea how to help her achieve it.

My goals weren't as specific as Lila's. Mainly, I wanted to be able to stand on my own two feet and stop relying on my sister for everything. Alicia was my big sister, married to Craig Bowersworth and living with their five kids in Seattle. Craig's job as a political campaign manager led them to many places, but Alicia fell in love with Seattle the minute she laid eyes on the rainy landscape, so they put down roots there. Alicia was a stay at home mom, and with Craig's income that he pulled in, money was not a worry for them. Alicia helped me stay financially afloat by sending me money each month. I held down stray jobs here and there, but still hadn't quite figured out what I wanted to do when I graduated. I was studying Business Leadership and Entrepreneurship at college and still waiting to see which direction the wind would take me.

"Fine, fine, a salad it is. Can you whip one up for me quick? I need to put my face on before Joel comes over."

"What time is he stopping by?"

"He said around five. He has some study group thing tonight so he wanted to drop by and see me before that." Joel Lohrbach had been Lila's boyfriend for just over year, starting when we were sophomores in college. Lila fell hard and fast for Joel, and the attraction still baffled me. Joel was short and geeky, with spiked black hair and big glasses that did not make a fashion statement, and always had his nose in a book. Lila was tall, blonde and gorgeous, with ambitions to live in sunny LA and schmooze with celebrities. Joel was not agreeable to Lila's future plans and I had no idea what would happen to their relationship if Lila actually made it in the entertainment biz. I wouldn't mind seeing them break up. I thought Joel was a dick to Lila more than a sweetheart. But she loved him, and who was I to say anything if my friend seemed happy. Enough.

"Okay. Get your makeup on and we'll eat some salad and change for the gym. And you can help me look at this job I'm thinking about applying for. Tell me if you get good vibes or not." Lila always said she got "vibes" about certain things, such as if the elective I wanted to sign up for would be a brain buster or if the new Chinese restaurant in town had bugs in their food. And she's usually pretty spot on.

"No problem. Are you thinking about leaving Tastie's again?" Lila's voice was muffled as she shouted out from the bathroom.

I put a healthy portion of lettuce in two plastic cereal bowls, quickly diced up the carrots and sprinkled those in, and shook the worn bag of croutons over the top. After smothering the salads with ranch dressing—officially taking them from a healthy snack to a questionable one with the rich, calorie-laden topping——I was satisfied. Finding two clean forks in our utensil drawer was somewhat of a challenge, since neither of us were big on washing dishes. After finally finding two, I took a seat at our two-person table shoved in the back corner of our minuscule kitchen and waited for Lila.

"Did you hear me? Are you thinking about leaving Tastie's?" Lila came back into the kitchen, her face glowing and her blue eyes popping, even though she looked like she had no makeup on. I had yet to master the natural look like she could—wearing two tons of concealer, highlighter, blush, shadow, liner and mascara, and looking like she had just woken up. Mine always ended up looking like clown makeup when I would put the effort in.

I dug into my salad, loading up my fork with lettuce and a crouton. "Yeah, just thinking about it, though. I'm getting tired of all my Friday and Saturday nights getting spent with sleazy guys. But the money is really helping me build up my savings account. I can't live off Alicia forever."

"I know, but look how good you're doing saving money. You won't be a waitress forever."

"I wish I knew what I did want to be. How hard is it to figure out a career, especially as a junior in college? Shouldn't I have this down already so I can stop taking all these electives?"

"Some people need more time. You'll figure it out. If you don't by the time I hit the high road out of this state, just come to LA with me. You could probably find a job out there in a heartbeat."

"As what?"

"A model! An actress! I could get all the exclusive scoops on which designer you're wearing and who you're making a sex tape with next. We could rule the world out there together. Come on, Alex! What do you think? Sounds good, huh?"

"Lila, I won't be making sex tapes with anyone in the foreseeable future. Or the unforeseeable future either, you perv." I dug out the last crouton from the bottom of the bowl, crunching it between my teeth. "Besides, that lifestyle just isn't for me. I don't like being the center of attention. I would rather be behind the scenes."

"What about a movie director? Or a screenwriter?" Lila kept firing off suggestions, and while I appreciated her trying to help, I knew it would never work. I was a painfully shy child growing up, always hiding behind my sister and keeping to myself. Our mother, Lisa Abrams, died when I was five, Alicia fifteen. She had been diagnosed with breast cancer and by the time the doctors found it, the disease was too far gone. She was only thirty-three. I didn't have a lot of memories from her, just little snippets—like the way her perfume smelled and how she loved being outdoors. I remembered that she used to push me around in a red wagon all the time, around the block or sometimes all the way down to the convenience store if she needed something. I missed her terribly, but sometimes I thought it was just the idea of a having a mom that I missed most. I didn't know her enough to miss Lisa the person, but I knew I missed Lisa the mom.

Our father, Marcus Abrams, was madly in love with our mother. Alicia would tell me stories of how they would dance around the living room at night when they thought she was already asleep. How Marcus was the kind of guy who never missed her birthday or forgot flowers on their anniversary. My parents were high school sweethearts and married just weeks after graduation, welcoming Alicia eight months later. Marcus went a little crazy after she died, not being able to handle the grief. He tried hard to stick around and be a good dad, but left right after Alicia turned seventeen. I really didn't miss him as much. My memories of him aren't very good ones. After Mom passed away, he took up drinking too much whisky every night to hide the pain, and I remember him yelling at Alicia all the time. He wrote Alicia and myself a letter when he left, saying he couldn't stand the physical reminders of Mom—which apparently were us. He eventually remarried and now lives in Georgia with his new wife and her children. I hadn't spoken to him since he left, and Alicia was no longer in contact with him, either.

Alicia was my hero. We had an aunt and uncle that took us in for a year, until Alicia turned eighteen. After that, we moved to Des Moines from our hometown of Baruva, Illinois, population just under 1,000 and not much opportunity. Alicia secured a job at the capitol building, starting as a typist and working her way up to secretary, then an office manager. It was there that she met Craig Bowersworth, and they immediately fell in love and were married. Alicia worked her ass off as essentially a single mother for years, helping raise me, enrolling me in school, keeping me clothed and healthy. I loved my sister with all my heart and missed her terribly. I had thoughts of moving to Seattle to be close to her again, but I loved Kaufman College and Lila and my other friends and really wanted to make it on my own. I wanted to stop relying on her for tuition and rent money and health insurance.

"Those are all great suggestions, just not for me. I was thinking about choosing a different major, maybe trying to narrow it down or something. Business is so broad, so general. Maybe that's part of the problem."

Lila carried our bowls to the sink, adding some dish soap and running water over them to "let them soak." Lila's version of doing the dishes. "That's always a possibility. Let me look at the job quick that you mentioned. What was it for?"

"A manager at a spa and salon."

"That would be perfect for you! You love those places. And see—your major could help you out here."

"Don't get too excited. I can't see a whole lot of owners putting an inexperienced twenty-year old in charge just because she loves getting pedicures." I pulled up the bookmarked page and Lila started reading, running her eyes across the page.

"Alex, are you kidding me? It says right here, 'no experience required, business degree preferred.' That's you! What are you waiting for?"

"First of all, a lot of job postings say they don't need experienced people, but if someone walks in and has ten years working at a spa under their belt, they will get the job. And secondly, I don't have a degree yet. Or have you forgotten that minor detail?"

Lila shooed off my concerns with a wave of her hand. "Big deal. You've nailed every interview you have been on. You're enthusiastic, hard-working, and personable. You have to at *least* apply for it. Just give it a chance. You'll never know unless you go for it."

"I already put getting my résumé together on my to-do list for today." I hesitated, weighing the pros and cons in my head. "And I do interview well." I once landed a job as a hotel clerk, even though I interviewed in a mini-skirt. In my defense, I never meant to interview, or even apply for the job when I left my apartment on the way to the mall that day. I saw the Now Hiring sign from the road and decided to stop in for an application. The manager was there and not busy, so I filled out my app, did the interview, and scored the job the next day. "I'll get it done by the end of the week," I decided, causing Lila to squeal and clap her hands together. "But I'm not going to get overly optimistic about this. And I'm going to keep job hunting. Waitressing is just not for me anymore."

"I agree. I'm getting tired of it too. I feel like something positive could happen here. You're focusing on getting a fab career, and I'm going to up my chances of getting discovered. I feel good. Things are about to change for us, Alex."

"I hope you're right, my friend. I hope you're right."

CHAPTER 2

The following day was a Friday, which meant the night shift for me and Lila. We worked as waitresses at Tastie's, which we described as a classy Hooters. It was a sports bar and restaurant, with polished wood booths in the restaurant part, a full circle bar in the middle of the lounge that was always full after nine at night, and pretty girls in short black shorts and tight white tops taking your order. At least we didn't have to wear the hideous orange hot pants and long socks, but the shorts were still short and our low-cut tops were designed to do the peek-a-boo bra thing. The tips were pretty decent though and the manager wasn't a sleaze, so Lila and I had stayed on for the past six months. Neither of us had managed to snag a job or internship in our majors—me in Business and Entrepreneurship, Lila in PR/Communications, but it was a job. For now.

"Where the hell is my bra? Alex, do you have an extra Tastie bra?" Lila was shouting in her bedroom while we got changed and ready to drive to work. I popped my head through my white shirt, adjusting it so you could just see the top of my lacy black boob holder, and approached Lila's disaster of a bedroom.

"My extra one is still on the rack, probably damp. How could you have lost both bras?" I questioned my friend, stepping carefully into her room to avoid stepping on a bottle of hair gel, a plate with a sandwich on it, or the mound of dirty laundry that was littered across her floor. Lila stood outside her closet, rifling through a drawer of bras and underwear. It was times like these that I was grateful we had lucked out and gotten a dorm with separate bedrooms. Our bathroom was tiny compared to others with only a toilet and sink—meaning we had to shower in the community bathroom—but I much preferred my own clean and organized bedroom.

"I don't know. They might both be at Joel's. I swear his bedroom eats my clothes." Lila stopped throwing undergarments out of the drawer, turning to face me. She wasn't wearing a shirt or a bra, but I was unfazed. Lila was a free spirit. I think all of the girls in our dorm had seen Lila topless multiple times by now.

"Well, we have exactly eleven minutes before we need to leave. I can check and see how damp my other one is. But we don't have time to find an open dryer."

"Maybe I'll get more tips if it looks like we're having a wet T-shirt contest night," Lila said, racing out of her room to grab my bra off the drying rack we had set up in the living room. She clasped it quickly in the back, then proceeded to feel herself up. "Yep, it's going to be a great night. I have a feeling. Big tips coming my way."

"All right, please stop touching your boobs. Let's just get out of here. Maybe Big Frank will let us cut out early tonight." Big Frank was our boss and the owner of Tastie's. He never missed a Friday or Saturday night.

"Doubt it, but I hope so. Carmen and Emma are having margarita night in their room, and we need to be there." Lila was finally dressed, and we grabbed our purses and headed out the front door, down the three flights of steps and out of Wacker, the laughable name of our dorm that was a constant source of comedy.

Lila's vibe was right, as that Friday night was one of the busiest yet. It was mid-October, and with the temperatures in the Midwest dropping by the day, more and more outside bars were slowing down and establishments like Tastie's were seeing more patrons come through the door. Lila and I bustled around our sections, and I smiled every time I saw her tugging at her chest. The damp bra could not have been comfortable. She was just lucky we were both a small C, or she really would have been out of luck that night. And Big Frank hates it when we show anything other than black underneath our work shirts.

"Hello, gentlemen. Welcome to Tastie's. My name is Alex and I'll be your girl tonight. Can I start you off with some drinks? We have two-dollar tall boys on special right now." I recited my opening line for about the fiftieth time that night to a table of four guys probably in their forties. Big Frank wanted us to say we were "their girl" for the night, not just their server or waitress.

"First round on me, fella's. Order to the pretty lady," one guy said, who was just slightly overweight and just slightly balding. All the men ordered Bud Lights, and I flashed them my perkiest smile, stuck out my chest like we were taught in training, and scooted away. I tapped their order with lightning speed into the machine and shouted, "Four tall Bud Lights!" at the bartender, Carl, who was on duty that night along with Brad. He gave me a nod to show he had heard me, and then I walked quickly across the floor to check on another table, this one also with four guys. I refilled one water, brought out ketchup and extra napkins for the messy eater, then shot up to the bar to grab the four beers. After delivering those and taking down the food orders, filing those in the machine that would spit out the ticket in the kitchen, I checked on my largest table, a party of six men in the back, who shouted more beer orders at me, plus two tequila shots. My evening went on like this—without a break—for the next four hours, and I could see Lila was having a similar night. We passed each other a few times on the floor or in the kitchen, giving each other the "will this night never end?" look each time.

Finally around 11:30, Big Frank started letting girls go. Lila was able to sweet talk her way to getting us to the top of the cut list, and just before midnight we were free to leave. We rushed out to my white Toyota Camry, a newer model but still practical enough when it came to safety and gas mileage that Alicia and Craig footed the bill, and sped back towards campus.

"I need a drink! Are you ever going to turn twenty-one so we can finally do damage at the bars?" Lila asked, tugging her long hair out of the elastic holder.

"Soon enough. I'm itching to get there myself. At least I won't be the last one who turns legal. Hannah's birthday isn't until June."

"Yeah, but Hannah barely drinks. She probably won't even do the bar scene when it's finally her birthday."

I took a right onto the interstate, increasing my speed and feeling the Camry smoothly chug along. "True, true. Oh, well. Less than six months now. We should start a countdown."

"I think you can do that on Facebook. I'll make one for you tomorrow."

"You're such a doll."

"What are best friends for?" Lila batted her lashes at me as her phone started ringing. She dug around in her purse, finally pulling out the device that was belting Black Eyed Peas. I fell silent as I listened to her phone conversation with Joel.

"I won't be over tonight. We're having margarita night with Carmen and Emma." Pause. I could hear Joel's voice but couldn't make out his words. "I told you last night that Carmen wanted to do this." Joel's voice got a little bit higher. "That's not true! I know I told you last night. And what's the big deal? We're not going to the bar; we'll still be at the dorms. And we have plans tomorrow anyway for brunch with Carli and Lucas."

I rolled my eyes, continuing the drive on the interstate while Lila and Joel argued. Joel always wanted to be around Lila from the moment they started dating, which used to seem sweet. But in the past few months, it had bordered psychotic smothering. Lila couldn't spend more than twenty-four hours away from him. And it usually ended up in an argument of some sort.

14

"Joel, I am not ditching my friends just to go to your place and sleep. I can't believe you would even ask me that." I drummed my fingertips on the steering wheel. I really wanted to compare tips with her, something we usually did at the end of the night. Lila's predication of a good tip night was certainly right for me. And Lila never had trouble raking in the dough. Her looks were gorgeous, even though she was always complaining about needing to lose weight. Her size varied from a very small four to a six, and I thought she was beautiful and didn't need to lose a pound. She wasn't necessarily voluptuous in a va-va voom way, but she certainly wasn't big-boned like she called herself.

"You're being ridiculous. I can't even talk to you right now. I'm going to Carmen's and I will be at your place ready for brunch tomorrow at 10:30, just like we planned. And don't you dare think of showing up and ruining girls' night for me. I don't barge in on your study dates." And with that Lila snapped her phone closed, leaning back in the seat and closing her eyes. "Why is having a boyfriend such hard work?"

"Wouldn't know, sista, haven't had one of those in forever," I replied, finally pulling into our parking lot outside of Wacker. We climbed out of the Camry, strolling with ease to the front door. "And from the way your relationship works, it's better that way." I couldn't resist a little dig. Lila knew I didn't enjoy Joel, especially when he was acting how he was that night. But I wasn't up for a fight right then.

"I know, you're right. I don't know why I stay with him sometimes. It's just this feeling that I have that he's the one. I can't shake that."

"Babe, your feelings aren't always right. Remember the scene you caused on the plane to Cancun?"

"I really thought there were snakes on the plane, Alex. I could practically feel them slithering up my legs."

"Or you had watched the movie too many times in one month. Regardless, our plane was delayed, on the news, and we missed a full day in Mexico."

"All right, all right."

"Or the time during our first year where you swore up and down that Professor Lytle had made all his multiple-choice final exam answers the letter C? Me, you, and Emma all practically failed his class because of that."

"Fine, fine, fine. I get it. My vibes aren't one hundred percent. Neither are psychics or fortune tellers."

Soon enough, we were back up in apartment 12, peeling off our work clothes that smelled of burgers and beer, and into comfy Margarita drinking clothes.

"I'm just saying—don't stick with one guy just because you have a feeling about it. Focus on how you actually feel when you are with him. Are you happy? Overjoyed? Blissed out?" I threw my black shorts and white top in my laundry basket, grabbing a pair of pink yoga pants and a white tunic from my closet and slipping into them. "Do you miss him when you're not together? Can you see a future with him?" I continued, walking into Lila's room and using her perfume to mask the stench of grease.

"Jeez, I get it, Al. But why do you think I should take advice from you? You said it yourself, you are one dateless sista."

"I did not say I was dateless. I just haven't had a long-term boyfriend in a while. I still go on dates," I defended myself, thinking about my lousy track record with men.

"It's because you got daddy issues. I'm telling you, just go on Oprah. She'll help you figure it out. Not all men will run away. Look at my dad. Still happily married to my mom. They even have date night a few times a month!"

Even just a few years ago that sentence would make my insides curl. I didn't like to be reminded of happy families when mine turned out to be such a shithole. I had taken therapy for it—obviously, who could survive a mother's death and father's hightailing without a few sessions—and the pain in my heart was slowly residing. I knew I was lucky that Alicia took me in. And paid for my school. And bought me a nice car and sent me a monthly allowance. Not everybody had that kind of support in their life. I never wanted to take my sister or my nice life for granted. But when it came to love and men, the idea of it freaked me out. It was hard for me to trust and fully let my guard down.

"Let's not dissect my love life now. I need a marg, and you need, like, seven so you can be black-out drunk to stop your snoring," I said, grabbing my cell phone and slipping black flip-flops on. Carmen and Emma lived just two floors down from us, so we didn't even have to bother with real shoes or sweatshirts. The perks of dorm life.

"I do not snore, you bitch. But seven margs will probably be enough to get my mind off Joel." Lila paused with her hand hovering over the doorknob. "Are margaritas healthy for you? How many calories do they have?"

"I'm going to go ahead and guess they are way unhealthy for you. Especially when Carmen makes her special spicy cheese sauce to go with all the corn chips we eat."

"I thought I read somewhere that spicy foods speed up your metabolism. Maybe I should work something spicy into my meals each day."

"You would need to use someone else's bathroom then if you did that," I responded, swatting her on the butt. "Now get going, I'm thirsty!"

Carmen Morales and Emma Burton were our closest friends at Kaufman. Carmen was a riot; a feisty Latina who always rolled her Rs and loved to stereotype herself. Her long black hair, coal eyes, smooth skin and painted-on eyebrows completed her look. She was on the chunky side, but on her it looked voluptuous instead of just large. And she loved her curves. She always had a drink in hand, usually a margarita, and no one was really positive if she attended classes. We always saw her in the hallways, lounge, visiting other dorms, but never in a classroom. I was sure she did attend class—otherwise how could she possibly live on campus—but it was the running joke amongst us anyway.

Emma was the complete opposite of Carmen, but they got along like margaritas and nachos. Emma's full name, Emma Burton, reminded everyone of the Spice Girl Emma Bunton, and weirdly enough, they could pass as twins. Both Emma's were petite, blonde, and had killer blue eyes. The nickname Baby Spice suited our Emma perfectly, and we treated her like our fragile, innocent daughter. Well, our twenty-one year old fragile, innocent daughter who loved to drink and whose sex life could only be described as promiscuous. Emma could drink everyone—except for Carmen—under the table, and she loved her men. All of them.

We gathered in their room that Friday night, and both girls were already well on their way to becoming toasted. They were arguing about the pros and cons of buying a gigantic wedding dress. Odd convo, as both girls were very single.

"At my cousin's wedding, she had to have two people lift up her dress to help her pee! Just what I want on my wedding day, someone other than *mi amor* to see *mi muchacha!*"

"But you're supposed to be a vision on your wedding day. A big white vision of Barbie Doll bliss. I want people to be able to fit underneath my dress!"

"I want something slinky, showing off all the proper assets. My husband should look at me and think I'm fuckable, even in the church. *Lo siento Dios!*"

"Whoa, whoa, ladies! You have company." I announced our arrival as we let ourselves in the unlocked door. "Emma, I'm with you on the big dress. Carmen, I'm not sure you're supposed to look fuckable on your wedding day. Aren't you supposed to look like a virgin?" I headed straight for the kitchen in search of our drinks.

"Nah, I'm with Carmen on this one. I'll be going for a sultry Barbie when I take the plunge. Think silk, tight, and low cut. That's my version of a perfect wedding dress," Lila said, taking a seat on the brown leather ottoman, provided for by Carmen's wealthy parents. Regular dorm furniture for their girl was not an option.

"Seeing as you're the only one with a man in this room, you'll probably be the first," Emma said, taking a sip of her strawberry marg.

"And we'll just be the single bridesmaids looking to get laid!" Carmen chimed in, causing all of us to laugh. Then quiet down as we thought about what she was saying. Would we all be single in a few years? Five years? Ten years? I quickly filled the rest of my glass with the regular margarita mix and took a big gulp, quickly ignoring my previous train of thought. The yummy yellow drink was ice cold yet warmed my belly. Much better.

Lila sighed, accepting her strawberry drink from me. "I don't know about that, ladies. I fear it's coming to an end for me and Joel."

"Oh, come on. You say that, like, every other week and you're still with him," Emma said, taking the words out of my mouth. Lila was always complaining about Joel, but did nothing to change their relationship dynamic.

"I know, I know. But I have a feeling that something is about to change with us. Or maybe just me. I don't know, but I don't think we'll last too much longer."

We spent the rest of our girls' night doing girly things—dissecting Lila's relationship, wondering who Emma would hook up with next, drinking way too many margaritas, and finally passing out in the living room. Not only could Lila and I not make it back up the two measly flights to our rooms, but Carmen and Emma couldn't even make it back to their bedrooms. In all, another successful college night with the girls.

CHAPTER 3

The weekend passed like it usually did: relaxed, uneventful, and full of drinks. Lila spent most of the day with Joel, so I tackled items left on my weekly to-do list: start marketing project, schedule a haircut, and finish laundry. My to-do lists were my best friends. I had daily, weekly and monthly to-do lists that I couldn't live without. My friends liked to poke fun at me for them, but I loved being organized.

Saturday night I attended a house party with Carmen, Emma, and Hannah. Hannah Lovington was the fifth girl in our group, the classic overachiever. Hannah was not one to imbibe often, so she usually acted as our DD when we went to parties. Her father was a neurosurgeon and her mother a psychiatrist, so she had a lot of expectations to live up to. She was attending Kaufman to get her generals out of the way, then transferring on to med school at the University of Iowa. When Hannah decided to let loose and party—which happened about once every other month—she was a blast. We still loved her even when she wasn't in Hardcore Hannah mode (she hated the nickname, said it made her sound like she was making a porno) and we understood why she didn't hit the bottle as hard as the four of us. A surgeon and psych for parents? Daunting.

Lila and I both had off from Tastie's on Saturday, which meant we had to work Sunday. Our shift wasn't bad that day, 11-4, and I even dragged Lila to the gym with me that night. I didn't know which was harder—getting her to the gym or getting her to make it onto a machine once we were there.

"Lila, get your ass on the treadmill. You can still read the magazine while you walk." I was jogging lightly on one of the five treadmills Kaufman had in their student gym. The place was quiet—most students probably still recovering from their weekends and frantically trying to finish homework for Monday morning classes. Only one other girl was stationed in the back corner, doing sun salutations on a yoga mat.

Lila was lying on the carpeted floor on her back, reading last month's People magazine. She was supposedly also doing crunches while reading, but I had counted maybe two so far. "I will, I will. I just want to finish this article. Did you know Lola Haloshi is pregnant? How could someone that skinny be knocked up?" She continued to read the article, engrossed about how the "allegedly" anorexic supermodel could be with child.

"What happened to the workout schedule we drew up for you? Are you following it at all?"

"Yes! I took a thirty-minute walk with Joel around campus last night and checked it off the calendar."

"What about your strength training? I thought Joel was going to accompany you to the weight room yesterday after your brunch date."

Lila groaned and got to her feet, reluctantly stepping on the treadmill and keying in her weight, age, and desired length of workout. "We got into an argument at brunch, so I did some shopping to cool myself down instead."

"But you won't be able to check that off your calendar!" I had helped Lila make a fitness calendar, similar to the one I had made for myself. I scheduled cardio days, strength days and workouts for Pilates and yoga. I marked days off as well so I didn't overexert myself. I had the day's color coordinated and left a little box next to each workout so I could check them off as I completed them. Lila called it my "anally organized workout death calendar." But since she wanted to drop some pounds, she asked me to make one for her. I was disappointed she was already wandering off schedule. Disappointed, but not really shocked.

"My calendar will survive. I'll try to make it up today," Lila said, barely shuffling her feet on the treadmill. She flipped another magazine page. Staying up to date with all things Hollywood was important to her. She wanted to be informed at all times, just in case she were to get discovered in little ole Des Moines. That way, she could spout off all her knowledge of fashion, baby names, and celebrity hookups and land her dream job.

"I wasn't going to go to the weight room today, but I can take a yoga mat down with me while you lift," I offered, upping my speed on the treadmill. Trying to motivate my friend to do the same.

Lila didn't take the hint. She continued at her snail pace, not even breathing heavy or breaking a sweat yet. "Hey, did you ever apply for the manager job at the spa?" Nice change of subject.

"I got my résumé all ready to go. I wanted to get Hannah to proof it for me before I send it off. I have it down for tomorrow to get it emailed. But I really don't think I'm even going to get an interview. Who hires a college student to run a spa and salon?"

"I bet it happens more than you think. They can probably get away with paying you a bit less if you don't have a degree yet. Then by the time you do graduate, you can get a raise and they have a fab employee who knows all the ropes already, so they won't be losing any money from the deal. It's basically a win-win for everyone."

I thought that over. Why didn't I think of that? I was the business major after all. "Well, I guess that makes me feel a little better. The worst they can say is no, right?" I continued without letting her answer. "And maybe I can at least get an interview, get some practice for my interviewing skills. That's never a bad thing."

"Right. I learned in class last semester that you're supposed to go on a job interview like twice a year or something, even if you're happy with your job. It helps keep those skills alive. Or something. Maybe it was more times a year. I don't really remember. But anyway, good plan. I say you can count on at least getting an interview."

"You don't have the vibe that I could get the job?"

Lila paused, putting her index finger in the air like the (non-existent) wind would give her the answers. "I'm sure if your

24

résumé is good and you fly through the interview like you always do, you could be a definite contender."

I smiled while continuing my run. I knew Lila was saying that as my friend, not as some hocus-pocus psychic. She was always one of my biggest supporters, and I was grateful for that. While Lila came from a close-knit family—mom and dad happily married, two younger sisters that were close in age to her—she understood my family complications. When I couldn't make it to Seattle to visit Alicia and my family over holidays or school breaks, Lila took me back to Okana to stay with her family. The Medlin's were like my surrogate family. And I loved them for it.

We finished up on the treadmills—me wiping sweat from my forehead, Lila still not breathing heavy—and made our way down to the weight room. I loved that Kaufman promoted health and wellness on campus. We had a workout room with plenty of treadmills, ellipticals, stationary bikes and a full weight room. In addition to those, we had a back room that had a TV and DVD player, and students could either bring their own workout DVDs or use the ones Kaufman supplied. There was also a gym that was used for basketball and volleyball games, and intramurals were popular on campus. The lounge on campus gave nutritional value of foods that were served, and only one pop machine was on campus.

Once we got back to Wacker and showered, I texted Hannah and asked her to come up to our room. Hannah lived by herself on the top floor of our dorm, where all the rich kids resided. No sharing a shower for her. She got her own bedroom, living room, kitchen, and full bathroom. Oh, to have parents with cash. Lots of cash. We could never hold that against her, though. Hannah was too sweet to dislike.

While waiting for her to arrive, I took a call from Alicia, who called every Sunday night regardless of what was happening in our lives. "Hello, sister," I said.

"Hi, honey. How is everything with you?" Alicia sounded upbeat, as usual, and I could just imagine her red hair curled to perfection and her green eyes bright even though she chased five kids around all day. My sister and I could pass for twins, if you ignore the ten-year age difference: identical red hair, though mine was almost to my waist and always frizzy, whereas Alicia's was just past her shoulders and always shiny; same green eyes and were both exactly 5'5" and weighed around 110 pounds. Did I mention she had given birth to five children—two of them twins? Maybe after I had kids my hair would finally be smooth. And I would still be skinny. I can be hopeful.

"Everything is good here. Lila and I just got home from the gym a bit ago. We both worked at Tastie's today."

"How is your work?"

I paused, debating whether to tell her about wanting to apply for the manager job. But I didn't want to get my hopes up any more than they already were, and telling another person—especially my cheerleader sister—would only crush me more when—I mean if—I didn't get the job.

"It was okay. Short shift. Friday night was one of the best tip nights yet, though."

"And how are your classes?"

"Good. Music Appreciation is more boring than I thought it would be. I thought we would be, I don't know, listening to music, but all we do really is just study the history of it."

"Is it too late to change your elective?"

"I think we can by next week, but I'll probably just stick with it. There really isn't anything else I'm too interested in."

Alicia and I chatted for a few more minutes about our usual topics, and then Carly got on the phone to say hi. Carly was seven, and I was pretty sure she was a fashion model in training. Alicia said that she had taken to stealing her digital camera and taking pictures of herself, and always strutting around the house, treating it as a makeshift runway in Milan. Alicia has thought about putting her into pageants, and I think the following year would be the first time Carly could finally get the go-ahead to compete. I would definitely be there to see my precious niece go for the crown if Alicia did decide to okay it.

Alicia and Craig's other four children weren't divas like Carly. Candace, the oldest at nine, loved to read and had very high emotions. I swear, if one of her brothers or sisters got hurt, Candace felt their pain and cried along with them. She was fairly quiet, and I think she took her role as the big sister pretty seriously. Their youngest daughter, four year old Caitlin, was the complete opposite of Carly. She was the tomboy and loved soccer. She refused pink clothing or wearing her red hair in pigtails like Carly often showcased.

Then there were the boys, Todd and Tyler, identical twins. While all three girls got the red hair and green eyes from their mother, the boys got their looks from their dad with dark hair and eyes. They were two, and it was no joke when people said they had the terrible twos. I had no idea how my sister handled them, especially with three other kids vying for her attention and rides in their brand new Lexus RX. Alicia would never be caught dead driving a mini-van. Neither would I for that matter.

After talking to Carly, who dominated the conversation about her new pink glitter shoes, Alicia got back on the line. "The other girls are still playing outside and the boys are in the bathtub. Maybe next week you'll have more kids to talk to."

"That's okay. My friend just got up here to help me with some, errr, homework, so I need to get going anyway." I waved to Hannah as she walked in. She looked very Hannah-like, wearing brown cords, a simple white sweater and brown flats, with her wavy blonde-ish hair pulled back into a ponytail. Her eyes were cornflower blue (according to her), and she always had an innocent look on her face. That was our Hannah. Innocent, slightly boring, but smart as a whip and a great friend. I disconnected with my sister, and we got to work on fixing up my résumé.

It was after eight when Hannah and I finally agreed that my résumé was perfect. She made me change the entire format, the bullets I had used, and rephrase many of my job descriptions. "Scheduling reservations for guests" under my hotel job became "Provided excellent customer service to all guests, handling all phone calls in a friendly and timely manner, and checking in guests with a positive attitude."

"Thanks for all your help, dear. You've worked wonders," I told Hannah after clicking 'save' for the last time on my résumé document.

"Not a problem. I hope you get the interview! I'm not a big spa person, but I would definitely come get something done if you were the manager."

"For half off!" Lila shouted from the kitchen, where I could hear popcorn kernels popping in the microwave.

"You wish!" I yelled back, smiling at my roommate as she came into the living room holding a giant pink bucket filled with buttered popcorn in one hand and a full wine glass in the other.

"How many calories does popcorn have?" she questioned, taking a seat on the chair opposite me and Hannah on the couch. I set my laptop on the floor, clicking 'save' one more time on my résumé to reassure myself, and settled in for a nice chat.

"It's not the unhealthiest thing for you to eat, but certainly worse than some fruits or vegetables. Do you have butter and salt on it?" Hannah asked her.

Lila paused with her hand halfway to her mouth. "Duh! That's the only way I can eat popcorn."

"You could cut a lot more calories from it if you didn't add salt and used low-fat butter instead. That spray butter is supposed to be pretty good."

Lila shoved one handful of popcorn in her mouth, followed by another. Then a gulp of wine. "Sure, right. What about wine? I heard it's good for you."

"Red wine is the best; it's good for your heart. But that's one or two glasses, not the whole bottle in one night."

"This is only my third glass!" Lila protested.

"How have you drank three already? We haven't been home that long. I'm still on my first," I said, holding up my glass as proof. Lila had bought some decorators earlier in the year when we decided we were turning into winos, and mine had pink and purple butterflies wrapped around the stem. Lila sported green butterflies on hers. Hannah was drinking a Powerade, no decorator needed.

"I don't know. This wine just goes down so smooth. I'm glad we splurged on a nice bottle this time."

"The four-dollar wine did not taste that bad!" Even though Alicia sent me money each month, I didn't think she wanted me to blow it all on expensive wine. I budgeted carefully, and had been trying to build up my savings account for months.

"Yeah, it wasn't terrible," Lila conceded, right as her phone started to ring. "Joel. Again. Are you guys keeping track of the phone calls?"

"I think this is call seven. Why don't you just answer the phone?" Hannah asked.

"Because I told him I was busy tonight and not coming over. He needs to learn that I'm not at his beck and call each and every night. Shut up!" she bellowed at the phone, hiding it in the couch cushions once it started again. We could only faintly hear the muffled chime.

"And we wonder why we're single, right, Hannie?" I asked with a chuckle.

"Right. No offense, Lils, but you don't make being in a relationship look like that much fun."

"I don't? No, I guess I don't. I'm sorry, guys. He's just been so overbearing lately. I don't know what his deal is. But I'm trying not to let it bother me. Let's talk about something else. Han—what do you look for in the perfect guy? Maybe it's time I put my matchmaking skills to work."

"Um, no thanks. I didn't know you had any 'matchmaking skills.'" Hannah said as she made quotes around the words.

"Well, not really, but I bet I could if I put my mind to it. Come on; let me find you the perfect man!"

"I don't have time for a relationship. I'm busy."

"Yeah, busy studying."

"Come on, ladies, no need to get into a fight over it." I felt the need to interject. "If Hannah doesn't want a boyfriend now, she doesn't want a boyfriend. And you can't magically produce someone for her. She'll find the right guy in her own time, someone who loves homework as much as she does." I threw Hannah a wink as she chucked a throw pillow my way.

"You guys make it sound like I'm so boring all the time. Am I that bad?"

"No, you're not. Sorry if it sounded like I was making fun of you. That wasn't my intention. Scouts honor." Lila held up her hand. "I think I just want to concentrate on someone else's love life other than mine. If you haven't noticed—it pretty much blows."

We discussed Lila and Joel for a while longer—getting nowhere on the matter—before Hannah bailed to head back to her room and get some shut eye. Lila downed another glass of wine, putting her at four for the night, and I had a midnight (well, ten o'clock) snack of a bowl of cereal, before we both headed to bed ourselves. My to-do list for the next day read: *thirty minutes of cardio, schedule eye doc appt, send off résumé.*

CHAPTER 4

"Could I speak with Alex Abrams?" an unfamiliar female voice asked over the phone, which had started to ring at 8:30 on Tuesday evening. Lila, Carmen, Emma, Hannah and I were all squeezed into my apartment, having a scary movie marathon to prep us for Halloween that was just around the corner. I took my cell phone and slinked into my bedroom so I wouldn't disturb my friends as I tried to figure out who the caller was.

"This is she," I answered, wondering who would be calling me so late at night.

"Hi, Alex. This is Dani Dohlman, the owner of Blissful Salon and Spa. I received your résumé yesterday and wanted to ask if you could come in for an interview sometime this week?"

Oh my God, oh my God! I was really getting an interview? I found my voice. "That's great! Thank you! Any day!" *Calm yourself. Stop speaking in exclamation points.* I cleared my throat to give myself a second. "I'm in class until about one each day, but anytime after that would work great."

"Let me pull up my calendar here, just a minute." Pause. Longer pause. Was she still there? I heard a kid shrieking in the background. "Brianna, put Cami down! Brianna, you better listen to Mommy!" Dani's sweet voice turned strict, and I could hear a little girl yelling but couldn't make out her words. "Sorry about that, Alex. My girls are running wild tonight. They should be asleep by now."

"Oh, that's no problem." What else could I say?

"How about we meet on Thursday? Say 1:30? If you want, we could do a late lunch at AJ's Bar and Grill?"

"Sounds good to me. Thanks so much for calling, Dani."

"You're welcome, sweetie. Thanks for applying. We're in desperate need for a manager, after the last girl quit pretty abruptly, and my husband has a lot of great contacts that came from Kaufman. I had a good feeling as soon as I opened your email."

I was thrilled, and silently thanked my college for its good reputation. "I'll be looking forward to meeting with you. Thanks again. And good luck with your girls!" I felt the need to add in a little personal touch.

Dani laughed. "Thanks. I'll need it. Their father isn't home yet, and I made the mistake of telling them Daddy would tuck them in. I didn't think he would be this late."

I hesitated, not sure what my response should be. I'm sorry? That's too bad? I stalled for a moment too soon, because Dani spoke again. "No worries, though. He'll either be home soon or they'll just tucker out before then. I have to rush now, looks like

Brianna is trying to shove something up her sister's nose. See you Thursday at 1:30!"

And then she was gone. I stared down at my phone for a moment, a little bewildered. Dani Dohlman of Blissful Salon and Spa seemed a bit all over the place. But her voice was friendly and she was offering me a job interview.

"I did it, guys! I got the interview!" I rushed back out into the living room, no longer caring about interrupting our movie. I stood in the middle of the room and did a little shimmy dance.

"Congrats, Alex!"

" Way to go!"

" When is it?"

" Let's drink!" My friends all started congratulating me at once, with Carmen suggesting a celebratory drink.

"Thank you, thank you. I'm meeting her at AJ's on Thursday after class. It was the owner, Dani, that called me. She said her husband knows some people at Kaufman, so they had to give me a chance."

"This college is good for something! I knew there had to be a reason we're all still here," Emma said, giving me a high five. "Way to go, girl. I hope you get the job."

"Thanks. Now I'm really nervous. What do I wear? What do I say? I have no experience managing but I really like to get manicures?"

"I'll help you with the interview part," Hannah volunteered. "I'm sure we can find some test questions online, and we can practice what you'll say."

"And I'll help you choose an outfit. Between the five us, we'll find something decent and professional for you to wear," Lila chimed in.

"And I'll go pour the wine so we can have a toast!" Carmen said, even though she was already drinking a margarita. Lila helped her get out the wine glasses and pop the cork on a new bottle, and we cheered to my good luck. And I crossed my fingers that I would impress Dani Dohlman enough to get the job.

I made sure to pay extra attention in my Entrepreneurship 2 class the following day. The lecture covered details about owning and maintaining businesses, and I wanted to feel extra smart for my interview the following day. I stayed up late on Tuesday night doing some research on Blissful Salon and Spa and Dani Dohlman so I could feel prepared for my interview. Turns out, Dani actually co-owned the spa with her husband, Kevin Dohlman. Blissful employed massage therapists, estheticians and hair stylists. You could walk in and get a massage, mani/pedi, eyebrow and bikini wax, and highlights all right there. They were open all week excluding Mondays, which was typical for spas.

I found a picture of the staff on their website, mostly women varying in age, but also two men. Dani and her husband Kevin were to the side of the picture, and were the only ones not wearing a black shirt with the Blissful logo on it. Dani looked petite, with long wavy brown hair highlighted with streaks of blonde. Kevin loomed over his little wife, looking full of confidence at the camera. Everyone was smiling, and the group looked fun.

I did more research on Dani and Kevin and found a few interesting things. Kevin, forty-four, had actually started his own company back when he was just eighteen. He opened a photography business—even though he had no skills as a photographer—hiring the models and photographers while he managed the business. He eventually went on to start his own magazine, which I had heard of and was a big deal a while back in the Midwest. Kevin had a degree in business and entrepreneurship and a résumé full of managing different companies, from restaurants to a small hotel. He still owned his photography/magazine business. Did I mention what that business was? The name of the magazine was Gropers and it was an adult magazine. As in, naked women. I was a bit shocked when I read that part, and when I clicked the link to the Gropers website, the pictures were quite. . . .revealing. It wasn't porn, just pictures of the women, but still. Not what I expected.

"So I don't get it. He's in the adult industry but runs a salon and spa with his wife?" Lila and I were walking back from classes on Wednesday. I had my purple notebook filled with what Professor Laman went over that day, and was feeling my confidence soar for my upcoming interview. I had an education, Kaufman, and great interviewing skills to back me up.

"Well, I'm not really sure. It says he still owns Gropers, but has considered selling it because of his children. They have three girls under the age of eight. That has to be awkward if they ever found out what daddy was doing at his job."

"I can't believe the wife is okay with it. That would just be weird to me. My husband goes off to work and oogles naked chicks all day. Do you think he gropes them?" Lila snorted with laugher at her play on words.

"Well, it actually gets a bit weirder." We continued walking through the parking lot, waving at friends and classmates as we neared Wacker. Lila got her keys out to unlock the front door. "Dani actually used to pose for Gropers. That's apparently where she met Kevin."

"What? Alex, I'm not so sure about this job anymore. You're going to turn into a porn star!"

"Lila! I'm sure Dani doesn't pose anymore. She's given birth to three children."

"That doesn't mean anything. Look at Amani. She went full frontal in her latest film just one year after delivering twins. Some woman can just bounce back. Look at your sister for crying out loud. She has a better body than me and she's had five kids."

"Yeah, yeah, I guess she could still pose. I just don't really want to think of her like that. . .you know, naked and stuff. It's a little weird."

"Do you think she'll talk about that business in your interview?"

I shrugged, stepping into our apartment and setting my oversized purse that doubled as a book bag on the kitchen table. "I don't know. I certainly don't want to bring it up. How uncomfortable would that be?"

"Definitely weird. But kind of fascinating at the same time if you really think about it." Lila stripped her heavy black sweater off, suddenly only wearing a flimsy red bra in our kitchen. "Do you think I need to get my boobs done?" she asked, cupping a breast in each hand.

Bewildered, I said, "Um, no. Are you crazy? You have frickin' C-cups; how much bigger would you want?" I couldn't even believe Lila was asking that question. She was always hard on herself about her weight, but she never mentioned plastic surgery before.

"What if I finally lose some weight, but it's all in my boobs? Silicone will keep them perky all the time," she answered, still not letting go of her girls. "And the main anchor on Buzzworthy has fake boobs and she's always flashing them around in those slinky dresses."

"You're crazy. Please don't get plastic surgery. You're beautiful the way you are. Trust me. And what would Joel say?"

"Speaking of Joel," Lila said, looking down at her cell phone, "he just texted and said he's on his way over. Want to have dinner with us tonight?"

"Nah. I think I'll head up to Hannah's and practice some interview questions with her. You kids have fun. And please— no more plastic surgery thoughts!" I pleaded one last time before we went our separate ways. Women shouldn't have to change their appearance for anything, whether it be for a guy or a job. I hoped Lila wasn't being serious about going under the knife.

I arrived at AJ's with five minutes to spare on Thursday. Generally I'd like to show up much earlier, but with class dismissing at one and then the fifteen minute drive, that was as close as I could make it. I knew what Dani looked like from her picture on the web, and hoped that it was current. I told the hostess I was meeting someone, then took a seat on the wooden bench beside the front doors to wait after not spotting her in the dining section.

I smoothed down my caramel sweater dress, knowing I looked professional but not stuffy after pairing it with dark brown tights, Emma's knee-length brown boots with just over an inch of heel, and a chunky gold necklace with a white flower attached to it. Lila had put hot rollers in my hair last night, so I woke up today with soft red curls framing my face and almost no frizz after a bottle of smoothing crème was ran through my strands.

At 1:30 on the dot, Dani burst through the restaurant doors. She looked just like her picture, except even smaller in person. I had a few good inches on her even though she was wearing heels, and I couldn't help but to admire her shoes. And by admire, I mean salivate. They were nude slingbacks with a peep toe and flecks of purple, and I knew if I could see the sole, the Louboutin red would be there. To own a pair of the coveted designer shoes was a fantasy of mine. Dani matched her outfit with her shoes, a loose fitting purple dress with a scoop neck and lots of gold jewelry. And her boobs. How a woman so tiny could have such huge breasts was beyond me. They must have been fake. How she didn't just tip forward was beyond me. But besides that, I was instantly in awe of her—from her fashion sense to her shoes to her manicured fingers that were holding onto a briefcase and the way she so confidently glanced around the room, extending her hand to me and introducing herself. I wanted to be just like her.

"You must be Alex. I'm Dani Dohlman. So nice to meet you! Thanks for meeting with me today." She stuck out one hand and I gave it three firm shakes, just like I learned in Kaufman's career class. No weak handshakes for this girl.

"Nice to meet you, Dani. And thank you for meeting with me!" I couldn't help my excitement. I just hoped Dani wouldn't think I was a supreme dork.

"Well, let's get a table and then we can do the interview and go over what we are looking for at Blissful. Cute dress by the way," she said, flagging down the hostess and requesting a quiet spot in the dining area.

I beamed in pride as I followed along, sliding in across from her at an oversized booth. Dani promptly turned off the mini TV that was at the table showing a basketball game, opening her briefcase and pulling out a few sheets of loose paper along with what looked like a handbook. It was that moment that I got a look at her wedding ring. Holy smokes, that ring was no joke. A giant square sat on her third finger, surrounded by even more diamonds on the side, and a band covering the top and bottom of the square with even *more* diamonds. I wondered how many carats her ring was, and just how much money she was wearing on her hand. "Okay then. Why don't we start by you telling me a bit about yourself?"

I hated that question. Almost every interview I had been on asked that. I never knew where to start. Where I was born? Did I talk about my family? My hobbies? "Well, I've been living in Des Moines since I was eight. I moved here with my sister from Baruva, Illinois. You've probably never heard of it. It's just a tiny town."

"Baruva? I used to live in Mapleton. That's just about forty minutes away from Baruva!" Dani exclaimed, her blue eyes lighting up. She jotted something down on the piece of paper in front of her. "What a small world. I moved away when I was still young though, so I'm not too familiar with the town anymore. Who are your parents?"

Ah, another question I hated. "Well, my mom was Lisa Abrams. She passed away though when I was five from breast cancer. And my father, Marcus Abrams, left me and my sister not too long after that. He couldn't handle Mom's passing, I guess." I stared down at the table, running a finger along the polished veneer. Why did my interviews always have to start off on this foot?

"Oh, Alex, honey. I'm so sorry," Dani said, the sympathy in her voice making my heart ache. "I know how it feels to lose a parent. I lost my dad in a car accident just four years ago. I think about him every day."

I looked up at her, noticing the way she gazed straight at me, not looking away or trying to change the subject like many people did when I talked about my mom's death. It was like everyone got so uncomfortable and flustered when I brought it up. But not Dani. She understood what I had been through. I felt an instant kinship with her and right then, and knew I wanted the job now more than ever.

Once we were able to move past the topic of our parents, she asked me a few questions about Kaufman and what classes I was studying. She was especially interested in my entrepreneurship class, which I knew would be the case. I flexed my brain and spit out the information I had learned over the past few weeks from my classes. I spoke about managing employees, how to handle the hiring and firing, how continuous training can be key in making the business succeed, and even some financial information. I gave ideas on marketing for good measure as well. I wanted Dani to see what I could bring to her business.

Through the interview, we found out we had more in common besides being from a small town in Illinois and losing a parent. Dani also held a job as a teenager at a hotel, and we shared some of our more outrageous stories with one another. She went on to tell me more about her life and how she began modeling when she was eighteen, which is how she met Mr. Dohlman on the set of a photo shoot. Since I knew she had posed for Gropers, I wasn't surprised to hear she did nude modeling, but tried not to let on that I already knew that information. From her beautiful face to oversized melons, I wasn't too surprised that an adult magazine snapped her up. I wondered if she ever considered Playboy? We all had a past, but now Dani was a buttoned-up (kinda) businesswoman, owning Blissful with Kevin and looking into opening multiple franchise locations. Dani was by far the coolest woman I had ever met.

"Well, Alex, I'm sorry for taking up so much of your afternoon," she said at one point, causing me to take a peek at my phone. It was already 3:30! The afternoon and interview had flown by. "Are you hungry at all? I could order us some food if you wanted to stay and chat for a while longer. I know I promised us a late lunch, but I didn't think it would be this late! I could tell you some more about Blissful and our staff, and we could set up a time for you to come in and see it and meet my husband."

Did that mean I had the job? She wouldn't offer to buy me lunch and keep talking to me if she was just going to toss me out, right? "I'd love that, Dani, thank you. I don't have any plans for the rest of the day. Well, some homework tonight of course, but that's typical."

"What's your favorite class that you're taking?"

"I would have to say entrepreneurship. I know that I would like to be my own boss some day, to own a business that I really love."

"Well, Alex, I'll tell you that I absolutely adore you. I think you would make a great addition at Blissful. If it were up to me, I would offer the job to you right now." I held my breath. It sounded like she was getting ready to turn me down. But what about lunch? That would make it awkward. She continued. "Once you meet with Kevin, I'm sure he will agree with me. We don't like to do any big hires without both agreeing to the person, but really, I can't see why he would refuse. You're just what we're looking for."

The waitress chose that moment to approach us, and Dani ordered us some spinach dip with pita bread, along with more waters. I couldn't wipe the smile off my face. Dani liked me. I was *this* close to getting a fabulous job and working with someone who I already considered to be a role model. She was successful, beautiful and seemed to overcome some hard times. I couldn't believe my luck.

"So, how about sometime this weekend? Can you stop by Blissful or do you have plans?"

"I can do this weekend! I don't have any plans at all."

"How about Sunday? It's still a pretty quiet day, but it should be busy enough so you can see some of the action without being overwhelmed. Kevin and I don't work a lot of Sundays ourselves. We reserve that day for church and family time, but we can definitely stop over so he can meet you and you can decide if you would want to take the job."

"That sounds perfect! Thank you so much, Dani. I really appreciate the opportunity," I said, hoping I sounded as sincere as I felt.

"You are so welcome, Alex. I have a feeling that my husband will just love you."

CHAPTER 5

I pulled my Camry into Blissful's parking lot on Sunday afternoon, the first real cold day of the fall season. The girls and I were keeping our fingers crossed that the weather would keep its semi-warm temperatures until next week—Halloween. We were attending a costume party together, and going as the Spice Girls. I mean, really, was there anything better suited for us? My red hair cast me as Ginger Spice, obviously, and I was looking forward to rocking a mini dress with some towering platforms.

Blissful Salon and Spa was a stand-alone business, meaning that it was not in a strip mall attached side to side with other businesses. Dani had told me when they first built Blissful just fourteen months ago, their original spot had been picked out, paid for, a done deal, then the owner of the strip mall decided to let a gym be put in right next to the spa. Dani and Kevin were appropriately peeved off. Who wants a gym with loud music right next to where a client is getting a relaxing massage? So they got out of that lease and into a new space, which had gone smoothly and opened up last year on Mayfair Lane.

A tinkling bell sounded as I opened the door, stepping inside the spa and taking my first glance around. Blissful was located in the suburb of Witte, almost a full thirty-minute drive for me from Kaufman, on the outskirts of town. Clients stepped into a beautiful reception area, open and inviting, with cream-colored walls and large pictures showcasing services they offered. I saw a picture that showed only a woman's back with stones placed along her spine, a beautiful blonde woman with bright blue eyes beaming at the camera while getting foils in her hair, and another picture just of someone's fingernails, each with a different design. A small waterfall in the left corner made soothing sounds as the water cascaded into the rocks, and the reception desk was made of blonde wood, the name and logo of Blissful carved in the center of it, lit up by pink lights. I fell in love that instant.

"Hi there, welcome to Blissful! What can I help you with today?" The young girl behind the front desk, who looked about my age, greeted me with a smile on her face. My first thought was that she was a bit plain looking, dark hair with no layers or highlights, no bangs framing her face and dark eyes with no eye makeup to accent them. Usually, salon receptionists sport a trendy haircut or at least some fun makeup products, but not her. Her smile seemed nice enough though.

"Hi! I'm Alex Abrams. I'm meeting Dani and Kevin Dohlman here for a second interview," I said, smiling as another gal popped up from around the partition leading to the salon.

"Oh, hi, you must be the one Dani was telling us about," the new girl said, extending her hand to shake mine. "I'm Allie Langtimm, an esthetician. This is Kamille, one of our coordinators. Dani is so excited for you to come today! How was your drive? You look adorable by the way. I love pencil skirts!"

Allie was the definition of bubbly. She seemed to be someone who had a permanent smile on her face, someone who just enjoyed life. She was petite, probably no taller than Dani, super tan, and had the blackest hair I'd ever seen. I thought there was one color of black, and that was black, but Allie's somehow seemed darker. Her eyes were an intense blue that had to be helped by colored contacts. She had her hair pulled back into a tight ponytail, and I noticed she had piercings all the way up her ears, seven in each, and also a nose ring.

"Well, thank you," I stumbled for words, trying to figure out what to say back to that barrage of a greeting. "I'm glad to be here and look around, and my drive wasn't too bad, thank you. I live on campus at Kaufman, so it was a little bit of a drive but nothing terrible."

"Do you just love Kaufman? I've heard it's a great school. Kamille here goes to Irving and just loves it, don't you, Kamille?"

Kamille seemed to have lost interest in our conversation, and was busying clicking around on the computer. She didn't even raise her eyes to look at me. "Yeah, it's peachy."

I nodded my head, not sure what to say when someone describes their college as peachy. Mine was like a plum? Cherry? So I kept my mouth shut, looking at Allie for help.

She clapped her hands together like a cheerleader waiting for that touchdown to happen. "Dani and Kevin aren't here quite yet, they might still be at brunch, but I'll give you a tour of the salon! I work as an esthetician, but I'm also the lead over all the salon and spa workers. I'll help the manager do scheduling for their shifts, and I do a lot of the ordering of supplies that we need. If anyone needs to call in sick or something, they call my cell phone and I try to help get someone to cover for them. It takes a load off the manager, who concentrates more on the coordinators, financials, and generally running the store. Have you ever been a manager before?"

"Uh, no. But I'm hoping my major will help me out here—business and entrepreneurship. The classes have given me some good ideas—well, what I hope are good ideas—to bring to this place." I followed Allie behind the partition and stepped into the salon. There were two rows of salon chairs hugging the walls, six in each row. A small table and oversized mirror furnished each hair station, and the tables were covered with an array of hair straighteners, curlers, blow-dyers and product. Black sinks lined the back wall, with bottles of shampoo and conditioner lined up like warriors ready to take on damaged hair and fight split ends. There were four girls on the floor, each wearing black pants and a black smock, working on a client. They all seemed friendly enough, shouting their hellos as Allie rushed me through and introduced me to the group.

"And this back here is our spa part. We do all the nail care, massages, waxing, and facials back here. Well, except for eyebrow waxes. Those can be done at the sinks, of course." Allie giggled as she led me through a set of double doors, with the words "Be Calm. Be Relaxed. Be Blissful." painted on them.

We entered into an oasis, a dim room with about a dozen plants placed strategically. The area reminded me of the reception out front but with darker lighting, soft music playing, and only the plants as decoration. The open room held six pedicure chairs and three manicure stations, one of those being occupied by a woman getting her fingernails painted.

Allie's voice dropped an octave or two when she spoke again. "We like this area to be as calm and relaxing as possible. We have a satellite music radio set to this station the moment we open until the last client leaves. Behind the doors are the treatment rooms," she gestured to the eight closed doors around the area, each numbered, "and certain rooms are equipped for certain treatments. That is a really important part when it comes to scheduling. The coordinators know which room can do what, so they schedule which rooms we will be in. It all needs to flow smoothly so there is no interruption or wait once a client comes in."

I nodded my head, understanding what Allie was saying. The client was the most important. When they walked through the doors at Blissful Salon and Spa, they would be treated with excellent customer service, from the front desk coordinator to their stylist or therapist. And it took a crew of people— the owners, managers, coordinators, everyone—to make their experience a good one. I could definitely appreciate that in a business.

Allie let me peek into the empty rooms to get a feel for them. The massage rooms held a bed, a chair for clients to place their belongings and one small table that held a microwave-looking thing. "A towel warmer," Allie explained when she caught me staring at it. "We like to start and end all our massages with a hot towel on the back, to help loosen and soothe the muscles. And if clients request a hot stone massage, we'll place the stones in there as well."

The facial rooms had a bed, chair, and small table as well, but also had what looked like a light that the dentists use to see inside your mouth. "This is just a magnifying light, so we can see your skin up close and personal. We can detect skin conditions, decide which type of products to use, and see if we need to do extractions during the facial by using the light," Allie said, flipping the light switch off and leading me out of the room. "Have you ever had a facial done before?"

I shook my head, wondering what the heck an extraction could be. Sounded painful. Like a tooth extraction. I'd had all four wisdom teeth removed, and that was not fun. I didn't think facials were supposed to hurt, but maybe it was like waxing. It hurt to be beautiful and fuzz free.

"We would let you try all the services here if you did get the position. We want all workers to know and understand the treatments so you can easily tell clients about them without stumbling over your words or having to grab one of us to explain them."

"Wow. That's pretty awesome."

Allie smiled at my enthusiasm. "It really is. And Dani and Kevin treat us so well. During your birthday month you can pick any two services and get those done for free. And you get half off all services any other time." *Score!* "But as a manger, you would also be in charge of hiring new staff, and that means letting them use you as a guinea pig."

"What does that mean?" I asked, a little worried. I didn't like the sounds of being a science experiment.

"It just means that if we have a massage therapist apply, you like their résumé and face to face interview, you would have them give you a practical interview where they demonstrate their service. So you would get a massage, or a facial or manicure, whatever it is they do. You want to make sure they are ready to be put on the floor and have a client right away."

I could feel the smile stretching across my face. I would want to be hiring all the time! "Wow, that sounds pretty good. But aren't they supposed to be licensed and graduated from a school? Shouldn't they all just be ready to go anyway?"

Allie led us out of the spa room and back into the bright and bustling salon section, where two more girls were now on the floor with clients. "You would think that, but actually it's not true. I've been helping Dani out with the practicals and we have found a few duds in there. It's shocking how the schools could let them graduate and get a license when they seem not to have a clue what they are doing. But you will come across a few here and there. I can pretty much guarantee that. Oh, look who's here!" Allie's blue eyes shone as she spotted Dani at the front desk surrounded by little girls. Well, just three little girls, but they were shrieking and shouting and running around, so they seemed to be multiplied.

"Brianna, lower your voice this instant! You know we're at work and we do not use loud voices here!" Dani was saying as we crossed the salon floor and approached the front. "If you sit down and be a good girl, we'll stop for some frozen yogurt on the way home." The little girl, wearing a long red dress, black tights and matching Mary Jane's, promptly flounced in one of the high-backed chairs, crossing her arms and sulking. Another little girl, wearing a matching outfit that was blue, followed suit, copying her face to form a frown like her sister's. And the youngest of the trio, wearing a pink dress, took slow steps around the reception area, looking a little unsteady on her feet. I guessed her to be somewhere around one or two years old.

"Oh, Alex, we're so glad you could make it today. Thanks for stopping by. Hi, Allie! Did you show Alex around?"

"Sure did. Filled her in a bit too, let her know some of the manger's duties that we discussed."

"Thanks so much, sweetie. This has been a day from, well," Dani cast her eyes downward, and I caught myself looking down at the polished marble floor, "just one of those days," she continued, and I guessed that she wanted to say "hell" but didn't for the children's sake. "Oh, here comes Kevin now."

I followed Dani's line of vision to the front door, where the bell tinkled as Kevin Dohlman came inside. Dani looked smaller in person than she did in her photo, and Kevin looked larger. He was tall, over six feet for sure, with a strong build and big hands. His black hair was spiked with gel, giving it that shiny look, which I thought was strange for a man in his forties. Didn't guys stop gelling their hair when they reach the big 3-0? His presence in the room commanded attention, I could feel it. The air seemed to shift and swirl around him, and he glanced around the room with authority, scanning the front desk area, reception desk, and then finally us minions that occupied the space.

"Hi, honey. Hi, girls," he said, giving his daughters a wave. He picked up the littlest girl in the pink dress, pulling her into his big arms. "Hi, Cami. You look so beautiful in your pink dress." The little girl giggled and squealed "Daddy!" while nuzzling against his neck. It was actually one of the cutest things I'd ever seen. This big beast of man with a soft heart for his precious daughter. Heartwarming.

"Hi, Allie, Kamille." He nodded to both of them with a smile, and they rewarded him back with high beams of their own. Even Kamille, who seemed a bit sulky when I showed up, flashed her pearly whites, her face lighting up. Even her dull eyes seemed to sparkle. "And you must be Alex." He stuck out his hand to me, easily holding Cami in the crook of his left arm.

I gave a firm handshake, showing my confidence and competence just as I had done with Dani. "Nice to meet you, Kevin. Thanks so much for meeting with me today," I said, hoping my voice didn't sound as shaky as I thought it did. Something about this man just screamed "Be on your best behavior! Stand up straight! Look sharp!" I threw my shoulders back and lifted my neck long, listening to the inner screams in my head.

Kevin's gaze swept across my body, taking in my black pencil skirt, tan blouse with ruffles along the buttons, and simple black pumps that I borrowed from Lila. I kept my jewelry minimal, just wearing my gold watch that was given to me as a gift from Alicia when I started college. My red hair was pulled back into a casual bun, with a few tendrils framing my face. I thought I looked classy and professional, but the way Kevin stared at me, I wondered if maybe my skirt was too tight or my blouse suddenly see-through. It was a very. . .intense gaze that he was giving me.

"Very nice to meet you as well, Alex. Welcome to Blissful. I hear you and my wife really hit it off the other day." He threw me a wink, and I wasn't sure he meant we hit it off professionally, or that he wanted us to mud wrestle in the nude. I didn't have senses and vibes like Lila, but something felt funny.

I glanced at Dani, wondering if she noticed the underlying sexual tone in Kevin's voice. But her smile was as bright as ever when she answered. "We sure did! We have so much in common. Alex is working on her business degree, and I just know she would make a fabulous addition here!"

I looked at Allie, my next, well, ally at the salon. She had the same smile on her face. Ditto for Kamille. This was getting weirder by the minute. Maybe I was the crazy one. Why would Kevin be hitting on me with his gorgeous, young, big-breasted wife standing beside me? I was obviously hallucinating. Maybe it was from all the hair and nail products in the air.

"Thanks, Dani," I said, pasting an identical smile on my face. "I absolutely love Blissful. From talking to Allie, it sounds like you are so customer driven, really focused on giving them the best treatment and experience, and I think that is excellent. I would really feel honored if you considered me for the position."

"Well, why don't we go back into my office and discuss a few more details, the fine print of the job," Dani suggested, taking Cami from Kevin's arms. "We have a few minutes until we need to get going so we could go over some paperwork, and then if you have any other questions, Allie can be your right-hand girl to go to."

I followed Dani and Kevin back, while Allie and Kamille stayed up front to keep an eye on their daughters. The office was through the spa doors and to the left and was a small square space that seemed efficient. Two computers hummed in opposite corners, file folders, loose papers and stacks of mail were piled on any free space available, and a family picture of Dani, Kevin and their three daughters was hung on the east wall. One computer had an email pulled up, the other showed what looked to be the salon schedule, with blocks of time colored different shades and names inserted at every hour. I felt professional just walking into the office, and could easily picture myself at the desk, monitoring the schedule, fielding phone calls, working payroll.

It only took about twenty minutes, and Dani explained to me the different job duties, hours they would want me to work, a salary and explanation of benefits. The work hours in the clinic were a little varied, Tuesday through Sunday three weeks out of the month, and then the last week Tuesday through Friday, with weekends off. They announced a salary that made my eyes bulge——I had never been offered a number like that in my life. And that included a pay raise once I got my degree—hello, making bank. The benefits were excellent, a 401(k) plan, health, vision and dental care, and even a free gym membership at a local facility down the street. I felt confident in my ability to perform the job requirements: scheduling employees, training events, marketing, dealing with unhappy customers, submitting employee hours to the payroll company, hosting monthly meetings with the staff, and generally being the face of Blissful. I needed to organize events around town to help drive in business, promote Blissful on the radio, basically "eat, sleep and breath Blissful," as Kevin put it.

I looked down at the large packet in my hands, which outlined everything we had discussed in a few short minutes. It was overwhelming. It was a real, grown-up job. It was everything I wanted. And then, Kevin threw in a few kickers. "We want our business to do well, and we want employees who can make that happen. And you, Alex, I believe can make that happen for us. You've lived in Des Moines for years, you know the town and the people, you have connections through your school and you're a beautiful woman. People will look at you and think your beauty comes from Blissful. Women will want to look like you and men will want their wives to look like you." I snuck another peek at Dani when he said that. She was beautiful. I wanted to look like her. "We'll have certain goals we will want you to meet each month—either an increase in appointments, product sales, treatment sales, whatever. You make the goal, you get a monetary bonus. And come on, who doesn't love some bonus money?"

I nodded my head, thinking of what I could buy with my bonus money. My savings account could really benefit from that. Kevin continued. "It's simple: meet your goal, we cut you a check. Bing, bang, done deal."

"That is so generous of you to offer that. I'll tell you, I love goals. I love being able to write things down and really go for them and—"

"Excellent, you get it then. Perfect." Kevin cut me off, leaning back in his chair and casually crossing one leg over the other. "And one more thing. Blissful is a franchise, and we're really interested in opening more salons in Des Moines and across Iowa. Maybe even dip in Missouri and Illinois. If you want to think of the future, you could possibly own a store yourself one day." My heart skipped a beat. Me—an owner of a salon and spa? "If you exceed expectations as a manger, understand the way the business operates, we could definitely help you open another store. More money for us, more money for you. Cheers all around. What do you think of that?"

It took me an extra moment to find my voice over the shock of realizing I could really be a business owner one day, with a man who obviously knew a great deal about owning and entrepreneurship. "Yes! That's my main goal is to own a store. And salon and spas are my niche—they're what I love. I can't believe I could really own one someday." I shook my head in disbelief. It was all so overwhelming. Everything was falling in place for me. Alicia was going to be so proud.

"I think you're the candidate for the job. Dani?" He raised his caterpillar black eyebrows at his wife, who had her signature grin in place.

"And I agree. Ooh, Alex, we're so happy to have you. That is, if you want the job." Her smile faded just for a second while she watched me pretend to go over their offer one more time, flipping pages in the packet. This job offered money, stability, a chance to get a real opportunity. What indecision?

"I say yes! I would love to come on as your manager. I will take great care of Blissful. Thank you so much," I said. Dani stood and reached her arms out for me. I leaned in to hug her, feeling her gigantic melons press against my own chest, and then reached on my tiptoes to hug Kevin. He secured his thick arms around my waist, resting them right above my tailbone.

"Welcome to the family, Alex," he whispered in my ear.

CHAPTER 6

Halloween weather was not on our side. By the time
Saturday rolled around, the nighttime temps wouldn't
budge more than forty-six degrees. Our tiny costumes
would not fare well against the blustering winds and teeth-
chattering cold.

"Hannah, please go start your car! The leather seats will
freeze my ass if you don't!" Carmen was trying to convince
Hannah, who was our DD, to start her car before we left for a
house party.

"Didn't your dad just install that automatic start? Just press
the button!" Lila chimed in, who sat on the couch covered in a
thick blanket. The heat hasn't been turned on yet at Kaufman, so
blankets and sweatshirts were scattered around our apartment.

"Chill out, would you? I will use my automatic start when
we're more prepared to leave. It doesn't take long to warm my
car," Hannah said, adjusting her black wig. Hannah was Posh

Spice, trumping Carmen who originally thought she should be Posh, due to her black hair. But Carmen ended up as Scary Spice, which she said was "blatant discrimination" making the Latina play the black singer. She got over it when Hannah said she would be the DD if she could be Posh (which she probably would have been no matter what) and Carmen agreed to the trade.

Lila was Sporty Spice, and while her black hot pants, skin-tight pink sports bra and towering platforms made her look more streetwalker than girl band, nobody was complaining. Emma was of course Baby Spice, who looked the picture of naughty innocence in a short white pleated skirt (the cheerleading fantasies guys would imagine that night), a pink baby tee that ended just a few inches past her boobs, pigtails (more fantasies) and white platforms.

"Someone help me take out these curlers, please!" I shouted from the bathroom, where I was the last one getting ready. I was at Blissful all afternoon learning the ropes, so I was behind schedule. I felt bad for holding everyone up, but I wanted to look my best for the party, not just a thrown-together Ginger Spice.

Hannah and Lila both entered the bathroom, Lila tripping over her blanket and Hannah tugging down the sides of her painted-on black mini dress. They got to work on my hair, rolling out the curlers, dousing the strands with holding spray, and chattering about the party. I sat quietly, letting them do their thing. I was horrible at hair and learned it was best just to keep my hands in my lap.

"Are you sure you know how to get there? I do not want to get lost tonight of all creepy nights," Hannah was saying to Lila, who struggled to reach my hair while trying to keep the blanket around her scantily clad body.

"I'm positive! I printed off directions from the Internet, plus confirmed them yesterday with Peter. And I have his number, so if it truly comes down to it, I can call him for help. But we won't get lost."

"And how well do you know this Peter?" Hannah wanted to know. My ears perked up. I wanted to know this too. Lila came home last week talking about a guy she met in the lounge, this Peter Gambil character. We couldn't figure out if she liked him, as in dump Joel and move on, or just thought he was a nice guy. But she immediately switched our Halloween agenda from the first house party we were going to attend to the one that would be taking place at Peter's house on the south side of Des Moines. And from what we gathered, Joel was not happy about the change of plans. The original house party had been at his friend's house, so now Joel and Lila were fighting. Again. I was surprised that Joel wasn't going to accompany Lila to the party. He usually just tagged along with her. To be honest, I was glad he wasn't. Lila needed time away from him.

"I've been telling you, Hannah, he's perfect! He's tall, good-looking, and smart. Plus, he's getting his generals here at Kaufman before going on to get his DDS."

"What's a DDS?" I piped up, curious.

"Doctor of Dental Surgery," Lila and Hannah replied at the same time.

"Right!" Lila exclaimed, pulling a roller out with a little more force than necessary. "He's got his own house—well, I think he rents it with some other guys, but still—he drives a nice car and he's super nice. Hannah, I think he's perfect for you."

So that's what it was. Lila wanted to play matchmaker. She was serious about the vow she gave Hannah a few weeks back.

"What? Come on, you're joking. Is this like a blind date house party or something? I thought you were kidding when you said you wanted to be my matchmaker."

"Hannah, when I see someone that is so obviously right for one of my very best girlfriends, I will not let him slip away. Let's just go to the party, meet some new people and have a good time. No pressure. If you hit it off, then send me gifts. If you don't, whatever. I didn't mention you to Peter at all, so he's not expecting any sort of hookup."

As I listened to the girls comment about the party and then segue into blind dates, I covered my mouth with one hand to hide all the yawns that insisted on escaping. Saturdays were usually reserved for lounging, catching up on TV shows, hitting the gym, maybe a little shopping. But I was at Blissful at eleven o'clock that morning, an hour before they opened on Saturdays, to start my training. I worked with Dani, Allie, and Kamille, who were getting me started on the basics: what Blissful offered and learning the computer system. I had an appointment scheduled with Allie on Tuesday after class to get my first facial. I caught on quick to the computer system, studied the services menu all afternoon until I could almost recite the thing from memory, and started interacting with the customers—introducing myself to the regulars who seemed delighted to see me. I was thrilled I was getting the hang of everything so fast. I just didn't account for how tired I would be after just a six-hour shift.

"You look fab, Alex, just fab. I still can't believe you found that dress." I snapped to attention when I heard Lila say my name and mentally shook myself awake.

"Thanks. It really wasn't even a bad price, and nothing says Ginger Spice more than the British flag dress," I replied, looking down at my outfit. I found the iconic dress that Geri Halliwell donned online, and instantly ordered it. Paired with fire engine red strappy platforms and my red hair bouncing in curls, I was full-on pop-girl group stardom. Tell me what you want, what you really, really want.

"I'm jealous you can pull off a dress that short. I swear, I feel like every time I move a leg one of my ass cheeks is going to pop out," Hannah complained, yanking down the hem of her dress.

"Come on, Hans, you are totally not in character. Don't you remember the scene from the movie where Posh walks out and says 'Is my dress too short?' and they say no so she hikes it up even more. Get in character!" Lila said, tousling my hair one last time and nodding in satisfaction.

"I must have fallen asleep before that part," Hannah replied, giving herself a once-over in the mirror. I stood, giving myself one more swipe with deodorant, a spritz of Lila's perfume, and threw a stick of eyeliner in my clutch.

"We've watched the movie three times in as many weeks. You could not have missed that part each time," Lila protested, also giving herself a glance in the mirror, frowning as she ran her hands over her bare stomach. "I need to do some more sit-ups quick." She exited the bathroom in haste, and Hannah and I rolled our eyes at each other, following suit. Lila looked fab in her costume, though we knew she didn't believe it when we told her.

After finishing our pregame drinks and making sure we all looked our best (and Lila finished yet another round of tummy-toning sit-ups) we finally moseyed our way outside and piled into Hannah's Audi. Lila read the directions aloud from her paper, and we actually made it to Peter's without getting lost, shocking us all. We walked right in the front door without bothering to knock, as we could already hear the music pulsating through the front door.

We stuck close together as we entered, grasping our clutches and still shivering from being outside for a few short minutes. We followed Carmen's nose to the keg, which was set up in the unfinished basement that screamed bachelor pad: hard cement floors, a pool table in one corner, two dart boards side by side on the wall, a big screen TV with what looked like two X-boxes, one Playstation, and one Wii under the entertainment stand, and a few worn couches scattered throughout. A group of guys were huddled around the silver keg, filling their red party cups with beer and laughing as one guy got too much foam in his cup.

One guy glanced our way as our group approached, and we made eye contact. When our eyes locked, the loud din of voices turned quiet, like someone turning the volume down quickly on the TV. The strangers in Halloween costumes faded away, until it was just me and Mr. Blue Eyes. Did I believe in love at first sight? If you had asked me three seconds ago, I would have said no way . . . but now. . .

"Alex! Come on, there's Peter!" Lila grabbed my elbow and firmly guided me out of my spot, leading me to the group of guys by the keg.

Oh, please don't let that be Peter, I silently begged the relationship Gods. I couldn't handle being completely entranced with the guy we were supposed to be hooking our friend up with.

The handsome stranger broke eye contact with me first, and I instantly felt goosebumps appear on my arm, like a gust of cool wind had flown through. He nudged the guy standing next to him, a shorter, friendly looking guy with glasses. Bespeckled man flashed us a grin and beckoned us over. I clutched my clutch even tighter, digging my fingernails into the black satin fabric. Why the hell was I so nervous over a guy?

"You made it!" glasses-man said as we finally reached the keg. "Did you find the house okay? Henry, get the ladies some cups. No charge tonight, these are our guests!"

Henry. It was Henry that I was so smitten for. Our fingers brushed together as he handed me my cup, and I swallowed back a nervous hiccup. He was the most delicious man I had ever seen.

"Peter! You don't have to do that. How sweet are you?" Lila was saying, giving Peter's arm a friendly pat. "We made it just fine, no troubles at all. It was mostly because of Hannah here," Lila shoved Hannah to the front of the group, who looked like a cat heading for a full bathtub. "She got us here with no worries. Hannah Lovington, meet Peter Gambill, our fabulous host for the night."

Hannah and Peter shook hands while the rest of us girls looked on amused, knowing that Lila was in matchmaker overload. Hannah looked painfully shy and embarrassed, while Peter was more laid back. "And this is the rest of our group: Carmen, Emma, and my roommate, Alex," Lila continued on with the introductions, and we all said hello.

"These are my roommates: Henry, Kyle, and Max. We're really glad you all could make it tonight. Does anyone know anyone?" Peter asked the group, and we all shook our heads. "How is it possible that we haven't run into each other before on campus? It's not that big of a school."

"True, very weird. But at least you're here tonight. Let me fill your cups up," Henry volunteered, taking my cup first. I let him fill it to the brim and pass it back to me, trying not to stare at his piercing blue eyes and the way his black hair flopped over his forehead in the most adorable way. It was then that I realized what his costume was, and finally found my voice.

"I, um, I like your costume." *Lame Alex, so lame.* I giggled a bit. "It's very unique." I tried again.

He smiled at me, showing a row of perfectly straight teeth that had to have been touched by braces as a kid. No one should have that great of teeth without some work. "Thanks. I actually hadn't planned on being here tonight. Me and Max," he indicted to his blonde friend, "were going to go back home for the weekend. So this was made in a pinch." Henry was dressed as a deer, with an orange ping pong ball that was probably swiped from the beer pong game attached to his nose, and a few skinny twigs perched atop his head as antlers. The camo he was wearing didn't showcase his body, but I could tell from his lanky yet lean build that I wouldn't mind a few layers being stripped off.

"Henry won in rock, paper, scissors so he got to be the reindeer," Max grumbled. "And I got stuck with this." He spread his arms out to show off his rabbit costume, which looked hilarious and a tad feminine. He wore a gray shirt and matching gray athletic shorts, with a bunny tail fastened to his tailbone, Playboy pink bunny ears, and someone had used a pink marker to color the tip of his nose. Even under the ridiculous fuzzy pink bunny ears, it was easy to tell Max was a hottie. Tall, blonde, blue eyes, with a surfer-look going for him. Peter and Kyle weren't bad either, and were both dressed as hunters in full camo and water guns. But it didn't matter how good looking they were. My eyes were still finding their way back to Henry between sips of cold beer.

Carmen and Max struck up a conversation about apple pie shots, Hannah was still struggling to get words out around Peter, Lila was trying to help their floundering conversation along, Emma was chatting with the last roommate Kyle, and I was staring into my cup, wishing I could be funny and witty and charming and sexy and convince Henry he was in love with me.

"Do you like pool?"

I looked up to find Henry looking at me, his dark blue eyes scanning my face. "Um, what?" I stammered, feeling my face start to flush. Why couldn't I be calmer around the opposite sex that I found attractive? *Think bold, Ginger Spice!*

Henry pointed to the pool table in the corner, now abandoned. "Pool. The table's open. Want to play with me?"

"I'm not sure if I'm any good," I said, trying to rack my brain to determine the last time I played pool.

"Well, I'm pretty good, if I may say so myself, and I can teach you a few tricks. Come on." Henry reached out and grabbed my elbow, since my hands were full of beer and my clutch, and steered me to the table. "My dad loves pool and we have our own table at home, so I get a lot of practice. I can give you some pointers."

"Okay. Thanks." *Say something! Make a real conversation, Alex!* "So you also go to Kaufman?" Finally. A real question made it out of my mouth.

Henry started placing the pool balls inside a triangle contraption. "Yep. I'll graduate in May with my Bachelor's."

"Hey, that's awesome! Congratulations. I still have another year to go before I'll be done. What did you major in?"

"I had some trouble deciding my major along the way. I changed it about three times. But I finally ended up with Entrepreneurship and Sales and Marketing."

My spine tingled. Similar majors? Could the signs be any more obvious? Clearly, we were meant to be. We would date, marry, own our businesses, have gorgeous babies and live happily ever after. Henry and Alex. . . .um. . . "What's your last name?" I blurted out before I could stop myself. Well, that was awkward. Why would I be digging for his last name for any other reason than to figure out what my name would be in a few years? I was sure Henry could see right through me and my wedding vision bliss.

But he didn't say anything, just flashed me another gorgeous smile and plucked a pool stick from the hanging wall rack, rubbing some blue chalk on the end. "It's Landon."

"Your last name is?" I was confused. Henry Landon? Or was Henry his last name, and that's what all his buddies called him?

Henry/Landon laughed, motioning me over towards him at the far end of the pool table. "That's right. My name is Henry John Landon. Three first names. Don't worry, you're not the first to question me on it. Some people call me Landon, like when I play sports, and that just confuses everyone even more."

Henry Landon. Alex Landon. It was perfect.

"Have you ever broke before?" I snapped out of my white dress fantasy and focused on the balls in front of me. The pool balls, of course.

"Um, no? Not sure what that is. Sorry, I've really never played a full game before," I apologized for my lack of knowledge and pool skills.

"That's okay. Everyone's got to learn sometime. Here, you stand here." He placed my body in front of his, with his chest slightly touching my back. My body was on fire. I had boyfriends in the past, even a few that I really cared about, but no one caused my body to react like this. I started to get scared of my attraction to Henry Landon. It could definitely lead to heartbreak.

"Here?" My voice came out in a squeak.

"Perfect." His lips were close to my ear, his baritone voice vibrating through my body. I shivered, hoping he couldn't feel me tremble. "And wrap your hands around the stick, just like that. Now you want to get low to the table, line up your shot, and pull back." His hand rested over mine, and together we pulled back and flung forward, smacking the white ball against the colored ones, sending them scattering around the table. A solid fell into the far right corner, causing me to whoop in delight.

"I got one in! I got one in!" I said, reaching to hug Henry. "Thanks for your help. That was fun." I kept my arms around his body for a beat longer than necessary. The beer was already starting to make me feel braver. Blaming the beer was always best.

We kept playing for a while, and it took Henry to be behind me for me to make a shot each time. We chatted about Kaufman, our roommates, wondered if Hannah and Peter would hit it off, and gulped glasses of cold beer. I felt relaxed, confident in my British dress, and none of the topics veered towards family, which I was thankful for. My complicated mess of a family life did not need to be discussed from the start.

When Carmen and Lila came over with a round of jello shots I didn't hesitate, grabbing two cherries for me and Henry. "Where's our Hannah?" I asked, sticking my index finger in the slimy jello and whirling it around, prying the red slime from the sides of the cup.

"She and Peter went upstairs so they could better talk to each other," Lila spoke up, her eyes shining with delight. "I just knew they would hit it off!"

"Your friend isn't some big jerk, is he?" I aimed my question at Peter's roommates, who had also joined us with shots in their hands. Carmen snickered at my drunk language.

"Nah, Peter's one of the good guys. He's one you don't have to worry about," Henry said, placing his hand on the small of my back. I drew a breath in and stood up straighter.

"And which one of you boys *do* we need to worry about?" Emma flirted, looking from Henry in his deer costume, Max the playboy bunny, and Kyle the hunter. Henry and Kyle pointed a finger at Max, who pointed a finger at himself. Our little group burst into laughter, with Max looking unabashed at being singled out. We cheered to our new friendship and downed the shots, and the party raged on. A new keg was brought in while I continued to play pool with Henry and tried my best to keep an eye on all my girlfriends. We were at a party at an unfamiliar house, an unfamiliar neighborhood, and with a bunch of people we didn't know. We knew to stick close, which is why I started to get worried when Hannah still hadn't appeared a few hours into the party.

"Carmen! Carmen! Come here!" I shouted across the busy room for Scary Spice, who started to weave her way between people to reach me. I was standing by the sliding glass door that led out to a concrete patio, where I could see plenty of party-goers standing and smoking. Henry had dashed upstairs to go to the bathroom, and I realized that I was feeling drunk.

"What up, chica?" Carmen asked as she approached, looking cool as a cucumber and not at all like she was drunk. I was sure my hair was starting to frizz and my face was getting the telltale red to it that happened when I drank heavily.

"Where a ish Hannah? I worried her 'bout," I said, growing confused when Carmen started to laugh.

"Girl, you are wasted! Slur your words anymore, could you? Oh, honey, I hope you don't have to work tomorrow."

I placed a hand to my forehead and felt the warmth radiate onto my palm. Ah yes, the drunkenness was there. Perfect. Henry probably couldn't understand a word I'd been saying for the past hour. "Damn nit. No, no work! None. Hannah?" I asked again, grimacing as I heard my words come out that time.

Carmen took her phone out of her clutch, showing me a text message. "She's fine. Just smitten with this Peter boy. Go upstairs if you want; see for yourself."

I walked unsteadily towards the staircase, pulling down my dress as I went. Lila intercepted me halfway across the room. "I knew my matchmaking skills would work on Hannah, but I did not see you and deer boy hooking up! What's the details, girl?"

"Not now, Lils. Need check Hannah. Really drunk." The room swayed, and I almost toppled over in my platforms. Lila caught me by the arm, keeping me upright.

"Maybe it's time for us to get going. Emma's upstairs on the couch passed out."

My body sagged in relief, happy I wasn't the first to succumb. "Me tired, Lils. Sleep."

"I know. Come on, up we go. Where's the hottie man of yours? I like him."

"No! I like him. Me like," I slurred, feeling the effects of all the beer, jello shots, and the tequila shot I shared with Carmen. We trudged up the stairs together, our platforms sounding like hooves, until we entered the kitchen. "My Hannah!" I squealed, running over to my friend and wrapping her in a hug. She was sitting at the kitchen table with Peter, a bulky sweatshirt covering her Posh costume and looking enviously sober.

"Oh, what do we have here? Little drunk, missy?" Hannah laughed, returning my hug.

I crawled into her lap like a little girl, resting my head on her shoulder. "Emma loser! I not pass out. I was so worried about you, Han. Don't worry," I tried dropping my voice to a whisper, which really didn't work, "his friends said he's the good guy." I tried to give her the thumbs up, but struggled to keep the rest of my fingers down.

Peter, Hannah and Lila all begin to laugh at my announcement, which clearly everyone heard. Henry walked into the room suddenly, appearing from around the corner. "So the party's up here now, huh?" he said, surveying us at the table, then seeing Emma sprawled out on the couch. Someone had been kind enough to slip some sweatpants on her so she wasn't on full display in her tiny white miniskirt.

"We think it's about time to get us out of here. Emma and Alex need their beauty rest. And to puke probably," Lila said. "Oh, it's going to be a long night for those two."

I jutted my lower lip out. "No! No puke. Gross. Just sleep."

"Let me go grab Carmen, then we can head out." Lila disappeared down the stairs and Hannah gently removed me from her lap. Well, aimed for gently, but my limbs were feeling like all the jello shots I had taken and I fell to the floor in an ungraceful heap. I frantically tried to keep my dress down, wondering which pair of underwear I had decided on that night and if I wanted to show Henry them at that moment. I wanted to get up, get to my feet and locate my clutch, which had fallen out of my hands at some point, but the tiled kitchen floor was just so comfortable. Just another minute down there. . .

Suddenly, I was being swooped into the air by a pair of strong arms. My eyes flew open, and I realized that Henry had picked me up off the floor, cradling me in his arms like a baby. Heaven. I snuggled into his broad chest, feeling giddy with excitement. I remembered feeling happy, tingly and maybe a tad sweaty. I didn't remember passing out in his arms, having to be carried out to Hannah's car, throwing up out the window on the ride home, having Carmen carry me into the dorm, throwing up more once I got home, and then throwing a fit when no one would order me a pizza. None of that was in my memories, but the girls were nice enough to fill me in the next day as I cleaned Hannah's car and suffered through my hangover. Halloween. Gets me every time.

CHAPTER 7

The Tuesday following Halloween, I headed to Blissful right after class for my first facial. I checked myself in for the appointment, and sat up front with Kamille until Allie was ready for me. I used my time studying the menu of services. I really wanted to get them memorized so I didn't have to always have one on hand when the phone rang.

"You ready, hon?" Allie appeared in front of me, clad in the usual Blissful uniform: black dress pants and the white-collared shirt with *Blissful Salon and Spa* etched in black on the left side. She had her black hair pulled back in a tight ponytail with a thin pink band holding back her bangs. I was going to be doing more training after my facial, so I also wore dress pants and a plain white top, as I didn't have my official staff shirt in yet. Dani had told me I didn't need to wear my work shirt everyday though, just to dress up on the days that I didn't wear it. I had planned to hit up the mall with Lila later in the week to help fill the void of non-professional clothes in my closet.

"Ready!" I slid off the stool and gave Kamille a friendly wave as I followed Allie behind the partition and into the salon part. Kamille just raised her overly plucked eyebrows at me and stared back down at the computer screen.

"I just don't think she likes me much," I said to Allie, waving hello to the other stylists that I passed. I had been introduced to all the staff at an employee meeting last week, and thought I would fit in just fine at Blissful. The stylists were mostly female, and the median age was probably twenty-five. There was one male massage therapist and one male stylist who seemed just as nice as the females. The only one that seemed less than thrilled with me was Kamille.

"Don't take it too personally," Allie said, opening the heavy doors that led to the spa area. I immediately felt a sense of calm when the busy chatter of the salon faded away and the soft music floating from the hidden speakers hit my ears. "She was being considered for the management job, so she probably wasn't going to like whoever ended up getting it."

Well, that explained a lot. "I get it. Why didn't she get the position? I mean, it makes sense to hire internally."

"I think there were a few reasons. She has a really busy schedule with her school and she's in a lot of extra-curricular activities. She's also pretty new to Des Moines—she just moved here from out of state last year to go to Irving—and Kevin was really big on finding someone who has a lot of connections with the city. And we've been able to watch her up front and see how she works, and she doesn't seem to connect with the clients very easily. The personality that's needed for the position just wasn't there. You can't tell me you think her personality is that of a winner."

I gave a slight nod but didn't say anything. That was a bit harsh, but Kamille never had been friendly to me.

Allie ushered me into a treatment room as she gave me the low-down on Kamille, then held out what looked like half a towel to me. "I'll slip out of the room, and go ahead and undress to your comfort level. Put this on over your body and lay face up on the bed. You'll want to make sure to either remove your bra or at least take the straps down, because I do a neck massage. Same goes for your pants. If you can take off your socks and slacks, I also do a foot massage while your mask sets in."

"Got it. Thanks." Allie left the room and I set out removing my socks, pants, bra, undershirt, and blouse. I also took off my watch and necklace, setting them carefully on the little table in the room, climbed into my towel/robe thing and crawled underneath the covers, eyes towards the ceiling. The soft music was soothing, but there was that scary-looking dentist-like contraption looming to my left. I wondered if I would be getting any extractions done and what the heck that entailed.

My thoughts wandered over to Halloween while I waited for Allie to come back in the room. I couldn't believe what a fool I made of myself. I threw up twice more on Sunday, thankful I didn't have class or work to attend, and cringed every time I thought of Henry Landon. I really thought we had a connection going, but now I seriously doubted it. I barely remembered what our conversations had been about, and I was sure he was just entertaining the drunk girl at his party, trying to help his buddy

Peter out. Peter had asked Hannah out for a dinner date this week, and all us girls were super excited for her once we found out about it. She deserved a nice guy. I wanted to ask Hannah to ask Peter to ask Henry what he thought of me, but I was sure Henry he would not be interested in a lush like me. I blew my chances on Halloween.

"Ready, hon?" Allie asked, tapping lightly on the door and entering, dimming the lights just a touch.

"Ready!" I responded, feeling the déjà vu from our earlier conversation at the desk. I wondered how many times stylists repeated themselves throughout the day. I wondered how many times I would repeat myself when working the desk.

"Do you have any make-up on, like foundation or blush?" Allie asked, sitting on the short black stool that was by my head.

"Um, yes and yes. Sorry, I didn't even think to take it off!" Duh, Alex. Obviously you couldn't wear make-up during a facial.

"No problem at all. Most women do, and I can easily remove it. We also offer a complimentary make-up session after all facials, just a touch-up to get you on your way. It's near impossible to go anywhere after a facial since we remove all make-up, so we just put a bit of foundation on, usually a bit of eye make-up as well so they can feel good about themselves and not have to worry."

"Wow, that's a great idea. I guess I don't know what I'll look like when I'm done, but I'm sure I'll want the make-up application."

"Our clients really appreciate it, and that's what we care about. Most other salons don't offer that." Allie wiped a cool cloth around my face then concentrated on my eyes, wiping away all traces of eye shadow, liner, and mascara. "I'm going to look at your skin under the light to determine what we need to use today on you. I'm just going to put these over your eyes so I don't blind you," I felt little pads cover my eyelids, "and just take a look. Now, what kind of skin do you think you have? Oily or dry? Any problem areas or trouble zones?"

The light flickered on but didn't really affect me thanks to the eye pads. I considered Allie's question. "This time of year I think I have really dry skin. I try to use a moisturizer a lot because sometimes it looks like my skin is just flaking off, which is really gross. I've never had the best skin and I still get breakouts, especially on my chin, but not many other problems that I can think of."

Allie ran the tips of her fingers along my forehead, both cheeks, my nose, chin and even felt my neck and décolleté. "Your temperature is nice and even, which is a good sign. You have fairly healthy skin, but I can feel little dry spots. It's important that you keep using your moisturizer, and aim for twice a day, once in the morning and again at night when you remove your make-up. We have a super-hydrating moisturizer that you could try as well that should help clear that up."

The light flicked off and Allie removed the pads from my eyes. I blinked a few times to get my contacts moist, then closed my eyes again as Allie began to smooth something on my face with what felt like a paintbrush. "I'm starting with an exfoliant first. This helps slough off the dead skin and reveal the sparkling skin underneath all those dead cells. Is the steam bothering you at all?"

"I really didn't notice it until now," I answered, feeling warm puffs of air reach my face. It was kind of nice actually.

"The steam helps open up your pores so I can really get down to what's beneath your skin and bring everything up and out. It's like a detox for your skin. If you use an exfoliant at home, the shower is a good place to apply it. Get in, shampoo up first and then put it on. The steam from the shower will be like giving you your own facial at home."

As soon as the gritty material was slathered over my face and neck, Allie promptly removed it, running a washcloth over the applied areas until my face was bare again. "I'm going to turn on the light again and just do a couple of quick extractions here for you."

"Uh, Allie? What exactly is an extraction?" I finally worked up the nerve to ask. Could I get some anesthesia or a Vicodin first?

"It's pretty simple. I'm just going to remove your whiteheads. I don't see any blackheads on your skin, which is great. It might be a little uncomfortable. I'm just going underneath the skin to bring everything up. It's a safer way than just popping pimples, which can cause irritation and lead to scarring."

Well, I felt like a fool. Good thing I hadn't asked for the Vicodin. The extractions didn't hurt too bad, just a mild discomfort like Allie had said. "Is training going good?" she asked, while squeezing a particularly sensitive spot on my chin.

"Oh, yeah, it's been great. I've almost got the menu down, and I think I caught on to the computer system pretty fast. I'm going to sit in with Kevin on a conference call on Thursday with other franchise owners, which should be pretty educational. Hopefully I can think of a few things to contribute so I don't just sit there in silence like a dope."

"I'm sure you'll do just fine. And Kevin will help you out. He's a man of a few words, but he cares about all of his employees. And the business. He loves to succeed."

"How long have you worked here?"

"Since they opened last year. I actually worked on the other side of town at a salon there, but Dani and Kevin made me an offer I couldn't refuse. And I love it here. My fiancé and I moved over to this part of town about eight months ago, and we just love it. More convenient for both of us, plus it's just a nicer area. It would be a good place to start a family."

"I didn't know you were engaged. Congratulations! When's the wedding?"

"Thanks, hon. I don't wear my ring a lot because I don't want to get product on it. But the wedding is going to be next summer, June 21st." I heard Allie fiddling with more bottles, then wheeling the chair back over to the bed. "I'm going to put the first mask on you now. It's a calming mask, and the second will be a hydrating mask to help get some moisture on your face."

"Okay." I felt the paintbrush running over my skin again, tickling me when she ran it under my nose.

"Did you work somewhere else before coming here?"

"Actually, I still technically work for Tastie's. Friday is my last shift there."

"Tastie's? I didn't really peg you as a Tastie's girl."

"Well, it was really just to earn some extra money while in school. And my best friend and roommate Lila also works there, so we did a lot of shifts together. Honestly, it really isn't that bad. Frank, the owner, is a really nice guy and the hours are pretty flexible. And the uniforms aren't as bad as what the Hooters girls have to wear."

Allie finished putting the mask on me, then started to massage my neck and shoulders. It felt amazing. All the stress and pressure that I didn't even know had built up started to melt under her fingertips. I closed my eyes and enjoyed the relaxation, but my thoughts wandered to Frank and Tastie's. Frank's reaction to my new career opportunity had puzzled me.

"Where is the job at?" I told Frank that I had gotten a manager position at Blissful Salon and Spa a week and a half ago, to inform him that I was officially putting my two weeks' in and hanging up my lacy black bra.

"It's in Witte, on Mayfair Lane," I had answered, taking a sip of my lemonade. I was sitting in Frank's office, which was messy with menus, design concepts, schedules, résumés and more. Frank liked to have his hands in every pot, and oversaw anything that went down at his restaurant.

"Who's the owner?"

His question caught me off guard, but I answered. "Kevin and Dani Dohlman. They're a husband and wife team."

Frank had sat back in his chair, one hand under his chin. "The Dohlmans, huh. You're going to work for the Dohlmans."

I hadn't known how to respond to that. Frank didn't seem happy about my new position. He looked concerned, mad, maybe a little confused. "Um, yes? I mean, yes, I am. At Blissful Salon and Spa. Have you been there? Do you know them?"

"I know the Dohlmans, Alex. I know them. I don't want to fill your pretty head with bad stories before you go, though. I can see what an opportunity this is for you. But, well, the Dohlmans might not be all you've cracked them up to be."

"What do you mean by that?" Kevin and Dani were successful entrepreneurs and business owners and wealthy and nice and welcoming. What could possibly be wrong with them?

"I've worked with Kevin before on a few deals and projects. Got burned one too many times. The man only cares about his money. Doesn't care about his employees, his partners, or his customers—though he'll try to tell you he does. He wants money and he wants it fast. You know, I really shouldn't even be saying anything." Frank halted his story, but I was salivating for more.

"No, you can tell me, Frank. I would appreciate knowing what I'm getting into. I did some research online about them but didn't really find out a whole lot."

After a bit more cajoling, Frank finally let it spill. He talked about bad business deals, disappearing money, multiple lawsuits involving Kevin, and many cases of sexual harassment brought on from Kevin's female employees. He discussed Kevin's background in nude modeling and the multiple affairs Kevin had since he married Dani, including one with Franks second wife—now ex.

I left Tastie's that day feeling a little sick to my stomach. I was overwhelmed with knowledge on my new bosses, and none of it was positive. Could Frank's stories be true? He made Kevin out to be scum, someone who only cares about dollar bills, women, and getting ahead no matter who he hurt. I remembered the odd feeling I had gotten when I first met Kevin, the intimate hug he gave me after offering me the job, Dani's frozen smile.

"Can I ask you a question, Allie?" I asked, as she wrapped up my massage and began removing the face mask.

"Anything, hon."

"Do you like working for Kevin and Dani? I mean, how are they as bosses?"

Allie paused, the washcloth hovering over my cheeks for just a moment before she resumed wiping the goop away. "They're great! Dani is the biggest sweetheart around. I just love her. A big heart, a great mom, and she's so focused all the time. And Kevin, he's not around as much as Dani, but we all still really like him. He's good to the employees, he's generous, and I think he's a pretty good boss. Why do you ask?"

"I was just wondering. I've never worked at a place where I'm so close to the owners, working side by side with them almost daily. It will be a new experience, that's for sure. So I just wanted to get some scoop, that's all," I lied. I wanted to see if Allie would offer up any details to back up Frank's allegations against Kevin.

"I think you'll like it. Dani seemed to take a liking to you right away. Kevin can be a bit overbearing at times, but you just need to stand up to him."

"What do you mean?" Like sexual harassment? Asking me to steal money from the cash drawer so he can pay strippers?

"Sometimes he thinks of his employees like personal assistants. When I first started, he was asking me to fetch his coffee, run to the store to pick up his orders, things like that. I finally put my foot down and said I am an esthetician, not his slave, and he stopped asking."

"Okay." I grew quiet as she slathered the second mask on my face, thinking about what she said. She didn't make Kevin out to be a bad guy at all. Maybe Frank had a different view on him because of some business deals gone wrong between the two of them. I started to relax, relieved that my worry was for nothing. And because Allie had started to massage my feet.

"Yeah, Kevin really isn't one to worry about. I think he's a great boss. Like I said—I think Dani is a big sweetheart. Most of the time. Sometimes she can be just as overbearing as Kevin though."

"Really? Like how?" I was surprised. I thought Dani was very real and down to earth. Kevin definitely gave me the overbearing vibes; Dani not so much.

"I shouldn't even say anything. It's our boss, you know? I don't want to seem catty right out of the gate."

"You can tell me, Allie. It's not like I'm going to run to her and start blabbing. I'm just curious about who I'm working for is all." I really did want to know Allie's opinion, even though she did come off just a bit snarky with her Kamille comments and now clearly wanting to dish on Dani. But this was a salon. Isn't that what always happened?

"I'd just say to watch out for her. She's someone who doesn't mind putting a knife in your back if it means she can get ahead. She puts herself on the top pedestal, and no one can come close to her."

I got quiet, thinking that over. Why would Dani stab someone in the back to get ahead? How much farther ahead could she possibly want to get? Was Allie serious that Dani would do something to one of her employees to make her look better? From what I knew of Dani so far, that just didn't fit. I stayed silent the rest of the facial, trying to make sense of what I had just learned. Could it be true?

I was feeling a little defeated, wondering if this position was really right for me. I didn't want to be around overbearing bosses who would take advantage of me or stab me in the back for their own selfish reasons.

"I'm sure you'll be just fine, Alex. I'll help take care of you, and the other girls are great too. Dani can be a sweetheart, and Kevin isn't around too much. Sometimes in a small salon the personal stuff can just get a little too personal, but you have to try to push it aside and focus on your responsibilities instead. Now, let me get this mask off you, and you'll almost be done. How was your first facial?"

"Um, it was great. I really enjoyed it. Thanks, Allie." Though I enjoyed the gossip more. Finding out why Kamille wasn't uber-friendly to me and the dish on Kevin made for a successful fifty-minute facial. I just wasn't sure how I felt about Dani now. Allie spritzed some toner around my face and declared me complete.

"I'll let you get changed and meet you up at the salon to retouch your make-up. I'm glad to have you on board, Alex. I think you'll make a great manager."

I put my clothes back on with a smile on my face. I knew my friends were supporting me, my sister was thrilled with my new position, and I had a friendship forming with Allie. If I had any troubles with Kevin, I knew I could go to her for advice. Now, I just needed to find a way to get Kamille off my case for losing out on the job, figure out how to sound smart and manager-like in the upcoming conference call, and get my homework done for Monday. And while I was making my to-do list, I thought of another one I could add: *stop thinking about Henry.*

After Allie reapplied my make-up (making me look better than the original make-up application I gave myself that morning) I headed into the office to study the menu and play around with the back office options on the computer. Dani had set me up with my own codes so I could get into the system, where I could pull up detailed tracking reports, find the order forms for products we needed, and even check out the numbers of competing Blissful salons.

I became engrossed in my work, jotting down notes for myself and marking down questions that I needed answered in my notebook. I kept flipping from the back office to the regular salon schedule, keeping an eye on how the appointments were moving and if my help was needed at all. Tuesdays were a slower day and I was pretty sure Tiffany, the front desk worker that night, could handle things. She was in her twenties, just a few years older than me, and liked to stay busy up front. Whenever there weren't customers, she could be found cleaning the area. She had admitted to me before that she was a little OCD about cleaning. I didn't have any problem with that.

I stayed in the back almost the entire night, but kept a close on the schedule. At busier times, right around six and then again at seven, I came out to help Tiffany at the front desk. Other than that I stayed in the office, fiddling with the back office controls, studying the menu that I almost knew by heart now, and re-reading parts of my employee handbook. At about 7:30 the office door opened, and I was surprised to see Dani enter.

"Hi!" I said, sitting up straighter in my chair and smoothing my hair back.

"Hi, honey," she said. "I just thought I would pop in and see how things are going tonight."

"Really well. It's not been super busy, but the stylists have been good with sales tonight. Everyone on the floor sold at least one product. Allie's sold three."

"Wonderful. Tuesdays are probably the slowest appointment day, so the more product we can sell, the better."

I made a note of that in my notebook. Maybe we should start a special, something that occurred only on Tuesdays during the week. Twenty percent off maybe? Help move the products off the shelf. I would have to think about it.

"Tiffany's been doing good out front, and I've been back here getting some studying in. I logged into the back office like you showed me and I've been playing around with the different features. It's pretty awesome what all you can see."

"It is. And that's something you can log on from home, too. You don't need to be on a Blissful computer for it. So that's nice for me and Kevin, we can easily pull up the schedule or numbers at home without having to call or stop in all the time."

"Oh, that's awesome! I'll definitely be checking things out at home." It would be nice to stay up to date on how the salon was running on my days off.

"Terrific. Hey, have you eaten dinner yet? I was going to see if you and Allie wanted to grab a bite after we closed up. Maybe just head down the street to Boomer's?"

I thought of all the homework that was waiting for me at home: studying for a test, finishing an accounting spreadsheet, and trying to decipher the difference between two songs that were written about fifty years ago. I knew I should have declined Dani's offer, but I really wanted to go out with her. I had felt us bonding over the past couple weeks and I really liked her. She was down to earth, fun to be around, and super nice. I hadn't gotten any of the vibes that Allie had warned me about. And Dani always seemed so nice around Allie and seemed to enjoy her company. I couldn't figure out Allie quite yet, but I hoped maybe she was just having an off-day when she gave me my facial. "Sure!" I heard myself say. "It shouldn't take too long to get everything cleaned up, so we should get out right around eight."

"And with Tiffany up front, you won't have to worry about cleaning the desk area," Dani said, making us both laugh. True enough, Tiffany had the front office area sparkling when I walked up there. Only Allie and one other stylist, Katie, were still working, and I let Katie go after her area was cleaned. I also let Tiffany head home, and quickly counted the money drawer and filed all the receipts. After double-checking that everything was set to run in the morning, we locked up and the three of us headed outside.

"Do you girls want to drive yourselves or pile in with me?" Dani asked, stopping beside Kevin's BMW.

"I'll just drive myself. I can't stay out too late, I have a bunch of homework still to get to tonight," I said, pulling my keys from my purse.

"Okay. Meet you down there then!" Dani gave a wave and piled into the tiny car. Allie and I walked together across the parking lot to the back spaces, where we parked to try to keep the closer spots open for the customers.

Luckily Boomer's wasn't busy, and we got a table in the dining area and put our orders in right away. I was grateful that Dani also ordered an appetizer of mozzarella sticks, because I was famished. I had to start remembering to bring more sufficient lunches than just a bologna sandwich or salad. I was even more grateful when they were delivered the sticks to our table within minutes.

"So, Alex, how do you like your new job so far? It's been about what, two weeks? How are things going?" Dani opened up the conversation with the focus on me.

"I think it's going really well! It actually doesn't feel like a job to me. I'm having fun with everything, I'm learning a lot, and I think I understand everything that is expected of me. I was telling my roommate just the other day how excited I was to come in to work. I think she thought I was crazy."

Dani and Allie laughed, and Dani said, "That's terrific. That's just what I want to hear from my manager. If you find something you really love doing, it won't feel like work because you enjoy it. I can see you thriving at Blissful, I really can. You've picked up quickly on everything. You've even surprised Kevin! He couldn't believe how fast you took to the system. It usually takes a new employee a lot longer to get it all down."

"I practice a lot in the office. I think that has really helped," I said. I grabbed my second hot mozzarella stick and blew on it. "Though I am a bit worried about payroll."

"I'll help you with that. Seriously, with the notes I have, it will be a breeze. It's just time-consuming, that's all," Allie said, giving my shoulder a reassuring pat. "Kind of like the schedules. It's easy, just a big ole puzzle that you have to figure out."

We continued to talk about Blissful until our food arrived. It got silent as we all dug in, me enjoying my loaded cheeseburger with abandon.

"Well, let's quit talking business!" Dani exclaimed at one point. "Alex, how is your school going? Are you able to balance your workload and school okay?"

Um, no. "Yes! It hasn't been too bad, really. I try to get most of my work done on Mondays for the week if I can." I should really start trying to do that. "And then at nights I can usually finish everything."

"Glad to hear. Do you have a boyfriend?"

"Oh, no." Thoughts of Henry Landon swished in my head. "Totally single right now."

"Nothing wrong with that. Men are trouble. Right, Allie?" Dani laughed and looked at Allie, who gave a chuckle and bit into her chicken sandwich, nodding her head.

I gave a laugh as well, though I was unsure what to say. Yeah, men do suck?

"My husband can be such a handful sometimes," Dani continued, ignoring her tuna salad sandwich. "Last Friday, he didn't come home until almost four in the morning! A friend of his just opened up a new bar, Sipps, and Kevin's been helping out there."

"I've heard of that place. My friend's are planning to check it out sometime. I won't turn twenty-one until January, though, so I have a while to wait."

"Oh, if your friends are ever going to stop by, just let Kevin know. He'll make sure you get in, and he can get your girls free bottle service, too," Dani said with a flick of the wrist.

My eyes widened. The girls would be seriously impressed if I could get us free bottle service at the newest bar in town. "Really? I don't want to inconvenience him or anything. . . ."

"Oh, he'll love it. Trust me. He enjoys doing that kind of thing for friends. He's very giving."

"Could I get another water, please?" Allie flagged down our passing waiter, who nodded his head and scurried towards the kitchen.

"Well, that is very generous of him. I'll be sure to let my friends know so we can plan that sometime. Thanks." I knew I would never ask Kevin to do any such thing for me. Asking my boss for bottle service just wasn't something I was comfortable with.

Dani smiled at me, then picked up her sandwich and took a bite. I concentrated once again on my own food, not surprised when I finished the entire burger. The three of us chatted for a bit more about Blissful, Allie's wedding plans, and how Dani was hiring a new landscaper for her lawn. I was shocked when I looked at my watch and saw that it was already a quarter to ten. My homework!

"Well, I think I should probably get going. Still have some studying to do," I said, pulling my wallet out of my purse.

"Oh, dinner's on me," Dani said, reaching into her purse as well. "You get going then, Alex. I'll take care of the bill and we'll just see you tomorrow. Are you in at two?"

"I am. But I can't let you take care of my bill. Please, let me," I protested.

"I won't hear of it. I'm happy to do it. Thank you for your company tonight. Both of you." She smiled at Allie, who was also getting up from the booth. "You girls get home. I'll see you both tomorrow."

"Well, that was nice of her," I commented as Allie and I walked out together, stopping to grab a mint at the hostess stand.

"Oh, get used to it. Kevin and Dani will pay for all your meals. I haven't paid for my own meal since I've started," Allie said.

"Really? Wow. That's sure nice of them."

"Yep. It's a nice perk to enjoy. So you can save your breath trying to protest each time. They'll never accept money from you."

We reached our cars, and I hit the unlock button on my key fob. "Wow. Okay, then. Thanks for the heads-up."

"Anytime. Drive safe, okay? I'll see you tomorrow."

"See you tomorrow!" I hopped in my Camry and let the engine run for a minute before putting it in drive. I fished a pair of mittens out of my purse and slipped them on—the steering wheel was freezing. As I drove towards campus, I reflected back on dinner. I had a great time and was happy that I got along with Dani so well. All the doubts I had about her from talking with Allie had evaporated. Sometimes I forgot that she was only eight years older than me. We had a smaller age gap than me and Alicia. It was strange to think that she was already married, had three kids, a thriving business and a successful husband. I decided that night that I was going to do my best to be just like Dani Dohlman.

CHAPTER 8

"There she is!" That was the greeting I came into on Thursday night, close to 9:30. I had a full day of classes, then whisked myself over to Blissful for a busy day at work that included a conference call with Kevin and a quick lesson on how to close down the cash drawer each night. I was scheduled to get off at eight—which was closing time—but with all the closing duties, it was impossible to get out right on time. Not only did I have to make sure the cash drawer balanced, I also had to make sure that the credit card receipts were filed away, all treatment rooms were cleaned and ready for the next day, all the windows were washed, floors vacuumed, salon floor swept, no appliances left plugged in, and the computers were shut down. Then I also had to prepare for the following morning, which meant pulling client folders, making sure enough towels were stocked in the closet, and any and all scheduling conflicts were dealt with. On top of being on my feet all day, dealing with clients, staff, learning the scheduling ropes, conference calls. . .I was exhausted. And I needed to get homework done for Bater's accounting. And sleep. I craved sleep.

"Alex, you are going to flip. Just die. Crack a smile would you. What's wrong? Want a marg?" Carmen held out her drink to me, but I just shook my head and threw myself on the couch next to Lila, snuggling against my roommate and closing my weary eyes.

"Hi, everyone. I'm just tired, sorry. What's up? Why am I going to flip?" I suddenly shot up straight, looking at Lila. "You're pregnant, aren't you?"

"What? Are you joking me? Why would you think I was pregnant out of all of us?" Lila pouted. "I would put my bets on Emma."

"Why me?" Emma shouted, but not looking the least bit offended.

"Don't make me pull a Fergie and spell promiscuous," Lila responded.

We all laughed, but I still didn't know what the big news was. "Well, if no one is pregnant, what's the deal? What have I missed?"

Hannah finally joined the conversation, her blue eyes sparkling. "Someone has a crush on you!" she said in a singsong voice.

"What? Me? Who?"

"Henry!" My four friends all shouted at me, practically causing my hair to fly back.

"Henry? He so does not have a crush on me. I almost threw up on the guy. Something tells me that doesn't exactly equal crush."

"But you didn't throw up on him. That's the important part, Alex. You simply showed him you like to have a good time, like your drinks, and can pass out like a good girl at the end of the night. He never even knows you vomited, like, seven times. Or that you had to clean Hannie's car for her because your puke was all over it. He doesn't know any of those things!" Carmen was trying to help me look on the bright side.

"How does anyone know he has a crush on me? And why do we have to keep saying crush? We sound like we're in high school again," I said, trying to figure out if the rumor was true. Could he really be interested in me?

"Well, Peter and I went out to eat tonight." Hannah's story was interrupted by a series of hoots and hollers from all of us. "Girls, really? You did that the first time I told this story."

"I know, but it's just so exciting! My matchmaking skills are genius. I'm already picking the wedding colors, and I think I look fabulous in purple," Lila said, blowing on her nails and rubbing them against her jeans.

"Let's just calm down a bit. Anyway, as I was saying, Peter took me out for dinner tonight and we of course started talking about the Halloween party. Which led him to ask me if you had a boyfriend, because his friend Henry is into you!"

"That's frickin' awesome! Amazing! I can't believe it, really. I thought I made such a fool of myself," I said, flashbacks from the night coming back to me. The beer, the shots. The games of pool we played and how I had hugged him on a whim. Then me falling to the kitchen floor and passing out. I shook my head to get rid of those later-in-the-night thoughts. "Well, what all did he say? And excuse me for being so rude. How was your date? Tell me about that first!"

Hannah launched into her story, saying how Peter took her out to dinner at Bon Sejour, a fancy schmancy French restaurant in the heart of Witte, where reservations were hard to come by. Turned out Peter was pretty well off, his dad being a successful investment banker who started his company in Truvista, then moved all his accounts to the booming Des Moines area, and now owned and operated his company in the booming Witte area. Hannah said she and Peter hit it off immediately at the party, at ease with one another right after meeting. Their date sounded horribly romantic, one that exceeded any date expectation I had ever conjured up, and made me just a touch jealous. But I was happy for Hannah, how could I not be? She was one of my best friends; she deserved all the attention and affection that came her way.

"I have a good vibe about this Peter. I do, Hannah. I knew it right when I met him that he was the guy for you," Lila said, the jealousy easy to spot on her face too. Not that any of us would begrudge Hannah. Carmen, Emma, and I were all single, and Lila's relationship with Joel had been constantly strained. We all wanted our fairy-tale ending. Nothing wrong with that.

"I'm not going to get too far ahead of myself. He's a year older than me, getting ready to graduate soon. And then there's the whole he's going to move away to continue on to get his DDS, so we would be living in different cities. And this is all brand new. I'm not about to rush anything," the ever-practical Hannah said.

"Yeah, but you'll be going to U of I as well just a year after him. That's really not that long when it comes to true love," Lila said, her eyes sparkling. I just knew she was giving herself major props for setting Hannah up.

"You guys will have the smartest babies ever," Emma chimed in.

"Oh, please. And hey—this story started with me telling Alex about her possible Mr. Right, not mine."

"Ooh, yeah, can we get back to me now. Can we, can we?" I pleaded, ready to break out in hives if Hannah didn't tell me what Henry was saying about me soon. I did the good friend thing, I let her have her moment. My turn.

"Well, it was when we were talking about the Halloween party. Peter just came out and asked if you had a boyfriend. I told him no, obviously, and he said that Henry couldn't stop talking about you the rest of that night. And get this—another girl at the party there tried to hit on Henry, and he totally ignored her! She even tried to 'pass out' in his bed," Hannah made quotes with her hands, "and Henry left her there and went and slept on the couch. Can you believe that?"

"All because he was interested in Alex? Who very well could have had a boyfriend, because he didn't know for sure yet. Wow. That's kinda hot," Emma said.

"That's fucking way hot! Are you kidding me? What guy pushes away a willing girl—who was probably dressed all slutty thanks to Halloween—for someone he barely knows? Why the hell did you girls get so lucky at the party?" Carmen asked, pretending to pout.

"Hey, I saw you talking to Max most of the night," Lila pointed out, causing the rest of us to nod and murmur in agreement.

Carmen brushed her hand through the air like she was swatting away a fly. "That was nothing. I am definitely not interested in skinny little Max. He was just fun to talk to, that's all. Trust me, nothing romantic or sexual there."

"Anyway, getting back to Alex once again," Hannah broke in. "Henry asked Peter to ask me to ask you if I could give Peter your phone number to give to Henry."

I somehow managed to get the gist that Henry was asking for my number and squealed in pure schoolgirl excitement. "Yes! Of course! Holy crap, this is insane! I thought I totally blew it after the passing out and falling off the chair episode in the kitchen. I can't believe he really wants my number!"

"Well, believe it, girl. I'm going to text Peter right now." Hannah punched in a few buttons on her phone, and the five of us sat in silence for a few minutes.

"Do you think he's going to call now?" Emma whispered, causing the rest of us to giggle.

"Do you have your phone on you?" Lila asked.

"Ah, no, it's in my purse. Oh, no. Where'd I put my purse?" I jumped up and scrambled to the kitchen table, finding it empty, then flew into my room where my pink bag sat on my bed. I quickly dug out my phone, right when it started to vibrate and light up with an incoming phone call from a number I didn't recognize.

I ran back into the living room shrieking at the top of my lungs. "I think this is him! I think this is him!"

My friends started shrieking right back.

"Answer it!"

"Hurry!"

"He didn't even wait five minutes!"

"This is so exciting!"

"Hello?" I answered, waving my arm to shush the hyenas, who were now all laughing at our outburst.

"Hi, could I speak to Alex?" Henry's deep voice came through the line, sending chills along my spine.

"This is," I spoke confidently, careful to make sure my voice didn't stutter. Never let a man know they intimidate you—a rule I learned from Emma.

"Hi, Alex. This is Henry Landon. From the Halloween party."

"Hi, Henry! How are you doing?" I spoke with a bit too much enthusiasm before I could catch myself. Never let a man know how excited you are that he called, because he should be calling. More Emma wisdom.

"Oh, doing okay. Still trying to put our house back together after last weekend," he chuckled, and I imagined his blue eyes sparkling as he laughed.

I shook my head, trying to get a grip on myself. I didn't think I'd ever been bitten by the love bug quite this bad. And so soon. "Oh no! That has to be awful."

"I guess that's the price we pay for hosting. We don't have to worry about drinking and driving, but our house is a mess for at least a week after."

"I bet it reeks too. I can't imagine how much beer and booze got spilled everywhere."

"You got that right. I stashed a bottle of cologne in my car because I'm afraid if I ever get pulled over, the officer will think I'm drunk because the brewery smell has seeped into my clothes."

We both laughed and the girls all smiled at me, even though they had no idea what we were discussing.

"Anyway, I wanted to ask if you had any plans for this weekend. I know it's really short notice but I was planning on going back home, but those plans fell through and now I'm here all weekend. I was just going to see if maybe you wanted to, like, grab dinner or something on Friday or Saturday night. If you want to, that is," he rushed to say, suddenly sounding awkward.

"I do! Yes, I do actually," I blurted out before I could say something coy like "let me check my schedule first." I wanted to go on a date with Henry and I obviously couldn't hide it.

"Hey, awesome! Which night works better for you? I know just the restaurant to go to, but I need to call and make reservations. Hopefully we can still get in. I know they're pretty busy on weekends."

"Well, I work both Friday and Saturday this week, but I'm off at seven tomorrow and six on Saturday. So that will give me enough time on either day to get home and get, er, ready." I wasn't sure what the rule was on telling a guy all the work you needed to put into getting ready for the perfect first date. "Maybe let's make it Saturday." That extra hour could come in handy.

"Saturday it is. I'll pick you up around 7:30. Would that be okay?"

"That would perfect." Oh, God, by the time I got home from Blissful it would be approaching seven already. I hoped all the girls could help me out, because I was going to need it.

Henry and I finalized our plans and I gave him my room number at Wacker, and then he was off. And I was in a daze that I had a date with Henry Landon in two very short days.

"We're going out on Saturday!" I screamed as soon as I hung up the phone, prompting immediate cheers and hugs from the girls.

"Wait a second. Saturday? What's with the super short notice?" Carmen asked.

"He said he was supposed to go back to his hometown this weekend but his plans fell through."

"Oh. I guess that's okay then. Yay, a date for Alex!" And the screaming began again until we were all out of breath laughing.

"You guys have to help me though. Are you all around on Saturday? I'm only going to have, like, forty-five minutes tops to get ready once I get home from work. And he didn't say where we were going, only that he hoped he could still get reservations. Do I go fancy? A dress? Chic casual? Who's going to do my hair? Thank God I just got a facial!" I was officially freaking out. Only forty-eight hours stood between me and my date, and I did not feel prepared.

"Al, don't worry," Lila said. "We all helped Hannah for her date, and we will all help you for yours. I did have plans with Joel, but I'll just cancel. It's okay," she broke in as I started to protest, "it's really okay. I'm not sure how much longer I can take this whole smothering act he's got going on. This will be a relief, really. You're doing me a favor. And who else can give you big sexy hair like I can?"

"We'll all be here to help, don't you worry your pretty little face off," Carmen said, standing and stretching her arms over her head. "But this chica needs to head off to bed. Got a big day tomorrow."

"Oh? A big test or something?" Hannah questioned.

"Test? No, no, love. It's the pancakes and beer breakfast down at Wiley's. Em's coming with me."

Emma stood as well. "It's true. While I will be stuffing myself full of yummy pancakes, I'm skipping the beer part this year. Got my 8:30 class to make it to, and I'm sure Professor Tallyman won't appreciate my beer breath."

"Well, you girls have a blast with that. I work until seven tomorrow at Blissful, but maybe we can all hang out after? Anyone know of anything going on?" I asked.

"Joel's friends are having a party at their house on Second Street. I told him I would go but. . .I don't know. If we can't find anything else to do, we could go over there," Lila volunteered, looking less than ecstatic about hanging out with her boyfriend.

After the girls left and it was just me and Lila getting ready for bed, I brought up her problems with Joel. "What's going on, Lils? You seem completely turned off by all things Joel right now. Did something happen between you two?"

Lila sighed, carefully plucking out her contact lenses and soaking them in solution. "Things have gotten, well, tense between us lately."

I slathered my nightly moisturizer over my face and neck, even adding some to my décolleté like Allie had instructed me to. "Why? What's going on?"

"Well, you know how I had those photos taken of me, right?"

"Right. For your portfolio."

"Right. The guy who took them was extremely nice, and he knows Mary Strubaker personally."

"Who is Mary Strubaker?"

"Alex! She heads IMAA—Iowa's Models and Actors Association. She's helped people like Carter Boss and Savannah Howe make it in Hollywood," Lila scolded me, naming two of the most popular actors currently gracing the big screen.

"My bad. So okay, he knows Mary. What does that have to do with you?"

Lila and I headed out of the bathroom and I followed her into the kitchen. She retrieved a big blue bowl out from the cabinet, swiftly dumping microwave popcorn in and popping the bowl in the microwave. I opened the fridge and settled on a pink PowerAde, reluctantly remembering my accounting homework. Damn. I would have to wake up early now to get it finished.

"Well, Mary runs these casting calls that are very limited throughout the whole Midwest. You have to have an invite from her, one of her employees, or a close confidante to even be considered by her. If you ace your casting call, she signs you to her agency, gets you jobs around here *and,*" Lila paused for dramatic effect, the popcorn kernels popping in the background, "gives you all the training you need to make it in places like New York and LA."

"So your photographer guy is going to introduce you to Mary?" I ventured a guess, actually a little impressed and thrilled for my friend.

"Yes! Alan—that's the photographer—got me an invite to her next casting call, which is in late November. If I can ace it and get signed, it would be huge for me! I could book real jobs around the area, gain experience and build up a portfolio. Mary also brings in teachers and other real actors and models to help give us more knowledge. Can you imagine if Carter Boss was giving me lessons on how to do a love scene in a movie? It would be magical! We could be the next Hollywood 'it' couple!"

"Excuse my ignorance," I said as Lila pulled her popcorn from the microwave, "but do you want to be a model or actor now? I thought you just wanted to be an entertainment reporter?"

"Well, yeah, but I can't just stroll up to the building in LA and think anyone is going to look at me. I have to have a presence first. And Victoria started off as a model."

"Who's Victoria?"

"The main anchor on Buzzworthy!" Lila was clearly exasperated with me.

"The one with big fake boobs that you are suddenly rivalling?"

"Yes, that's her. And I haven't even scheduled a consultation yet. I just don't know for sure if I would do the surgery."

"You've thought about a consultation?" I yelped, nearly spitting out my drink. "Have you researched doctors? What if you get a quack with a fake diploma who makes your body look like that chick off that '90s sitcom?"

Lila shook her head at me. "You are pathetic when it comes to celebrity knowledge. Sometimes I wonder how our friendship has survived."

She wandered out of the kitchen still clutching the popcorn bowl, and after a beat of silence, I ran after her. "Lila Medlin! Do not ignore me! Are you truly thinking of going through with the surgery?"

"Alex, calm down. I haven't decided yet. I started making a list of doctors. Haven't contacted them yet, don't even know the prices yet. This is like preliminary prelimits. . .or something along those lines. So just hush. Let's finish this episode and then crash."

I silently took a seat next to Lila on the couch, dipping my fingers into the popcorn bowl. We watched the rest of Buzzworthy—where I paid close attention to Victoria and her assets—said our good-nights and went into our separate bedrooms. I was still excited about my big date with Henry, worried about how to pull it off due to my time constraints, and now terrified that my best friend was going to go under the knife. With all my fears crowding my mind, I thought for sure I would toss and turn for hours, but exhaustion from my hectic schedule won out and I was asleep in minutes.

CHAPTER 9

"Thank you for calling Blissful Salon and Spa. This is Alex, how may I help you?"

It was only ten in the morning on Saturday—the Saturday of the big date night—but I was already at Blissful. I agreed to come in early for training with Allie, this time about payroll. We didn't open for another two hours, but I decided to answer the phone when it started ringing at five after ten. Might as well get as much practice now as I could.

"Alex? Hi, it's Dani. How are you doing?"

"Oh, hi, Dani! I'm doing fine, just waiting for Allie to get here and start learning the payroll process." I paused, a little confused as to why she was calling the salon so early in the morning.

"Great. It's actually a pretty simple process. You shouldn't have a hard time picking it up. Anyway, I wanted to ask—is Kevin there?"

My brow wrinkled. Why the heck would Kevin be at Blissful before it opened? "Um, no. I don't think so. I'm pretty sure I'm alone here. And I didn't see his vehicle." There was no way I could have missed either of the cars Kevin drove—a Porche and a BMW—sitting in the parking lot.

"Have you been in the office yet? Maybe if you could just pop your head in quick and see if he's there?" Dani's voice was starting to become strained.

"Okay, hold on just a sec. I'll be right back." I set the receiver down on the desk and hustled to the office in the back. I knew Kevin wasn't there, but was afraid I would make Dani upset with the news. But why couldn't she find her husband?

After confirming the office was indeed empty, I trotted back to the front, just in time to see Allie walk through the door. I waved to her, then scooped the phone back up. "Dani? He's not here. I checked the whole back area too. He's not there, either."

Allie's eyes flickered over to me, and she cocked her head while listening to my conversation.

"He didn't come home last night? Do you think he's okay? Have you checked the hospitals?"

Dani sighed. "No. I'm sure he's fine. He went out with some friends last night; he probably just crashed at one of their places so he didn't have to drink and drive. He'll show up today, he always does. Well," Dani's voice suddenly brightened, "I hope you have a great day there. We'll try to stop in this afternoon and see how everything is going."

"Oh, okay then. Please call if you need me for anything else, if I can help in any other way," I stuttered, baffled by the conversation I was having with my boss. "I hope everything is okay."

We hung up, and I turned to face Allie.

"Good morning, sunshine!" she exclaimed, thrusting a waxy white bag at me. "I brought us bagels."

"Yum, thank you! I just had a slice of toast for breakfast this morning. Mmm, these are still warm." I eagerly grabbed a chocolate chip bagel and bit into it, feeling the warm chips melt on my tongue. Bliss. I laughed inwardly at my own play on words.

"What was that phone call all about?" Allie asked, opening a packet of cream cheese.

"I don't know; it was so strange. Dani was asking if Kevin was here, then she said that he went out with his friends last night and never came home. Is that. . .normal for around here?" I suddenly flashed back to my facial, when Allie told me that Dani has called looking for her husband at the salon from time to time. And that sometimes Kevin slept on the beds at Blissful instead of going home.

Allie sat on the stool behind the desk, playing with her short black ponytail. "Well, unfortunately, that answer is yes. I'm surprised Dani is starting in with you already. She should have just called my cell phone."

Goosebumps sprinkled my arms. What did that mean? Was Big Frank right about Kevin? "What do you mean?"

"Well, sometimes things can get a bit tense around here with Dani and Kevin. And of course there are rumors always floating around, but I try not to get involved with that."

I was practically salivating, and not from my bagel. "Allie, I'm begging you, please tell me what's going on. I can't be the manager here without being informed."

"I'll tell you what I know, but you have to promise me that you won't freak out. Or quit."

"Okay, now you're scaring me. Just tell me!"

After I begged and pinky-swore I wouldn't just up and quit, Allie launched into story after story regarding Kevin and Dani. I thought I had gotten some juicy bits from her the day of my facial, but this—this was so much more.

Allie told me how Kevin had met Dani—who was sixteen years younger than him—on one of his magazine photo shoots about nine years ago. Dani was modeling topless, Kevin walked in and saw her, and apparently it was like love at first sight. Except for the tiny detail that Kevin was already married. In fact, the ink was barely dry on his marriage certificate when he started his affair with Dani. He was married for two months and two days before filing for divorce, and the day after it was approved by the courts, he whisked twenty year old Dani off to Mexico and they were married. Nine months later, Brianna was born.

"Two months and two days? Come on, Allie. You have to be exaggerating," I said, wide-eyed at the story. We made it to the back office, and were waiting for the computer system to get pulled up before we started the payroll training.

"Cross my heart, hon. The poor first wife who married him didn't stand a chance."

Allie's story continued. Kevin was a well-known playboy, who was thought to be settled down after he married Dani and she gave birth to his first daughter. While he was able to keep it his pants for some time, his old ways eventually got the best of him.

"Dani has to know about his affairs. He's really not that secretive about them. He tells us girls here all the time about sleeping with the strippers in Vegas and Dani's always calling around looking for him. I think unless she sees it with her own eyes she'll keep denying it."

"But why? How can she let him get away with that?"

Allie tapped her ring finger, where her engagement ring sat glowing. "It's all about the money honey. You've seen what Kevin drives. You've seen the five-carat rock on Dani's hand. You can't tell me you haven't seen Dani's humongous fake boobs. I've been to their house—their mansion, rather. Dani wears designer brands. Would you give that lifestyle up?"

Would I? We both fell silent for a minute, while Allie hit a few keys and different spreadsheets started popping up on the screen. Although she had already moved on from the topic of conversation, I couldn't get her question out of my head. Would I give up that lifestyle? I thought only celebrities like that basketball player's wife stayed with their man even after their affairs became headline news. Kevin lived in Iowa, ran a few small businesses. Was that level of financial security enough to make someone like Dani stay with him? Could I even marry for love, or were people only looking for a way to succeed? And how could I have looked up to Dani, considered her someone I wanted to be like? The confusion I felt was making me more and more uncomfortable.

"Allie?"

"Yeah, hon?"

"Why are you getting married?"

Allie looked at me, her deep blue eyes open in alarm. "What? Why are you asking that?" She sounded like I was trying to accuse her of something. I quickly backtracked.

"No, no! Sorry if that sounded rude or like I was accusing you for something. I guess, well, I haven't really ever thought about marriage a whole lot yet, but when I do. . .I guess I just don't want to end up that way. Only marrying for money like a Playboy rabbit or something."

Allie let out a chuckle. "They're called Playboy *bunnies,* hon, not rabbits."

"My bad. But really, I mean, it's something to think about. I thought people got married for love and because you want to be with someone so badly for the rest of your life. It's just so strange to think that isn't true. Maybe I'm just too naïve."

Allie sat back in the office chair, looking deep in thought. She twirled her engagement ring around her finger a few times as she stayed silent. When she spoke, her words had a surprisingly hard edge to them. "I love Jordan. I do. We've been together for five years, and I fell in love with him on the first day. We are getting married next year because we love each other. He might not make the same amount of money Kevin does, but I know he's a good man. Kind and loving, and someone who will make a terrific father one day. That's why I'm picking Jordan. I'm picking love."

We fell silent again, and I absorbed Allie's words. She was saying great things. Awesome things about her soon to be husband. So why was I getting the feeling that something was off? The tone of her voice, the edge in her eyes, the lack of her usual sparkle and bubble. It almost seemed like she was trying to convince herself, rather than me.

The subject of marriage, or Kevin and Dani, didn't come up again that morning. We worked on the payroll training, and I learned how to import all the employees' hours into the spreadsheet and send it off to Houston to get processed. I was taught how to enter new employees, their names and address, bank account numbers and exemptions. Numbers swam in front of my eyes, and my training notebook was filled with my shorthand on tips and tricks to making payroll go as smoothly as possible. Allie showed me how to mark in the dates on the calendar so I knew when the pay period was, when pay day was, when the payroll was due, and when any exemptions needed to be processed by.

By two o'clock, I felt that I was in full-on manager mode. It was one of the first days that I felt in control of the salon. That might have had something to do with Kamille being off that day. She never brought cheerfulness to Blissful and always made me feel that I was stepping on her toes. But I got along with the other employees like a charm. The first staff meeting I had been a part of, I made sure to make everyone aware that I was their manager and that I was capable and knew what I was doing. Was I faking it the whole time and secretly trembling beneath my pencil skirt and Blissful shirt? Of course. But I had read in one of my management books that I checked out in the library that it was important to establish power right from the get-go. Not to come in shy and hesitant and give the employees the opportunity to jump all over you.

So I had walked in on that Monday morning (Dani had changed the time so the meeting was held over my free hour) with my head high, my best skirt on (or Lila's best skirt) and fabulous pumps (borrowed from Emma). I carried a briefcase that held all sorts of documents—my employee handbook, a list of all the employees, Blissful information on the hours and services, and even a few school notebooks for if I ever got down time to study at the salon.

Kevin introduced me—even though I had already met the majority of the employees—and when he turned the floor over to me, I felt confident and ready. "Thanks, Kevin," I had said, flashing him my winning smile. "It's nice to meet everyone, some of you for a second time." I turned my smile on to my new employees. I had employees. "I'm really excited to begin working here at Blissful. From the wonderful comments I've heard in the community" (I hadn't really heard any, but I frequented college house parties, not lady luncheons), "to the drive and passion that I've already seen in so many of you" (that much was true), "I think I will feel right at home here. Kevin asked me to put together a few new marketing strategies, and I'm going to run over them with you quickly."

On cue, I handed out sheets of paper that outlined a few of my plans, such as up-selling and the goals I implemented that day. "Based on your hours and previous client load, I have put together sales goals that I will be expecting you to meet. These will be monthly goals, and if you successfully hit each goal in a three-month duration, you will receive a monetary bonus." I had watched the estheticians, massage therapists, hair stylists, and the front desk gals skim over the sheet and the individual index cards that listed their goals. No one said much, but when Kevin piped up in his booming voice about my academia background and professional skills that I had already showcased, I felt a boost of pride. And when a few of the hair stylists came up to me after the meeting to let me know that they appreciated being given a direction and clear cut goal to strive towards, I knew I was on top of my game.

I had rushed back to Wacker to change out of my business clothes and into something more casual for the rest of my day in classes, but when I went to work that night, I put my pencil skirt and heels back on and walked into Blissful ready to show my stuff. I was the manager. I was going to help be a part in making Blissful a successful salon. I had the confidence and the knowledge.

From that day forward, all my fears about being good enough seemed to evaporate. Was it hard work putting together the schedules? Yes. The calendar seemed like a giant jigsaw puzzle at times, with Mary needing these days off, Carolyn only being able to work morning hours, and Twila wanting every other Friday off. When Kevin gave me a deadline to come up with a new advertising design or wanted me to put together a written commentary for a radio ad, did I stress about it and stay up until two in the morning trying to get it finished? Of course. But did I love every second of my new, grown-up life? You better believe it.

So that Saturday, everything was running smoothly in the spa. I was helping man the front desk along with Julia, a sweet high school student who could up-sell better than anyone I had ever seen. Since I implemented the goals to be achieved she had outshined everyone, even though she worked significantly less due to her school schedule.

At least one day a week I liked to be up front at the desk instead of in the office—which is where I was the majority of the time—and I had chosen Saturday earlier in the week to be my day. Now I was grateful for that decision, because it kept me busy and kept my mind off constantly glancing at the clock to see if it was closing time yet and time for me to head home to get ready for my date with Henry. The phone calls were steady, the appointments flowed with precision and there were no major emergencies such as the computers crashing and the cash drawer getting stuck (both which had already happened to me on the job). Since it was Saturday, we had a full staff of stylists on board, with Mandy, Lindsey, Katie, Sophia, Jewel, and Carolyn working full shifts. We had four massage therapists kneading clients—Courtney, Alyssa, Vicki, and Shawna—and two estheticians on board as well—Allie and Morgan—who were embedded in their own hectic schedules filled with facials and peels.

At three o'clock, we hit our busiest hour. Each salon chair was full, all massage therapists were booked, Allie and Shawna were facialing their tails off, and we had a wait list going for late afternoon appointments. I started to worry that I wasn't going to make it out of there even close to when I wanted. As much as Julia and I were trying to keep everything clean and in order, the sheer volume of clients was making that task impossible.

"Hi, welcome to Blissful! How can I help you?" I greeted a trim brunette as she walked through the door.

"I have an appointment at 3:30 for a massage," she answered, hoisting her purse up on the counter. "I have this gift card to use as well."

I took the gift card from her and set it on the computer, opening up the massage therapist's schedule. "And what's your name?"

"Clarissa. Clarissa Butley."

"Okay, Clarissa, I have you all checked in. Since this is your first time here, I'm just going to ask you to take a few minutes and fill out this form. All basic questions, some health questions, and any areas you want Vicki to pay special attention to. Just bring it up to me when you're finished."

I flashed Clarissa a smile as she took the clipboard and settled into an empty chair, scribbling on her form. I quickly pressed the check-in button on Clarissa's name in the computer, which would send out an alert to the back room where the staff could see who had checked in. The system was quite efficient. Instead of me having to call back or walk back to tell them, they could easily tell from their own computer.

The bell jingled again as two young women walked in and approached the desk. They checked in for pedicures, and I sent them to the nail racks to pick out their color. They looked to be in the mid-twenties and sounded like they were in a heated gossip session.

Clarissa came back to the desk with her completed form, which I unhooked from the clipboard and placed in a file folder. "Do you need to use the restroom before you start?" I asked, a standard question for all massage clients. Nothing is worse than lying down for sixty minutes when you have a full bladder. Clarissa declined the offer and was just about to take a seat when Vicki came to the front. I passed off Clarrisa's folder to her, and the pair disappeared into the salon.

Just as they walked away, another massage client appeared from the back, looking sleepy and relaxed. Julia set to work checking her out while I slipped into the salon part to make sure no one needed me. I noticed some hair on the ground that hadn't been cleaned up yet, and swiftly took out the big janitor-like mop/broom and got to work. Then I re-aligned the shampoo and conditioner bottles along the back wall and wiped away any excess product that was dripping out. I was just getting ready to head back into the spa section when Mandy, one of the stylists, approached me.

"Hi, Alex. Are you real busy right now?" she asked, intercepting me before I walked through the spa doors.

"No, I'm just trying to keep the place tidy is all," I answered. "I can't believe how unorganized it can get—and so fast!"

"I know. It can be hard to keep up with sometimes. I was wondering maybe if I could speak to you? Privately."

I studied Mandy's face, trying to figure out if something was wrong. "Sure thing. Let's just slip into the back office, okay?"

She nodded and followed silently behind me. I held the spa door open for her to pass through, and we walked through the treatment room section to get to the office. I sat in the big chair in front of the computer and held my hand out to indicate her to sit in the smaller chair next to the printer.

"What can I do for you, Mandy?" I opened the floor to her, still unable to guess what she needed me for. Mandy was a natural redhead like me, her pale skin sprinkled with freckles and a tall and lean frame. I knew that she was twenty-four and had been working as a stylist in the Des Moines area since she graduated beauty school and came to Blissful with commendable

117

references and also brought a slew of clients with her. I hoped that she wasn't quitting. She was one of our top sellers and most requested stylist on the floor.

"I've had a little problem come up. And I guess I—I need to talk to someone. And I thought you might listen to me." Mandy spoke slow and with hesitance, not making eye contact with me.

"Well, sure. You can talk to me anytime. About anything. That's what I'm here for," I reassured her, trying to make my voice sound more comforting than authoritative.

"I've really enjoyed working at Blissful. I've been here almost since it's opened and have had some great experiences."

My heart sank. She was going to quit. One of my best employees! How could I make her stay on? My mind started racing with bonuses, more flexible hours, maybe an Employee of the Month system? Make her feel wanted and needed. Actually—Employee of the Month wouldn't be a bad idea overall. That could help make all the employees feel like they are striving towards that goal.

"I just don't know how much more I can take." I snapped out of my management thoughts when I realized Mandy had started to speak again.

"I'm sorry, Mandy. How much more of what?" I asked, focusing solely on my employee.

"Of Kevin. His comments and actions are really starting to get to me. Nothing has been completely inappropriate, but they are getting borderline. I just feel I need to let someone know."

Shit. I remembered Frank's words to me about Kevin and sexual harassment cases. Was this really happening?

"Can you tell me a little about what he has said to you? Do you mind if I take notes?" I grabbed a notebook from under a pile of mail and flipped to a blank page. My heart was pounding in my chest. What had Kevin said to Mandy? Who did I need to tell? The franchise president? The police? Dani? I could feel a line of sweat start on my forehead.

"That's fine. At first it just started out as little things. Complimenting my clothes or hairstyle. Sometimes I found his—*stares*—to be weird, but I thought I was reading too much into it." My mind flashed to the weird gaze Kevin gave me the first time I was at Blissful. I could feel my skin begin to crawl as Mandy continued. "Then it morphed into more questions— where do I hang out at on the weekends, what's my favorite drink. I answered them not thinking anything of it. We all know Kevin likes to party." Kevin was known for taking employees out for parties and footing the entire bill.

"Right. I've heard," I said, my pen hovering over the page. Not sure 'likes to party' needed to be recorded.

"I told him I usually went out with my girlfriends on Saturday nights to The Dragon House. Last Saturday he showed up there."

"With Dani?" I knew that was a dumb question.

"No, he was with just one other guy. They started hanging with me and my friends, buying us shots. My girlfriends were loving it, but I was a little weirded out. I mean, my boss hanging out with me and my friends at the club? Shouldn't he have been home with Dani and his kids? I mean, sure, there's nothing wrong with having some guy time. But The Dragon House? I just thought it was weird."

"Yeah, I see your point," I said, making a few notes. I still wasn't sure I had anything solid to go on though. "Is there anything else from that night?"

"Well." Mandy took a deep breath, and I noticed how uncomfortable she looked. "Kevin and his friend stayed with us until bar close. None of us could drive, so we started to get in cabs. I went to hop in with one of my girlfriends but Kevin started calling out to me, saying one of the cabs was going right by my place. I didn't really stop to think, I just said bye to my friends and walked towards that cab. But I realized then that it was just me and Kevin in there."

"Where was Kevin's friend?"

"He must have gotten in a different cab. I had been drinking a lot, so some of my recollection is blurry. Sorry."

"You don't need to apologize to me," I said immediately. "You weren't doing anything wrong."

"I know. It's just when alcohol is involved. . ." she trailed off in a sigh. "I just wish I could have all the details down perfectly."

"Is there anything more after you got in the cab? You did go home—right?" I was suddenly afraid of how the story ended. She wouldn't have gone back to Kevin and Dani's house. Would she?

"There's more. This is where it gets. . . .bad."

"Bad?" I heard my voice wobble over the word. *Please just spit it out.*

"We were in the cab—just the two of us—and I gave the cab driver my address. But Kevin said maybe we should have afterhours." I continued to stare at Mandy. "I said I really wanted to get home. I said I had to get up early, which was a lie—but

I just really wanted to get home. Kevin gave the cab driver a different address and said that he knew I would want to keep partying with him. I was 'his party girl.'" She used quotes with her fingers. I felt sick. "I said no again, that I really needed to go home. He wouldn't listen. The cab driver was listening to Kevin because Kevin slipped him some money. I didn't know what to do."

Mandy's eyes started to fill with tears. I grabbed her hand without even thinking about it. "It's okay, Mandy. You can tell me. I'm here to help," I whispered, worried I was about to start crying. I was terrified about what she was going to say.

"This is all just really silly. I'm sure it was just a misunderstanding. I shouldn't even be making a big deal over it." Mandy's demeanor shifted suddenly. But she wasn't fooling me.

"Mandy, if it makes you uncomfortable or upset, it is a big deal. Just let me know, and I can figure out the next step," I said firmly.

"Well, we were in the cab and he—he put his hand on my knee. Like this." She put her hand on her own knee, closer to her thigh. "I shifted away from him, thinking he would understand that I was uncomfortable. But the hand went higher." She ran her hand up on her leg, and I felt my stomach flip. "Before anything else could happen, we were being dropped off at Blackout."

"The afterhours nightclub? He really meant afterhours like— afterhours?" I asked, baffled. Blackout catered to the younger crowd, the ones who thought they were invincible and could stay out until five in the morning. Even Mandy at twenty-four would be considered old at that club. And Kevin was in his forties!

"The one and only. We walked in, he got us a table and ordered some drinks. I was sure something was going to happen there and knew I needed to get out."

"So what did you do?" I had no idea how the story would end, and was aching to find out.

"I went to the bathroom, called one of my friends, and snuck out."

I sat in my chair in disbelief, mouth agape. "And Kevin?" I had to ask, had to complete the story.

"I'm sure he realized what happened. I had a tough time debating whether to come to work this week."

"Why did you?" I asked honestly. I was shocked. I wasn't sure I would go to work after something like that. Her own boss had practically forced himself on her, imprisoned her in a cab, and took her somewhere she didn't want to be. Jesus. Where would I even start my note-taking? Who the hell would I tell?

"Well, I couldn't decide if it was a big deal. Technically, nothing happened."

"Technically. But what if you didn't get out of Blackout? What if your friend wasn't able to pick you up? It could have been bad, Mandy. Really bad," I repeated, emphasizing the words. Frank was right. What had I gotten myself into?

"Yes, but then with the alcohol. . .I had been drinking. . .maybe I led him on? I didn't think I had, but I don't know. Maybe it was just as much my fault. And he never said anything to me about it. He was here on Tuesday and greeted me like everyone else. I figured it was all just in my head. No big deal. But then. . . ."

"There's more?" I practically shouted, on the brink of falling off my chair. What the hell could happen next?

"There's more," Mandy confirmed. "He—he paid me."

Not what I thought was coming. "He paid you? What does that mean?"

"He came in last night, right before closing time. I was in the front sweeping. You and Allie were here in the office doing the closing reports."

"Okay." I remembered being in the office with Allie. I didn't know Kevin had stopped by.

"He said that he would appreciate if I kept Saturday night on the down low. Then he handed me an envelope and just walked out."

"And there was money in the envelope?"

"Two hundred dollars."

My eyebrows shot up in surprise. That was a lot of money to me. And probably to Mandy, too. "Two hundred dollars? Wow."

"Yeah." Mandy just looked at me, the disgust clear on her face. My thoughts raced. Was it hush money? Bribe money? Prostitution money? What was Kevin's deal?

"So," I tried to pull myself together, act like I had a plan, "what do you want to happen next?"

"Well, I really considered quitting. That night in the cab freaked me out. And then the money. . .it made me feel like a hooker or something. Even though we didn't do anything. I swear to you, Alex—what I told you was the truth. We did nothing."

"I believe you, Mandy, I believe you." I didn't want to mention the stories Frank had warned me of. "I just need to figure out what I need to do next." I stared down at my sheet of paper, the words swirling in front of my eyes. "So, you said you thought of quitting. But you aren't going to?" I questioned.

Mandy dropped her eyes down to the floor once again. "I just found out I'm pregnant."

I scrambled through my mental employee rolodex. Did Mandy have a boyfriend or husband? I couldn't remember.

"I just started seeing a guy not too long ago. I haven't even told him yet. I haven't told anybody yet. I had pretty much made up my mind to quit, then I took the test and now. . . .I need a job. And I need my benefits." Mandy's eyes started to fill with tears again as she tried to speak. "I need this job. I need to get past this. I'm hoping that Kevin understands that I don't want anything. . .a relationship or anything like that from him. He's my boss, he's married and has children and I'm not attracted to him at all. Hopefully by sneaking out and leaving him at the club alone, he'll back off me now."

I nodded my head, absorbing Mandy's story. What a hard place to be in. I didn't know what step I, as her manager, was supposed to take next. "Are you going to tell the guy you're seeing about the baby?"

"I am. He deserves to know. I'm going to keep it too. I'm twenty-four. I need to be responsible for my actions. And he's a good guy. Well, I think he's a good guy anyway. I really haven't known him all that long." Mandy paused, straightening her shoulders and sucking in a deep breath. "If he doesn't want to be a part of it, then that's fine. I'm not asking him for anything. Well—probably child support down the road. Or maybe not. I don't know." Mandy looked at me with helplessness in her eyes. I was sure I mirrored her expression.

"Well, we can always work through that part in a bit. Let's focus right now on Kevin, and Saturday night and the money.

Since you told me this story, is there something you would like me to do? Speak to Kevin about it?" How the hell was I going to pull that one off? And then Kevin would know that despite paying her, Mandy still told someone what he did. What if he fired Mandy because of it? She needed her job.

Mandy was shaking her head. "No. I really don't want to bring it up. I guess I was just hoping for. . .protection maybe? I just feel better knowing that someone else knows, so you can maybe keep an eye on it. Make sure he's not doing it to the other girls."

In addition to my regular work duties, school and social life, I now had to make sure Kevin didn't hit on his employees. Slap that on the to-do list. "Mandy, have you heard of anything like this happening before? Have any other girls said similar things?"

"Sometimes I've heard people talk about the strange comments Kevin can make, and I've heard stories about him and Dani being swingers."

"What?" I practically shouted. Swingers? Seriously?

"I don't know if that's true or not," Mandy rushed to say. "Only a rumor that I heard."

I dropped my head in my hands, massaging my temples. "Okay. For now, I'll do my best to keep an eye on Kevin. While I know what he did on Saturday wasn't right, I'm not sure it's technically illegal or sexual harassment. And you don't want to go that route anyway, so we'll just leave it at that for right now. Please come to me again though if something else happens. I'll need to figure it out then. I just hope that time doesn't come." Mandy nodded. "And for your situation, if you ever need someone to talk to, feel free to come to me. I have an open door policy. I hope everyone knows that. Would you like more hours scheduled to try to bring in some more money? Do you have a savings account or plan in place for financials?"

"I've always had a savings account, and it has a decent amount in there right now. I'll just keep making that grow. And I would appreciate the extra hours. Better to get them in now before I'm too pregnant to be on my feet all day," Mandy said.

"Right. Well, I'll help Allie do your schedule and slip in that you are looking for some more hours. I won't say why. I won't say anything until you do. You have my word on that." Mandy nodded again. "Okay, so that's where we'll leave it for now. I'll have my eyes and ears open. Don't hesitate to come to me again if you have another incident," I said firmly. "It's my job to run this salon smoothly and to make sure my employees are happy. And safe," I added.

"Thank you, Alex. I feel so much better telling you. I really wanted to get that—all of that—off my chest." Mandy stood, and I got to my feet as well. "I should probably get back out there. I have a 4:30 highlight that I haven't started preparing for."

I gave Mandy a little squeeze before she left, wanting to assure her that I had her back. I would want the same from my manager. After Mandy left the office I sat back down in my chair, staring blankly at the computer screen. The salon and spa schedule was on the screen, showing who was checked in, which rooms were in use, and what employees were about to be done with their clients. For ten minutes I sat alone in the office, trying to understand what Mandy told me. Was I making the right decision by not confronting Kevin? I knew I needed to respect

Mandy's wishes—and protect her job. I struggled back and forth until the office door opened again and Allie peeked her head in.

"Hey, Alex? I think Julia might need some help at the front. She's having a problem redeeming a gift card."

I popped out of my chair, straightening my shirt and patting my hair. "Okay, thanks for letting me know. I'll get right up there."

"Everything okay?" Allie questioned, peering at my face.

"Yeah, everything's great." I wondered briefly if I should fill Allie in on what Mandy told me. She had been here longer and might have more insight or an idea on what I should do next. But, no, I promised Mandy it was between me and her. "Actually," an idea hit me, "I'm not feeling well all of a sudden. You're closing tonight, right?"

"Yep. Do you need to go home?"

"I might try to get out a little early. Do you think it would be a problem?" It was a total lie. I suddenly wasn't feeling great, but it wasn't physical sickness. I was sick over Mandy's story. And I needed to get home and get ready for my date and try to get this icky feeling lifted off me.

"No, that's fine. I can run the reports. I've done them before and I do it with you all the time. I'll just call if I have any questions, but it really shouldn't be a big deal."

"Thanks. I appreciate it." I knew that Dani had told me before that she expected me to close every night that I was working, but that was impossible, right? And the salon had managed for months without a manager prior to me coming on board. I was sure it would be fine.

"I'll just come in earlier on Sunday to make up for my time," I told Allie as we walked out of the office and towards the spa section. "And I'll just run through the reports when I get here and work on the schedules. That will keep me busy until opening time."

"I have tomorrow off, but you work Tuesday, right?"

"Correct." I opened the heavy spa door and was greeted with the active bustle of the salon. "I'll say bye before I leave. I'll try to make it as long as I can." I flashed what I hoped was my 'I'm so brave to work through this sickness' smile and headed to the front desk.

I helped Julia with the gift card problem, checked in Mandy's 4:30 highlight, closed down and cleaned treatment rooms 1-5 since they would no longer be in use the rest of the night, and did some more sweeping to remove hair off the salon floor. At 5:15 I decided to call it a night. After saying my good-byes and continuing to fake a stomachache, I climbed into my Camry and headed to Kaufman. I felt bad for lying to everyone, but I seriously needed to get out of there. I trusted Allie to close the salon, had my cell phone on me if there were any problems, and needed some time to unwind from Mandy's story. I knew I had given Mandy my word not to tell, but I had to go to the girls for advice. Hopefully between the five of us we could figure out what I should I do.

But most importantly, I wanted to get Kevin and Blissful out of my mind and concentrate on one thing—Henry Landon.

CHAPTER 10

"Hey, you're back early!" Lila greeted me when I walked through our door, setting my purse and work bag next to the kitchen table.

"Yeah, I was able to slip away a little early. I have so much to tell you guys. And I figured having more time to get ready would only help me."

"I was just getting ready to jump in the shower, but I'll wait 'till after you leave now. I'll text the girls that you're ready. Everything okay?" Lila peered at my face, which I was sure still showed the dismay from Mandy's story.

"Yeah. Kind of. Maybe not. I'll tell you when everyone gets here. It's quite the story."

"Okay, then. Are you hungry? I know you're going out to eat, but I was just going to munch on some grapes."

"Grapes? Not a piece of cake or something?" I teased her.

Lila opened the fridge and pulled out a bowl of green grapes, easing the lid back and heading to the kitchen sink. Turning on the faucet, she replied, "Funny. And no. My casting call with Mary Strubaker is in three weeks, so I'm putting my best foot forward from here on out. Watching what I eat, paying attention to the workout calendar you made me, and I need to schedule an appointment for a facial. I'm thinking next week. Could you get me in?"

"I'm sure we could. Have you ever had a facial before?"

"No, why? Are they scary?"

"No, not at all. But sometimes if you haven't had them you can be prone to breaking out. I would just hate for that to happen right before the big day. When did you say it was?"

"The 25th. The last Friday of the month."

"Okay, that should work then. I would suggest about two weeks before. That way you're skin will have time to react and leave you fresh and beautiful for your call."

"Casting call."

"Right. I'll get you in the books tomorrow."

"You're the best!" Lila gave me a squeeze as our door opened and Emma, Carmen, and Hannah all walked in.

"Girls gone wild in a dorm room! Action!" Carmen said when she saw us.

"You're so hilarious, Ms. Morales," Lila said, tapping Carmen playfully on the bottom. "Nothing wrong with showing the roommate love for giving me a discount on my facial. Grape?" She offered the bowl of fruit.

Carmen wrinkled her nose, looking at the healthy snack. "Yeah, no gracias, chica. Brought my own refreshments." She pulled a bottle of wine from her bag, handing it to me. "Happy first date present."

"Thanks, Carmen! Thanks all of you for coming. I have some major news to share, and I need your help. Badly. Let me just open this quick and we can get started." I pulled out the wine opener from a drawer, swiftly popping the cork and pouring glasses for everyone except Hannah.

"I still have to study tonight," she said when I offered her a glass.

"Study? Hannie, love, it's a Saturday night," Carmen said, eagerly taking her own glass.

"Yes, well, I would leave it for tomorrow but. . . .I have a date." She barely got the words out before we all started squealing.

"Shut up!"

"Another date with Peter?"

"So quickly after the first one, I love it!"

"Where are you going?"

"I will not shut up, yes with Peter, I know it's so soon, and we are going to an early movie and then to Demetri's for fondue."

"Demetri's? You're so lucky, I've always wanted to go there!" Emma exclaimed. "All the guys I go out with are too cheap to take me. You're a lucky one, Hannah. This Peter seems pretty awesome."

"I'll let you slide on the studying tonight then. Only because I am *muy* excited for you," Carmen said.

"I wanted to ask you, Alex, do you think I could get in for an immediate haircut and style tomorrow? I've been putting it off forever, but I think it's necessary."

"Not a problem. I just looked at the schedule before I left and I'm pretty sure Jewel had a pretty open schedule. Can you come in right at twelve when we open?"

"I can. Thank you so much."

"Pleasure's mine, Hannie." I smiled at my friend. It was odd seeing Hannah so excited over a date and actually thinking about her hair and appearance for once.

"Alex, do you know where you are going tonight?" Lila asked, changing the subject. "And let's continue our convo in the bathroom. We need to help this one get ready."

We shuffled our way into the tiny bathroom, which wanted to explode once the five of us were in there. "Maybe we should just do this in the bedroom. Lila, you have a bigger mirror on your vanity. Can I just sit there?" I asked. We were shoulder to shoulder and could barely move.

"Good idea." We picked up our wine glasses and made our way into Lila's room, where she shoved all her stray clothing and whatever else hid in her room under the bed. I took a seat, and Lila plugged in her curling iron.

"And to answer your question, no. I have no idea where we are going. Henry said he had a place in mind, but he wasn't sure he could get reservations at such a short notice," I said, staring at my reflection in the mirror. "To be honest, I'm a little nervous. I don't do good with fancy food. What if I don't like anything on the menu?"

"I'm sure you'll be fine," Emma said, sprawling on Lila's bed and picking up one of the many rag mags that covered it. "Every place has to have chicken strips. Those are plain enough."

"Not necessarily. I've been out to eat where you can't find anything plain. Everything is stuffed or smothered or comes with weird stuff baked on it," I countered.

"Everything will work out. Stop being so nervous about it," Lila scolded me, running a comb through my hair and spritzing my strands with a heat protector spray. "I would also like to take credit for this date."

"How do you get credit? I'm the one that told Peter that Henry could call Alex," Hannah argued.

"Yeah, but I'm the one that set you up with Peter. Alex meeting Henry through Peter would have never happened if it weren't for me. Voila—I'm the winner."

"Fine, fine. I'll let you have this one," Hannah conceded, nudging Emma over so she could sit on the bed as well.

"Alex, I'm thinking big, curly, sexy hair. Lots of volume. Agreed?" Lila asked, meeting my eyes in the mirror.

"Sounds perfect. Who's working on my outfit?" I asked my friends behind me.

"I am. I brought another pair of Emma's shoes for you to borrow," Carmen said, reaching into her bag and pulling out a pair of black strappy sandals with a tall heel. "It's a little difficult to dress you since you don't know where you are going, or even what type of restaurant it is. We have to nail a casual outfit that can look formal if need be. But not too formal in case you end up at a McDonald's."

"I will trust whatever you pull for me," I said truthfully. Carmen had a good eye for clothes and fashion.

"Alex, didn't you say you had something to discuss with us? Is it about your date?" Hannah asked.

"Actually, no. It's about work. You guys will not believe what one of my employees told me today." I launched into the Mandy/Kevin story, repeating all the details Mandy had shared with me just hours before. The comments, the cab ride, the money envelope. By the time I finished, Lila was done curling the bottom section of my hair and the girls were looking at me with wide eyes. Emma spoke first.

"Um, let me go ahead and say it—what the fuck?"

"I second that," Carmen said. "What is this guy's deal?"

"I'm a little concerned for you, Alex. What if he tries to pull that on you?" Hannah asked.

"How much money did he give her?" Lila asked.

"Lila! Why is that your response? And it was two hundred dollars. Probably pocket change to him, but a lot to someone like Mandy," I said.

"And she doesn't want you to turn him in?" Hannah asked.

I shook my head, causing an immediate squeal from Lila as she tried not to burn me. "Sorry! But no, she doesn't. She's afraid that she was leading him on and the alcohol makes all the events a little fuzzy for her. But I seriously doubt it was her."

"And even if it was, he's her employer and he's married. It shouldn't matter if she takes her top off and makes him motorboat her, he should still be the one to walk away."

"I could do without that visual. Thanks, Carmen," I said, resisting the urge to shake my head again. "But I do agree with you. So I'm just not sure what to do. What do you guys think? Who would I even turn him in to if I wanted to?"

"That's a tough one, Al. You don't want to go behind your employee's back and make things worse for her. But you need to be responsible for keeping them safe." Emma blew out a breath. "I don't even know what I would recommend. Ladies?"

"As much as I want to say turn him in, I think you need to do what Mandy is suggesting," Carmen said. "It's her wishes. If she were raped, that's a different story. I'm not trying to downplay what happened, because it sounds awful enough. Let's hope it was a one-time thing. Kevin got a little out of hand and it can be moved on from. Maybe Kevin paying her was his way of saying he's sorry. Maybe not the most traditional way—or best way— but maybe that really was his way of trying to make things right. Now, if it happens again, that's a different story. Then he clearly didn't learn his lesson, and some kind of action would need to be taken."

"But what kind of action?" I asked. "I feel helpless. If I'm having a problem with the salon or an employee or even a customer, I would go to either Dani or Kevin. I just don't know what to do in this situation. Obviously, the Dohlmans are both out. So who does that leave?"

"Maybe you could ask that esthetician for help. The one that you like a lot," Lila suggested, clamping another piece of hair between the prongs and twisting it up towards my scalp.

"Allie? I guess I could. I just would feel bad after telling Mandy I wouldn't tell anyone. I mean, you guys are fine. Obviously you're not associated with Blissful. But I worry about the gossip and rumors, you know? I don't think Allie would do that, but I'm just not sure. I really haven't known her all that long."

"I would say keep an eye on the situation. If Kevin does something like that again, tell Allie. She could probably at least point you in the right direction," Hannah spoke up. "Or maybe you could just go to Kevin and tell him straight out that he is making Mandy uncomfortable. Maybe he just doesn't get it."

"Yeah, maybe he's used to women falling all over him. He doesn't understand being refused," Emma said. "Didn't you say that Allie told you about strippers in Vegas and a bunch of affairs? I bet Kevin just doesn't realize that he can't get away with it all the time."

"But still, Mandy is an employee. Not a stripper or some floozy who's looking for a good time and wants to be paid for it. She's a good worker who was just out on a regular weekend night with friends. And said no to Kevin, repeatedly. What doesn't he get about that?" Lila argued, giving my hair a final blast of hairspray.

"I'm just saying. Some guys, especially ones with money and a big ego, can't handle the fact that not every woman wants them. It could be true in this case," Emma argued back.

"I think you both are right," I interjected. "Actually, I think you all made excellent points. I will keep an eye on the situation for now and if I see or hear anything else that isn't kosher, I'll go to Allie for help. Maybe we can confront Kevin together. Power in numbers and all that. But thanks for listening to me. I knew I couldn't keep this inside."

"You're most welcome. Now, do you want to see the outfit I picked for you?" Carmen disappeared in the closet and came back out with clothes slung over her arm. "Ta-da!"

A few minutes later I was attired in black leggings, a long blue dress with a cowl neck, black heels and had my bouncy curls held back from my face with a sparkling headband. Due to the headband and bling effect it offered, we kept my jewelry simple—a plain silver bracelet of mine that was a Christmas gift from Lila last year. Emma helped give my eyes more of a pop by mixing together silver and blues and applying them to my lids, giving me the classic smoky eye that I was unable to do for myself. All in all, I thought I looked pretty good for my first date with Henry Landon.

At 7:20 my cell phone started to buzz. Carmen flipped it open for me and read the text message from Henry aloud. "Just leaving my place. See you soon!" We all started screaming again and rushed out of Lila's bedroom and into the living room. I sat on the couch and struggled into the heels, Emma started pacing around, Hannah sat next to me and patted my hand, Lila brought me a bottle of her best perfume to spritz, and Carmen headed into the kitchen, presumably for another drink.

"How far was his house?" Emma asked. "I can't remember."

I looked at Lila. "You were direction-bitch. You should remember."

"I don't think it was that far. Maybe like ten or fifteen minutes," she replied.

The silence stretched on. "He'll probably just text when he gets here so I can head downstairs. I should get my jacket on," I said, standing to retrieve my light jacket in the coat closet. I had just started to shrug it on when the buzzer rang, indicating someone was at the front door and wanted to be let into the building.

I ran back into the living room, where all four girls looked at me expectedly. "Do you think that's him?" I shrieked, no longer able to play it any sort of cool.

"Buzz him in, buzz him in!" Emma shouted.

I pressed the 'talk' buzzer on the intercom. "Hello?" I asked.

"Hi, Alex? It's Henry," came the reply.

I hoped he didn't hear the shouts of excitement in the background. "Hi, Henry. I'll be right down."

"That's okay. I can come come up."

I looked at my friends, confused. Why did he want to come up? "Uh, yeah, sure. Okay. Come on up. Number twelve." I looked back at the girls, who were staring at me. "Um, are you guys supposed to hide? Act casual? What? Why does he want to come up here?" I was on the verge of freaking out.

"It's cool. We'll just wait here and see you off. We'll tell him we're getting ready for a party ourselves. It's fine, Al. Keep it cool," Lila advised, and I followed her deep breathing. It was just a first date. No biggie. Right.

A knock on the door had me jumping out of my skin. Hannah let out an excited yelp, then looked at me sheepishly. "My bad."

I scolded her with a frown, then yanked open the front door. Time stood still as I locked eyes with my date. With Henry Landon. Scrumptious piece of man meat. Who happened to be holding a bouquet of red roses. I felt faint.

"Hi," Henry said. Was that shyness I detected in his voice?

"Hi," I responded, grinning at him and the flowers like a dope.

"These are for you." He thrust the bouquet my way and I gathered the sweet-smelling roses in my arms.

"Henry! You didn't have to do that. How sweet of you." I remembered then that we had an audience. "Um, you remember my friends from the Halloween party? Hannah, Carmen, Emma, and my roommate, Lila."

"Of course. Hello again, ladies," Henry said, stepping fully into the living room.

"Hi, Henry," they chorused back.

"Let me just put these in a vase for you. You kids get out there and have fun. We have lots to do here tonight," Lila said, standing and hurrying over to me. She collected the roses from my arms, burying her face in the petals. "Mmm. Henry, you have scored some major points already. Kudos to you, man."

The living room tittered, and Henry smiled easily. "Well, I'm glad to hear that. The points might come in handy when I break the bad news."

He was calling off our date already? His parents were going to supervise us? What was the bad news?

"What bad news?" Hannah piped up, then slunk down in her chair when Carmen glared at her. Hannah's unusual behavior wasn't upsetting me, more making me laugh then anything. She almost seemed more nervous than me for the date.

"I was really hoping to get reservations at Bellini's Magnifico, but they were already booked up when I called. I've been calling back the last two days to see if they had any cancellations, but still couldn't get in. I'm sorry, Alex." Henry looked so contrite that I just wanted to hug him and tell him it was okay. Would I have loved to visit the number one Italian restaurant in not only Des Moines but in Iowa? Yeah, sure. Would I survive? As long as I could still go out with Henry, that answer was a yes.

"That's okay! I'm sure we can find another place to eat. It's no big deal, really," I tried to assure him.

"Maybe next time we can go there. I'll do better on the planning," Henry responded, flashing me a leg-wobbling grin. I heard Hannah suck in her breath. Was he really already asking me out on a second date? Our first date hadn't even officially started!

"Well, you kids should be off. Henry, I think Bellini's sounds like the perfect spot for your second date." Lila winked at me, still holding my flowers. I could tell she was just as excited as I was.

Henry and I slipped out the door to a wave of good-byes from my friends and walked down the flights of stairs to reach the main entrance of Wacker. Henry held open the door for me and led me to a black SUV parked near the edge of the lot. I knew nothing about cars or trucks or SUVs, but this looked like a nice one. I was taken aback when Henry opened the car door for me too, and held his hand out for me to help me climb up and in.

The interior had smooth black leather seats and smelled strongly of cologne. "Sorry if the smell is too much for you. I wasn't kidding when I said I stashed cologne in here to try to help mask the booze smell. I swear the scent traveled from the house onto my clothes and into my car. I figured an abundance of spray would smell better than the disgusting alcohol."

I laughed, settling into my seat while Henry started the engine. "No problem. I completely understand. I would much prefer this over booze."

Henry turned and smiled at me, and I realized I would be just as happy sitting in his car in the parking lot all night if we had to. Who cared about fancy Italian restaurants? I just wanted to talk to him, be around him.

"So I guess we should figure out where we are going, huh?" he asked, pausing with his hand over the gear stick.

"I guess so," I replied, racking my brain. Did I suggest something fancy, along Bellini lines? Something more laid back and low key? My stomach rumbled then thinking about food, and I wanted to die of embarrassment. I cringed, hoping Henry hadn't heard it.

"Well, whatever we decide, it should be soon," Henry said with a laugh. Of course he would hear my angry tummy.

"Sorry. Work today was extremely crazy, and I didn't get to eat much for lunch." I remembered munching on some carrot sticks and celery in the break room while talking to Allie about ordering more lotions. Not the most substantial meal.

"Well, let's think of what's close by," Henry said, turning the heat up a bit and making sure all the vents were open. The temperatures dropped low at night, and the digital car thermometer in his rearview mirror announced it was a whopping forty-six degrees.

"Um, let me think. There's Chinese right down the street that's pretty good. Or a diner, Nancy's, just a few block away. A dive bar that I could get into and drink at without a problem. Or, oh! An Applebee's is just a few streets over. That actually sounds really good."

"Applebee's?"

"Is that lame? That's a lame date spot, right?" I said, immediately scolding myself for suggesting it. What a dope.

"Not at all. I love Applebee's. As long as you're down for it, I'm in."

"Really?"

He nodded, shifting gears to reverse. "Absolutely. What's your favorite menu item there?"

"Oh, man, that's hard. I always seem to order something different. Salad, steak, their chicken strips. They have an excellent pasta bowl with all sorts of vegetables and different noodles that would probably be my favorite. What about you?"

We continued to discuss the menu and our favorite foods in general on the short drive. I found out that Henry Landon hated chocolate (seriously!), gets craving for spinach (I liked spinach, but to crave it?) and could easily live off frozen pizza.

"I'm not kidding. I've been through three different Pizzazz machines since I've been in college. Between me and my roommates, we go through about ten or fifteen pizzas a week. No joke."

"Holy shit. That is a lot of pizza. I can't even remember the last time I had pizza." I paused a moment to think. "Nope, can't remember. Lila and I make a lot together, like easy pasta dishes. Carmen can make some mean enchiladas. Emma is best away from the kitchen. Hannah can do anything she puts her mind to."

"Your friends seem really great," Henry observed, taking a left onto Grandview Road.

"They are. I'm a lucky one," I smiled at him, hoping he understood that I wasn't saying I was only lucky because of my friends. I felt lucky to be on the date with him as well. "But what about you? You seem to have plenty of great friends and roommates as well."

"I do. Peter and Max are both from Truvista. We've been friends for years. Have you ever been to Truvista?" I shook my head. "It's a pretty small town. It's impossible not to know everyone and their business. I'm glad I got out of there. I needed a bigger city. Peter and Max are good guys, though. It's not like they're just from my hometown so I know them that way. I'm glad they came to Kaufman. We met Kyle during the first week of orientation."

We pulled into the Applebee's parking lot, which didn't look overly crowded for a Saturday night. Hopefully we had missed the dinner rush hour. "I met all the girls on campus here. I came to Kaufman alone, but I lived in Des Moines for a few years before going to school here. My sister worked at the capitol."

Our conversation stalled as we got out of the vehicle and walked through the door. We were promptly seated at a cozy booth in the corner, which actually seemed somewhat romantic—as romantic as an Applebee's could get. When the waiter came by we both ordered sodas, then browsed the menu.

"Are you going to get your pasta dish?" Henry asked me, his eyes meeting mine over the menu.

"I think so. Since I mentioned it in the car I haven't been able to get my mind off of it. What are you thinking?"

"I might go for a steak. With some onions and cheese on top."

"Yum. Smothered steak. Sounds delicious." We smiled at each other once again, and I thought about how goofy we might have looked to other patrons, grinning wildly at each other over menus.

Our conversation resumed after we placed our orders, and went right to the area that I was hoping would get bypassed. "So your sister worked at the capitol? How about the rest of your family—are they from around here?"

I paused, taking a sip of my drink for an added pause. Then stayed silent a beat longer.

"Alex?" Henry prompted.

"Well, my family . . . . My mom passed away when I was five and my dad took off shortly after. It's just been me and my sister for a while. And she lives in Seattle now with her husband and kids."

"Oh." I knew I took Henry by surprise with the abundance of information. Everyone always got surprised and flustered when I told them about my family. It was like no one had ever heard of death before or something.

"Yeah. Shucks. But we don't have to talk about that. How is your family?" I desperately wanted to change the subject, try to make Henry feel less awkward.

"My family is fine. Parents together. I have an older brother and sister. But I'm boring. I'm sorry to hear about your mom. Was it. . . .?" he trailed off, waiting for me to fill in the blank.

It took me a moment to respond. Usually when I tried the change-the-subject tactic, people pounced on it. But not Henry. "It was cancer. Breast cancer," I answered softly. "By the time they found it, it was so far advanced there wasn't much left to do except prepare. I was only five, like I said, but Alicia—my sister—was fifteen and more aware that she was about to lose her mom."

"I can't imagine what that would have felt like. It was probably so tough on Alicia. Alicia, right?" I nodded. "Alicia. Such a young age. She was probably just starting high school then. Oh, man." Henry looked absolutely devastated, and I was in shock. Typically people respond with "oh, I understand." No, they didn't. Not unless they went through it themselves. It was refreshing to hear Henry say he didn't know what it felt like. That was the truth. And to immediately pick up on Alicia's feelings? If I was telling the story, everyone focused on me. Poor little girl who lost her mommy. I really didn't get what was going on after she passed. I just knew Mom wasn't there to tuck me in at night or take me for wagon rides or sing with me in the shower. I didn't understand she was gone forever. That pain came later in life.

"Thanks, Henry. Most people try to avoid the subject because clearly it's an uncomfortable one. Sometimes it can just be a relief to talk about it. Not try to dance around it."

"Of course. I mean, it's a part of you, your life, your history. You can't change your past. I know it's not something you would have chosen for yourself, but you still have to embrace it. It is what it is."

"It is what it is," I repeated, feeling suddenly euphoric. This man got me. He understood me. He didn't judge me.

"And you said your dad left? How come?"

"He left about two years after Mom died. He wrote us a note saying he couldn't handle seeing us." Henry's eyebrows rose in surprise. "He really loved our mom. I mean, he *really* did. I guess he couldn't handle the pain or the reminders of her. Both Alicia and I look so much like Mom it's almost spooky. Red hair, green eyes. Alicia and I are even the exact height now that she was when she died. I've wondered sometimes if Dad got freaked when he would see Alicia in the hallway at night, wondering if he thought he saw Mom's ghost. So he ran. He lives in Georgia now and started over with a new family. Alicia and I don't keep in touch with him."

Our food arrived at that minute, and the waiter carefully placed our steaming plates in front of us. "Both are really hot, so be careful," he said. "Can I get you anything else?"

Henry and I shook our heads, rolling the silverware away from the napkin and preparing to dig in. "Wow. Another thing I can't imagine. How does a father just walk away from his family? Didn't he understand his kids were hurting too? They—you— lost your *mother.* I mean, come on."

I dug into my pasta bowl, carefully blowing on the shells and cheese to cool it down. "I know, right? I'm really not sure I could ever find it in my heart to really forgive him. I mean, really forgive him. Sometimes I'll think 'oh, sure, he missed his wife.' But Alicia and I lost our mother and father within two years of one another. I hope I am never that selfish."

"Selfish is the perfect word. I can't imagine my dad ever leaving our family—for anything. No matter how terrible. I guess I just realized how truly lucky I am." Henry cut into his steak, then paused and set his fork and knife down. "In fact, remind me to call my parents after we eat. Just to say hi."

I smiled at him, feeling my heart do a weird flutter thing. *Stop thinking love! You cannot love this guy after a first date!* "I will. It's always nice to remind those we love how much we care about them. Alicia calls me every Sunday, no fail, just to say hi and lets me talk to the kids. I am an aunt times five, if I haven't mentioned that."

"Five! Wow, that is a lot of kids. I'm not an uncle yet; probably won't be for a while as neither my brother nor sister are with anyone. They are both too career-focused than family-oriented."

"What do they do?"

"My brother Jacob is an architect. He lives here in Des Moines and works for a large architect firm. And my sister lives in Milwaukee. She owns a few fashion boutiques."

"Wow, that's really neat. Lila would probably be fascinated by your sister. She loves fashion and celebrities and all that stuff."

"Kate has told me she's had some celebrities visit her shops. And baseball wives come in from time to time. We go up to visit her quite a bit—Jacob and I—and she seems to be pretty happy. And we love to watch the Milwaukee Brewers play."

"Maybe I should plan a trip up there with the girls. I've never been to Milwaukee. Sounds like it could be fun."

"Maybe we could all road-trip together. Your girlfriends, my roommates. I don't think Peter and Hannah would have a problem with that."

A shiver ran up my spine. A second date and now a road-trip—to another state? Was Henry Landon really that into me, or simply yanking my chain? I found my voice. "Yeah, that would be awesome. But I thought baseball season just got over?"

"It did. Did you watch any of the World Series?"

"I watched a few games. Believe it or not, Emma actually loves sports and she watched all the games. I know she would go to Milwaukee in a heartbeat."

"We could go maybe sometime in April. Or May. There should be nicer weather during that month. Give us all some time to save money."

Before I could open my mouth to respond, a strange hush seemed to fall upon the restaurant. Voices dimmed, the lights dimmed, and all the hair on my arms stood at attention. Henry was still happily cutting into his steak, people were walking around like normal, but something was happening to me. It was almost like I could feel my life changing, that I knew on a deeper level I was in the right place and the right time with the right person. Before I could react to what I was feeling, the moment was over. Everything was bright and loud and my arm hairs settled down. I gave my head a shake, trying to clear the fog. That was seriously bizarre.

"I think May sounds perfect. A little vacation before we have to settle down and cram. I'll talk to the girls about it tonight." And tell Lila that I thought I was getting some of her psychic abilities. We'd been roommates for three years; it was about time I started picking those up!

"Awesome. It will be a great trip. I know it." Henry grinned at me. "I'm glad you girls came to the party."

"I'm glad we did too, Henry. I'm glad we did too."

CHAPTER 11

"I'll have the avocado salad, hold the dressing. And just a water, please." Dani dug around her oversized purse, triumphantly pulling out her wallet.

"Is that all, miss?"

"And whatever she would like too." Dani gestured to me.

"Um, I'll just have what she is having. Thanks. And thank you for lunch," I said, turning my attention away from the complicated menu board to face Dani.

"My pleasure. I should be thanking you for coming out to lunch with me. I need a break from the girls every once in a while or I'm afraid I would constantly talk in baby language!"

It was a Wednesday, and Dani had asked me out to lunch before I started my shift at Blissful. Lunches were becoming a common occurrence between us. We even had a few dinners together, and trips to the mall. I had been to Dani and Kevin's house twice and was starting to feel more comfortable around my bosses. Kevin still gave me the creeps sometimes, but nothing further had been said from Mandy, so I was assuming everything was okay with that situation. And Dani really was becoming a true friend. Well, a friend in the way that a boss can become a friend. I still got nervous around her and tried to always say the right things, but I could tell I was slowly becoming more at ease with her.

"So I haven't really talked to you in a few days. How's everything going? Classes all right?" We settled into a booth in the corner, Dani shoving her briefcase in first and then sitting down. I also shoved my briefcase, smaller than Dani's but still professional looking, into the corner and took a seat across from her.

"Classes are good. My friends are good, and I think everything else at Blissful is going really well. And—" I was bursting to tell her about my date—"I had a date on Saturday night!"

"You did? I didn't know you had a date lined up. With who? Where did you go?" Dani leaned her elbows on the table, pushing her body forward. I made sure to avert my eyes from the cleavage that was spilling out of her lavender blouse.

"It was kind of last minute. His name is Henry Landon, and his friend Peter is kind of seeing my friend Hannah. We met at a Halloween party." I paused as our food was brought out. The salad looked. . .interesting. A little sad with no croutons or dressing, but it was healthy and Dani swore by them. I tucked in with only somewhat abashed enthusiasm.

"Henry thought he was going home for the weekend, then he didn't, so he decided to take a chance and see if I was free.

He wanted to get reservations at Bellini's but they were full, so we actually just ended up at an Applebee's."

Dani's perfectly plucked eyebrows rose. "Applebee's? On your first date?"

"To be fair, he let me choose the restaurant. And I love Applebee's and it's simple and wouldn't put as much pressure on me as Bellini's." I hurried to defend Henry. I loved our first date. I thought it was perfect. "But he did say for the second date he will make sure to get that reservation at Bellini's."

"Wow, so you already have a second date planned?"

"Yep. It's going to be this Saturday. And I'll have the whole day to get ready since I have the weekend off!"

"If things go well, maybe the four of us could go out together sometime. Kevin and myself, you and Henry. I would love to meet him."

I nearly dropped my fork. "Yes! That would be excellent. I've already talked so much about you and Blissful. I would love that!" It was almost going to be like a meet the parent's scenario, which made me nervous. Maybe after the third date—if there was a third date—would I mention it to Henry.

"Tell me more about Henry! What does he look like? Where is he from?"

Dani and I had an enjoyable lunch, where I spilled all the details on Henry and how excited I was over a boy—the first time in a long time. Dani gave a few stories on her daughters and the hassle they gave her over the weekend, and mentioned a few sales reports that she wanted to go over with me back at the salon.

When we left the deli, I imagined what we looked like to others as we bounced out the door—Dani, petite yet full of confidence, dark hair tucked under a stylish wool cap and a dark red peacock coat protecting her from the cold. Me with a lighter coat on because I still hadn't dug up my proper winter coat from the storage box, a white stocking cap covering my red hair. We ran towards Dani's vehicle to get away from the cold, laughing and out of breath by the time we reached the doors. I imagined that people thought we were sisters, or maybe just best friends. Perhaps business professionals out for a casual lunch before heading back to the office. Being around Dani gave me newfound confidence. I had the power to make decisions, to run a full-scale salon and spa, and be in charge of employees. Dani made me feel level with her. We were a team, and our main goal was to make Blissful as successful as it could be. I was falling in love with my new life.

"Alex, can I talk to you? Are you busy?" Kevin opened the door to the office and took a seat.

I swiveled my chair around so I was facing him. "Yeah, sure. I was just looking at the sales reports for the goals I assigned everyone."

"Yeah, yeah, the goals. That was a great idea if I haven't mentioned it. Great idea." Kevin was his usual self—all over the place and seeming to be in a rush. "Buy, hey, listen—did you leave here early on Saturday?"

That wasn't what I was expecting. I thought back to Saturday. Date night with Henry. The chat with Mandy regarding the man standing before me. "Um, yes. I left about forty-five minutes early. Then I came in an hour early on Sunday to make up for it and to work on schedules." I gestured to the schedule board, where my hard work was pinned to the corkscrew.

"That's really not acceptable. We need a manager on duty at all times, and you need to stay to do the cash drawer."

I felt as though I had been slapped. "But Allie was here. . .?" I trailed off meekly. Allie had been here, right? And she told me it would be okay to leave, I was sure of it.

"While Allie helped us for a while, she is not the manager of the store. Either you, Dani, or myself need to be here to close. Every. Night."

I stood still for a moment, wondering if I was going to cry. The tone of voice Kevin was using made me feel like he was belittling me. And every night I had to close? That meant I could never cut a night short during the week or weekend—ever? "Okay," I said slowly. "I see what you mean, and I apologize. I wasn't aware that Allie wasn't capable of closing. I do have one question though."

Kevin had already turned his back to me and was powering up his laptop in the far corner of the office. "Yeah?" he said, distracted and already uninterested in me.

"What about the days I come in early? Or do work away from the salon before my scheduled time?"

"You're a manager. You're going to work more than forty hours a week. That's why we pay you salary and give you those nice bonuses when the salon does well. Didn't they teach you anything about managing at Kaufman?"

My face went crimson. How dare he undermine me! A question is a question. And no one said anything about working more than forty hours a week when I signed on. I swiftly turned back to the computer, the sales reports going fuzzy as tears filled my eyes. *Do not cry in front of this dick. Do not cry,* I repeated to myself. How I so badly wanted to snap, to tell him his disgusting behavior towards Mandy helped me reach my decision to leave early on Saturday. See what excuse he could come up with then.

But I didn't. I calmed myself down, focused back on my reports, and Kevin and I worked in silence for about ten minutes until his phone started ringing. First, it sounded like a business call. I could only hear Kevin's side of the conversation, but it didn't sound like a good one. "Did you get him to sign the paperwork? I told you—the paperwork has to be signed! What are you not understanding? Get the fucking paperwork signed and to me no later than five o'clock tomorrow!"

Sheesh. And I thought he talked down to me. Another phone call right after that. "This Kevin." Kevin and Dani both answered their phones that way, like they were too busy to include the "is." "Well, hey, stranger! I just spoke to Chris and it sounds like everything will work out fine. The paperwork should be to me by tomorrow, no problem. She'll be ready to be on set by next week, and the photographer and shoot location are good to go. Yeah, it was nothing. Come on, you didn't think I would let this opportunity slip, did you? She could be a potential Playmate, and I want her to have her first real shoot to come from Gropers. Yeah, buddy, we'll get it!" A hearty laugh that sounded more evil than anything to my ears. "Yep. Yep. Friday night again? I'll be there. Make sure she is too." His cell phone flipped closed, and Kevin started whistling a tune. I kept working, shifting my focus to preparing the next payroll batch, trying to ignore the slime that dripped from my boss's words.

"Hey, you doing anything for dinner?" Kevin asked, and I turned my head slightly to see if he was on the phone again. He wasn't.

"Me?" I asked.

"Well, yeah! I think I'm going to stick around for a while and keep an eye on things. I could go grab us something if you didn't bring anything."

"Um, sure. I mean, no, I didn't bring anything. So sure, that would be great." I was confused. Was he not just berating me for leaving the store? Now he wanted to buy me dinner? And he wanted to stay at the salon all night? That was really going to cramp style. I felt like I was under a microscope now with my leaving-early mistake. I would have to put on a top manager performance that night.

Kevin left shortly after to pick up some Chinese, and I went out into the main area. Wednesdays were a hit or miss busy night, but that Wednesday the schedule had seemed full so I scheduled more staff than usual. Perhaps people wanting to get in before the Thanksgiving holiday made the schedule busier. Tiffany was at the front (Windexing the counter when I checked on her) and Allie, Morgan, Jewel, Katie, Sophia, Alyssa, and Vicki were on the books. From the schedule it looked to be a steady night, and that was not including walk-ins. I was thankful that Mandy wasn't scheduled. Even though there hadn't seemed to be any more problems, I didn't want her and Kevin together all night long in case it made her uncomfortable.

"Hey, Tiffany. How is everything going up here?" I asked when I reached the front. Tiffany flicked her brown bangs off her forehead and threw some paper towels in the garbage.

"Not too bad. A little busy."

"Well, I'm going to eat dinner soon, and Kevin will be here the rest of the night, but if you need help up here, don't be afraid to get me. I'll be up in a jiff."

"Kevin's going to be here? All night?" A flicker of panic crossed Tiffany's heavily made-up brown eyes.

Shit. Please, oh please, do not be another Mandy situation, I thought to myself. "Yes. We have some work to do in the office." Total lie, I was pretty sure Kevin just wanted to keep an eye out on me, but I certainly didn't want to tell one of my employees that. "Is everything okay?" I dared to ask.

"What? Oh, sure. Sure, yeah." Tiffany grabbed out a bottle of Pledge from beneath the counter and ripped off another handful of paper towels. "Just was wondering. Want to be on the best behavior if the big man is around!" She tittered, a cross between a laugh, a screech, and a choke.

Fuck. Clearly something was rattling Tiffany. And I would bet money that it involved Kevin being inappropriate in some way towards her. Did he follow her to a club too? Try to pay off her in some way?

I stood for an extra beat at the front, watching Tiffany furiously scrub down the wooden panels of the desk. I didn't want to push her or make her more uncomfortable than she clearly already was. I just needed to remind her that I was here. "Okay, well, I'm going to alert the others that he'll be around tonight so we keep everything extra clean. But, Tiffany, if you ever need anything, work or personal-wise, my door is open. Okay?"

Tiffany looked up at me then and seemed ready to say something when the ringing of the office phone cut through the tension. She just nodded at me and picked up the phone with a brisk, "Thank you for calling Blissful Salon and Spa. This is Tiffany, how may I help you?"

I walked into the salon, wondering how to get Tiffany to tell me what was up. Wait? I didn't make Mandy come to me, but then again, I hadn't known any of this before Mandy told her story. Now that I knew, I was afraid every time an employee acted rattled around Kevin I was going to assume he was harassing them in some way. Maybe he was just firm with Tiffany once, like he was with me earlier. Maybe she made a mistake with an appointment, or forgot to clock-in, or left cleaning supplies out. Just because she was jumpy didn't automatically mean Kevin tried to hit on her. I was jumping to conclusions.

After satisfying myself with that pep talk, I walked around and alerted the rest of the staff that Kevin and I would be having a business dinner in the office while going over stats (another lie, but I didn't want to make it sound like we were having a cozy dinner together) and that we would both be around the rest of the night if they needed anything from us. That seemed to go over well enough for everyone, so I retreated back into the office to wait for Kevin to return with my Kung Pao Chicken and egg rolls.

Friday. I arrived at Blissful two hours before opening time. Kevin stayed at Blissful the entire night on Wednesday, even staying to count the drawer and organize receipts with me. Then Dani stayed all Thursday night with me. I felt terrible. I felt that they didn't trust me with their business, all because I left early one night. One night! And it wasn't like I skipped an entire shift at work; it was a measly forty-five minutes. The eggshells I was walking on were delicate, and I felt sure I was going to lose my job any day now. I needed to work extra hard to prove that I was a capable manager for Blissful Salon and Spa.

I shuffled my way into the office first, placing my winter coat on the rack behind the door and unwinding the blue and pink scarf from my around my neck. Placing my briefcase on the desk, I snapped it open and took out a few reports. Even though I was slammed with homework last night, I still took a stack home with me to work on. I was afraid for my latest Musical Appreciation assignment. I couldn't concentrate on my report about the elements of opera when our hairspray sales were in desperate need of a boost. How could I think about libretto and supernumeraries when a real crisis was happening in the store?

The more I went through the reports on Thursday night, the more I saw that sales were slipping overall. The bonus idea that I had for the employees helped raise the numbers from previous months before I was around, but they still needed help. Especially during the week.

I sat at the desk and tapped a pen against my mouth. Something was nagging me, an idea I thought I had. . . .I flipped through my notebook, where I would often jot down passing ideas or tasks for me to complete. There, written in pink pen: "Have specials on Tuesdays? Wednesdays? 20% off? SLOW DAYS!"

I sat up straighter in my chair. Okay, this was good. This gave me a start. I could put together an advertising plan for the slow middle of the week days. Help move products off the shelf.

Before I could start outlining my ideas, Blissful's phone rang. I picked up the office extension, shaking the computer mouse alive so I could pull up the schedule if necessary.

"Thank you for calling Blissful Salon and Spa. This is Alex, how can I help you?" I cooed into the phone.

"Oh, Alex, hi. Wow, you're there early." Dani.

A satisfied smile spread across my face. I was trying to think of ways to casually mention my early start, but this worked perfectly. "Hey, Dani! Yeah, I have some new marketing ideas that I wanted to try to plan out before next week. Since I have the weekend off, I figured I could come early and get a jump on it."

"That's great, hon. Lots of initiative, that's what we like to see." Score! "Hey, sweetie, is Kevin there by chance?"

My euphoric feeling dropped. Not this again. "No, I don't think so. I didn't see his cars anywhere, and I've been through the whole salon this morning." A white lie, but I think I would have realized by now if Kevin was in the store.

"Well, shoot. He didn't come home last night and I need help with the girls." Awkward pause. "I'm sure he was just staying at his buddy's house," she quickly interjected. "Kevin got a DUI last year and is really careful now not to drink and drive."

Something was telling me that wasn't the whole truth, but I still said, "I see."

"Shoot, shoot, shoot. I don't know how to be in two places at once. Do you know what time Allie comes in?"

I didn't have to check the schedule. I practically knew it by heart. "She should be in around 9:30 for set-up."

"Alex, sweetie, I hate to ask this of you, but I think you're my only hope. Would you be able to help me out today for a little bit? Allie can handle the store I'm sure. Who's at the desk this morning?"

"It's Kamille." Again, no checking needed. "What do you need me to do?"

"I have to drop Trinity off at her daycare in ten minutes. Camilla's baby-sitter is in the daycare center as well, so both girls will be there. But Brianna was supposed to bring snacks to her school party today, and I put her on the bus without them. They're sitting on my kitchen table."

I was still unsure about what she needed me for. And did she really want me to leave the salon—on a Friday? What happened to always being here? "Okay."

"So I need to get the girls out the door, but they are in the opposite direction of Brianna's school. Would you be able to swing out here and grab Brianna's snacks and take them to the school? I don't want her to get in trouble for not having them. Or have the other kids give her trouble. Kids are so angry these days."

Dani and Kevin's house was a good twenty minutes away from Blissful. Twenty minutes there and back, plus picking up the supplies, driving to Brianna's school, finding the classroom, making small talk with the teachers. . .I was looking at being gone for over an hour from the salon. And right when I was in the middle of a brainstorm. But how could I say no? This was Dani, my boss and my pseudo friend. I had to do it. "Okay, sure. How do I get into your house?"

"The code on the garage is 17456. Just type that in and the door will open. The door to get into the house is unlocked. Just be sure to close the garage door when you leave."

"And where is Brianna's school?" I stood up and shrugged my coat back on while listening to Dani spout directions.

"Thank you so much, Alex! I owe you one. And of course I'll pay you gas money for all your troubles. Just leave a note for Allie and let her know one of us will be there shortly."

We hung up and I scribbled a note for Allie, letting her know I had to help Dani but one of us would be back at the salon near opening time. I left my notebooks and briefcase on the desk, grabbing only my purse as I rushed out, making sure the salon doors were locked behind me.

The early morning traffic didn't help me get to Dani's any faster. I jumped out of my car, leaving the engine running, and scrambled to the garage. Punching in the numbers that I scribbled on the piece of paper, I ducked under the door and tromped up the three wooden steps leading into the house. Luckily, the plate of cookies and box of juice boxes were on the table like Dani said, so I scooped them up and rushed back out of the house. With my hands full, I had to first drop the boxes off in my car, then run back to close the garage.

Speeding to get to Brianna's school and trying to carefully read my directions, I heard my cell phone ringing from the depths of my purse. The ringtone alerted me that it was coming from my Blissful phone. Dani and Kevin had given me my own cell phone my first week on the job and paid for the phone bill. They told me I could get rid of my regular cell phone but I hadn't had the time to cancel my service yet. It was on my to-do list. . . .somewhere.

I missed the phone call and pushed harder on the gas pedal. My car clock read 9:45. Blissful opened in fifteen minutes. Damn it. It was going to be closer to eleven when I finally got back.

After successfully delivering the cookies to the classroom, waving at Brianna who gave me an eyebrow raise back (really? A seven-year old can do the one eyebrow raise?) and jumping back in the car, I finally dug out my company phone and listened to my voicemails.

9:28. "Hey, Alex, it's Allie. Just wondering if you're coming in today. I figured you would already be here by now. Let me know!"

9:34. "Me again. I checked the schedule and it said you would be here at nine. Everything okay? Are you sleeping? Wake up, silly!"

9:46. "I just called Dani and she said you were running a favor for her. Glad to hear everything is okay. See you when you get here!"

All three messages from Allie. I must have not heard my phone ringing when she called the first two times. But didn't she go into the office and see my note? Allie always left her belongings in the office as well; she should have seen the note taped to the computer. I shook my head and continued driving.

Pulling into Blissful at 10:48, I parked over the line but didn't care. I would fix it later. I jumped out and hightailed it into the salon, throwing open the front door and hearing the bells chime. I was greeted by Kamille's smiling face. Weird. She never smiled at me.

"Hey, Kamille," I said breathlessly. "How are things going in here?"

"Great!" she trilled, making me even more suspicious. Kamille did not trill. To anyone, especially not me.

"Great," I echoed. "Is Dani here?"

"Yep. Her and Kevin are in the back." More smiles.

"Oh, um, okay. Great. Thanks. I'll just head back there then." I walked past the desk and into the salon, where I was glad to see Lindsey and Carolyn with clients in their chairs. I waved my hellos and continued back, once again stripping off my winter coat and scarf.

"I'm back!" I announced, opening the office door. Dani, Kevin, and Allie were all in the office, hunched over some papers on the desk.

"Alex, sweetie, I'm so glad! Thank you so much for your help. This day would have been a disaster without you." Dani put her arms around me and squished me into her chest. I patted her on the arms, feeling slightly uncomfortable that her enormous boobs were all over me.

"No problem. It all worked out and Brianna's teacher was thrilled that the kids wouldn't have to miss snack time," I said. "Allie—I got your voicemails. Did you not see my note?" I asked, shoving my purse in a desk drawer.

163

"A note? No, I didn't see one from you." Allie looked confused.

"It was right here, taped on the computer screen. You sure you didn't get it?" I pressed, looking at the computer for my note. Then around the computer. On the desk. The floor. Where the hell was my note? I knew I wrote one.

"No, sorry. I didn't see anything." I studied Allie's face. She looked genuinely confused. I believed her.

"Huh, that's strange. I know I left one. I even taped it on the computer." I shook my head, trying to figure it out. "That is so weird."

"Kamille got here before me, but she said she didn't see anything either. And I don't know why she would have come into the office for anything. I think she just looked around up front," Allie said.

Kamille. Would she have thrown away my note? Is that why she was all smiley at me when I came in? But what would be the point? Obviously, she had to deduct that I was doing something for Dani since the note stated so. Did she really think she could try to pass me off for being late on my own accord?

"Actually, speaking of Kamille, she came to me this morning with a great idea!" Dani interjected.

I turned my attention to her. "Well, that's wonderful. What's her idea?"

Kevin piped in. "Our sales tend to suffer during the middle of the week. Less appointments, people aren't getting their paychecks yet, blah, blah, blah. Tuesday and Wednesday seem to take big hits on sales."

"I don't know how Kamille figured that out. She must have overheard us chatting about it," Dani said.

I started to get a cold feeling throughout my body. No. It couldn't be. She didn't.

"So Kamille came up with some plans, some advertising strategies to try. Check these out." Kevin thrust some loose-leaf papers my way, and I scanned them over. Kamille had taken my ideas. She had outright stolen my plans for Take Two Tuesday and Want Me Wednesday.

I was speechless. I stared at my plans, taking in all the details. She hadn't changed anything. Not one idea on here was hers. They were all mine. She hadn't bothered to change a fucking thing. My mind raced. Did I tell Kevin and Dani that these were my ideas? How would I get proof? My briefcase!

I turned around to face the desk I had been working on before Dani called. All my papers that were scattered around were gone. I opened up my briefcase. Nothing in there except my notebook and usual folders. She must have found the papers, copied everything, then disposed of them. She must have found the note I left for Allie and got rid of that too. That sneaky little bitch!

"Alex? Hello! Come on, don't you think this is great? We decided to start it next week and see how it goes," Kevin said, snapping me back to reality. I couldn't tell them the ideas were mine. I had no way of proving it. I would just have to play along.

"That's great. Very wonderful." I forced a smile on my lips. "Let's roll it out on Tuesday. I'll contact Peter and see if he can make up some new signs for us to put around the salon. And I'll bring it up on Monday's staff meeting as well so everyone knows to push it." I started moving around the office on auto-pilot, hastily scribbling a to-do list.

"Terrific! Maybe we should think about giving Kamille a little bonus as well. Such a fabulous idea. I wish I could claim it myself!" Dani said, and Kevin and Allie chuckled. I forced myself a small laugh, all while thinking, *yeah, me too*. I didn't know how, but that bitch was going to be called out on this.

Alex's To-Do List:

> *Peter—signage*
> *Prepare for Monday staff meeting*
> *Manicure for Henry date*
> *Take Kamille down!*

CHAPTER 12

"You're home! Finally. We didn't think you were ever coming back." I was greeted by Lila's scolding on Friday night when I finally walked into our apartment just minutes before nine. Even though my shift ended at seven I had all the cleaning duties to take care of, and tried to work on even better marketing ideas. And figure out how to show Kevin and Dani that Kamille stole my original ideas.

"Home. Finally. Hi, ladies. What's everyone doing here?" Lila was sitting in the living room along with Emma, Carmen, and Hannah. All were dressed casually, so I assumed there was no partying happening that night. Though everyone but Hannah was holding a margarita.

"Well, it feels like ages since we've seen you last. What the hell have you been up to?" Emma said.

I quickly dumped my purse and briefcase on the kitchen table, then wedged myself between Lila and Hannah on the couch. "I know, I know. I've been a terrible friend lately. I've been so busy at Blissful. And when I'm not physically there, I'm either taking work home with me, thinking about work or. . ." I trailed off, rubbing my eyes. I was exhausted. Usually my Friday nights were filled with drinking, getting ready to go out, and then parties. Now, it was barely nine and all I wanted to do was sleep.

"I figured you would be tired tonight—since you usually look like you're dragging when you get home—so I invited the girls up so we could just hang out here. No need to get dressed up or be anywhere. Just the five of us tonight."

I looked at my roommate, my eyes softening. "Thanks, Lila. You don't know how much I appreciate that."

She picked up my hand and gave it a squeeze. "It's nothing. But we have some serious catching up to do. These guys have barely heard about Blissful, you have a big second date tomorrow, and Hannah has some news of her own to share."

My head whipped over to my left side where Hannah sat. "What? What's your news?" I practically shouted. I knew it had to be something with Peter.

Hannah giggled. She never giggled. "It's nothing, really. Peter just asked me to go home with him over Thanksgiving break. He wants me to meet his family." Her blue eyes were bright and alive, a look I'd rarely seen on my friend. I was thrilled.

"Oh, Hannah! That is a huge step. Wow, meeting the family. Are you nervous? Excited? What will you wear?" Questions shot out of my mouth, all while I envisioned Hannah and Peter's wedding. It would be a spectacular occasion, with both Hannah and Peter's families coming from money and having important jobs and all. Carmen, Emma, Lila, and I would be her bridesmaids, of course. I wondered who she would choose as the maid of honor. Lila and I would be each other's of course, Carmen and Emma would probably pick each other, but what about Hannah? Maybe it would be me!

"Hello, Alex? Please stop planning my wedding." Hannah snapped her fingers in front of my face, cutting off my daydream.

"What? I wasn't planning your wedding. I was, um, thinking about Blissful. And schedules and facials and stuff. Duh," I said, not convincing Hannah.

"Sure, sure. But I don't really know what I'm going to wear. We're going back on Wednesday night and leaving on Friday. That means I am spending the night there—twice. Are we supposed to sleep together? Separate bedrooms? What if I can't think of anything to say around his mom or dad? How much food do I eat on Thanksgiving? Not enough might offend his mom, too much will make me look piggy." Hannah looked terrified. "I've never had a real boyfriend before. Or met anyone's parents. I'm scared."

"Don't you worry, girl. We'll make sure you are totally prepared before you leave. We'll get you the right outfits, go over some topics you can bring up, everything. You will not leave this city unprepared," Carmen vowed. The rest of us murmured our agreements.

"Thank you." I could feel Hannah relax into the couch cushion. "It's just so nerve-racking. But enough about me. Alex, you have a second date tomorrow? Is this the Bellini's one?"

I nodded, thinking about my date with Henry tomorrow. Backstabbing bitch Kamille had almost drained all my euphoric feelings about my second date. The energy and enthusiasm was slowly being pumped through my body after just minutes of being around my friends. "Yep. Bellini's it is. And I'm kind of freaking out, no lie. I don't know if I've ever been to such a fancy place. What if I don't know how to order? What if I can't find anything normal to order on the menu? I don't want to look like a complete tool in front of Henry."

We chatted about my date for a few more minutes, where I got all kinds of advice from my friends. Start with the fork farthest from the plate—Hannah. Casually rub my foot against Henry's while we are chatting—Emma. The salads would probably not come with ranch dressing, instead something fancier—Lila. To limit myself to one dinner drink in case I don't like my food and get bombed at the table—Carmen. Carmen's advice probably wasn't needed. I didn't want to bust out the fake ID and get kicked out of Bellini's. Nothing like cops and an arrest to ruin a date.

Our chat then segued into Lila's love life. "Joel is pissed about the meeting I have coming up with Mary Strubaker. Doesn't want me to go, says it's a waste of time. Good to know the person that is supposed to love me has no faith in me." Lila picked at a piece of lint on her purple socks.

"Lila, please break up with him. You know it's supposed to happen. Why are you holding on?" Carmen demanded to know.

"I know you think I'm crazy, but I had a feeling once about us getting married. Not all relationships are perfect all the time. There's going to be rough patches and fights. But I really do love Joel. We've been great together and happy for years. How can I just throw all of that away?"

"Answer me this," Emma said. "Say you meet with Mary and nail it—which I'm sure you will." Agreements all around. Lila smiled at us. "And then say she wants you to hop on the first plane to New York and meet with agents and do a photo shoot or whatever it is you need to do. You come back and tell Joel. What do you think he will do?"

Lila was silent. We all stared at her. I was sure that the four of us were thinking the same thing. Joel would flip. "I think he would be happy for me."

Giant room sigh. "Do you really think that, Lila? Or is that what you hope will happen?" Hannah asked gently.

"It sounds to me that if he doesn't even want you to go to the meeting, he sure as hell wouldn't want you to go to New York or LA, or anywhere for that matter," Emma said.

Lila was quiet for a beat longer. "Well, it doesn't even matter now. Who says that Mary will like me or want to help me? She could laugh in my face and show me to the door. Then I will have caused a big ruckus over nothing. I'll just go to the meeting, I'm sure nothing will happen, and then we can all just forget about it."

"Wait a second. So if one woman doesn't think you have what it takes, you're just going to roll over and play dead?" I asked. "Lila, you've been talking about this dream for years. You want to be an entertainment reporter. Don't let Joel or Mary bring you down. Don't bring yourself down."

"Alex is right. If you give up, it's over. All your dreams and planning and hard work down the drain. Don't do it, Lila. Keep fighting." Carmen added her advice to the fray. I looked around the room, immensely grateful for my awesome friends, their unwavering advice and support. We all stood by each other no matter what.

"Thanks, guys. I won't give up. I really won't. And I will nail this meeting with Mary. I know it," Lila said, her voice only warbling a little.

"That's more like it! That's the Lila we love," Carmen exclaimed, holding up her margarita glass in a toast.

"Speaking of—do you have me scheduled for my facial at Blissful?" Lila asked, turning towards me.

"I put you on the books today with Allie. You're scheduled for Tuesday at 6:30."

"Perfect! Thank you much."

"You're welcome. I'm sure you will love it," I said. "I'm going to get a full body wrap thing done in the next few weeks too."

"A full body wrap? What is that?" Emma wanted to know.

I explained how a wrap worked—painting lotion all over the body, then wrapping the body up like a giant cocoon and letting it sit there. I was getting the wrap meant to soften skin, but there were wraps that are said to actually slim the body. Blissful offered both. Emma asked to be scheduled for one herself, and I made a note in my phone to check the schedules and book her.

The rest of the night passed quickly. I joined in on the margarita scene, grateful for the weekend off. I planned on sleeping in, catching up on a few homework assignments that I kept pushing off, and preparing for my date with Henry. Hannah and I were going to participate in Kaufman's annual food day festival on Sunda—which was just a big to-do on campus that featured healthy foods, recipes, and lots of yummy snacks to munch on while you went from booth to booth. Lila and I discussed a possible shopping trip, which I was up for. I had barely used any of my hard-earned money since I was too busy to have a social life anymore. My bank account was happy, but I was having some shopping withdrawals. Lila, Hannah, and I also promised each other we would make it to church on Sunday. I had been slacking in the religious department lately as well.

Lila and I said our good-byes to the rest of the girls around one in the morning. I sure hadn't planned on staying up that late, but with the combination of alcohol, a late-night delivery pizza, awesome friends and some trusty board/drinking games, I couldn't let myself fall asleep early. I shuffled into my bedroom after closing the front door, not even bothering to remove my makeup or brush my teeth. I just wanted to shut my eyes.

The ringing of my cell phone woke me up the next morning. My eyelids creaked open, matted together by the eye makeup that I didn't feel like removing the night before. My mouth felt like the hangover fairy was shoving cotton balls in overnight and the room was spinning. Or it just felt like it was spinning, courtesy to the four margaritas I drank the night before.

I rolled over, looking for my phone. Before I could answer it, the ringing stopped. It was the Blissful phone. I squinted at the clock. 10:34. Check for sleeping in. The phone started ringing again. This time I flipped it open right away. "Hello?" I croaked out.

"Alex? Are you okay? You sound terrible." Dani's concerned voice came over the line.

"No, I'm fine. I was just sleeping."

"Sleeping? It's almost eleven o'clock. Wake up!"

"I'm awake now. I was just lying in bed, trying to wake up." I changed my story after hearing Dani's disapproving voice. I was sure she had been up for hours, getting her girls ready for the day, probably already running a few errands. Mothers didn't get to sleep in. Neither did professionals. Or at least I didn't think they did.

"Well, we have a problem at the salon today," Dani continued. We did? Blissful wasn't even open for another hour. What could have gone wrong? "Kamille was scheduled to work a full today and Julia was going to do the partial. Kamille called in and Julia said she can't get there until her scheduled time of two o'clock. So we have no one at the desk at noon to open. Tiffany hasn't returned my call yet."

My hungover brain was trying to keep up. Kamille—called in. No one to open. Did Dani mean. . . .

"Kevin was going to cover my shift for me today so I could get some shopping done for the holidays. Remember, I mentioned that the other day? I shouldn't have gone out of town without reaching Kevin first, but I left at six this morning and now I'm in Iowa City. I can leave right away, but it's still about a two-hour drive.

"And where's Kevin?" I asked, feeling my blood start to boil.

"I can't get a hold of him and I'm worried he's not going to be there in time. He—he didn't come home last night and I can't reach him on his cell."

What the fuck? I looked at the clock again. 10:38. Blissful opened at noon. The opener was supposed to be there at least thirty minutes prior to opening. I would never make it by 11:30.

"Alex? You there?"

"Ugh, yeah. I'm here. I don't think I can get there by 11:30," I said meekly, feeling my day off evaporate into thin air. My day to relax, to catch up on homework and shop with Lila. To prepare for my date. "I would still need to get ready and drive over."

"Allie should be there shortly. She can help with opening duties and cover the desk until you get there. Keep trying to call Tiffany. She might be able to come in and help. I was going to be there by five tonight to close up, but I can try to be there earlier. I'll leave right away, but that doesn't help the situation now. We need someone to open."

I sat up in bed, a wave of dizziness crashing over me. Not only was I getting called into work on my day off, on a Saturday, but I was going to have to do it hungover. Perfect. "Okay. I'll be there as fast as I can."

"Excellent. I'm so sorry for this, Alex. I hate to make you come in on your day off, but I really thought Kevin would be good on his word today. I'll keep in touch on my drive back. See you this afternoon." And Dani was gone. I couldn't believe my ears. What a hypocrite Kevin was. I had to be there at all times when it was my shift, but when he agrees to cover for his wife he just goes MIA?

I made my way through my morning routine in warp speed. Toothpaste speckled my mirror as I brushed without abandon, my shower was under two minutes and I skipped conditioner, opting to simply scrunch some mousse through my hair and twist it up in a clip, and I only added blush to my cheeks and mascara to my lashes. Running back into my bedroom, I pulled my black pants from my overflowing laundry basket and grabbed a light green sweater—one of the last articles of clean clothing I had left. I skipped all jewelry and even forgot my perfume, walking out of my bedroom and into the kitchen to grab my purse and briefcase. Lila was lounging on the couch watching TV when I walked by her.

"Hey, where are you going?" she asked, struggling to sit up. I was sure she was battling a hangover as well from the looks of her puffy eyes and the bowl of mac n' cheese on the floor. Lila swore by it for a hangover cure.

"I got called in today. The regular gal called in sick," I said, pulling my winter coat on and yanking a hat over my head.

"What? No! This was your day off, Alex. You need the rest." Lila finally managed to stand upright, swaying slightly as she walked over to join me by the door. "There isn't anyone else that can cover?"

"No, there isn't," I snapped, immediately feeling contrite. "Sorry. Not trying to take it out on you. I'm just pissed. Kamille called in and I guess Kevin was going to cover for Dani today while she was out of town, but now no one can find him and he's not answering his phone."

"Seriously? No one can get a hold of him?"

"Seriously. Dani's in complete panic and driving back now from Iowa City. I feel so bad for her. Her husband can't even make good on his word so she can have a day off. What a fuckhead!" I couldn't believe the anger burning through me. I had been bending over backwards for that salon since I signed on, working closer to fifty hours a week, running errands for Kevin and Dani that I didn't see anywhere under my job responsibilities, taking work home with me and this is what I get? My day off to be called in?

"I'm so sorry, Alex. I know you were looking forward to this day. And what about your date tonight?"

My spirits sunk lower. "I just hope Dani can get there at a decent time to relieve me. Hopefully I can still make myself look somewhat decent for tonight." Tears pricked behind my eyes. "And I'm hungover, Lil. I feel like shit!"

"Here." Lila scurried into the kitchen, opening a cabinet and removing a bottle of Ibuprofen. "I already took two this morning. Take these and be sure you eat something. Stop and get breakfast somewhere if you need to. We don't have anything that you can just grab. Unless you want me to make you a sandwich or something?" She shook two pills out and handed them to me, rapidly filling a glass with tap water.

I threw the pills in my mouth and took a long drink, spilling water on me in the process. Wiping the water from my chin, I said, "No, that's okay. I really need to get going. Thanks for offering though. I'll try to be home as soon as I can."

"We'll all be here to help, remember! Don't worry—this date will go smoothly. No worries." Lila gave me a quick hug, and I squeezed her back gratefully.

As I pulled into the Blissful parking lot, I decided to park around back. Sometimes I parked in the back to leave open spaces up front for the customers. I typically did this on weekends, when I knew we would be busier. I pulled around back and was driving slowly down the bumpy street when I noticed Kevin's car up ahead, about three spaces down from the Blissful back door entrance. Did he make it to Blissful in time? Would I be able to go home and sleep off this hangover? I noticed someone in the car with him, and something told me to stop my car. I braked, and watched horrified as Kamille got out of the BMW. My eyes traveled to her beat-up blue Honda parked in front of Kevin's snazzy ride. What the hell was going on here?

Without thinking, I grabbed my cell phone and flipped it open with shaking hands, tapping at the camera icon. Kamille walked around to the driver's side and leaned down. Kevin's face appeared out the window, and he gave Kamille a lingering kiss. My camera phone snapped pictures. Finally, Kamille pulled away, said a few words, then got in her car and drove off. Kevin did the same moments later.

I sat frozen in my car for a few minutes, staring at the incriminating evidence on my phone. I tried to piece everything together. Kamille had worked at Blissful last night. Did she leave her car here and go off with Kevin after her shift? Dani said on the phone that Kevin didn't come home last night. Kamille called in this morning. My mind was on overload. I felt sick. Kamille and Kevin. Kevin and Kamille. Kevin was having an affair—with Kamille?

With shaky legs, I managed to drive the few feet forward and park at the Blissful door. I shoved my phone back into my purse and made my way into the salon. I had to put on a happy face. So what if I was hungover? So what I just caught my boss cheating on my other boss with an employee? I had to pull it together and get through the day.

The afternoon passed quickly enough at Blissful. Allie had gotten the front desk ready to go for me by the time I walked in, which I was extremely grateful for considering the scene I had just witnessed. Allie, Mandy, Sophia, Courtney, and Jewel were on the books for the day. The schedules were pretty full, so walk-ins would be limited which was typical for a Saturday, but Allie and I still discussed calling in another stylist just in case we got even busier. She got a hold of Katie who agreed to come in around two. That would open up our availability and help get a few more appointments squeezed in.

I wasn't able to work on any of my regular manager duties since I was the only one at the front desk. The phones remained constant and the stream of clients checking in and out helped the time pass quickly.

"Thank you for calling Blissful Salon and Spa. This is Alex, how may I help you?" I sang sweetly into the phone, at the same time smiling at the woman that just approached the counter from the salon. I could tell she had just been massaged by her smudged mascara, rumpled hair, and sleepy gaze. I held up a finger to let her know it would be just a minute.

"I would like a massage." A gruff female voice came over the line. Definitely a smoker.

"Sure! When were you thinking of coming?" I pulled up the schedule, my pulse racing when another client walked in the door and stood behind the first lady. Shit. I hated getting backed up.

"I don't know. When do you have?"

"Were you thinking today or tomorrow? Or someday next week?" I smiled at the new customer, a distinguished looking man probably in his thirties.

"Tomorrow is fine. Someone told me there are different types of massages. What does that mean?"

Sigh. I didn't really want to explain everything with a line happening in front of me. "The basic types of massages are Swedish and deep tissue. The Swedish is focused more on relaxation as opposed to the deep tissue which is a firmer massage that focuses on target areas that you want addressed."

"Hmm. Give me the deep tissue. I like firm!" the lady barked over the phone, then started hacking in my ear. It took all my willpower not to hold the phone away from me in disgust.

"Okay. Could you hold for me for a minute while I look up tomorrow's schedule for you?" I asked, desperately wanting to address the clients in front of me.

"Yeah, sure. No mornings! I like to sleep in."

"Sure thing. Please hold." I jabbed the button on the receiver and set the phone down. "I'm sorry for the wait, ma'am. How was your massage?"

"Wonderful. Courtney does a terrific job," she said, slipping a sparkling wedding ring back on her finger. "Can I reschedule with her in two weeks?"

"You sure can." I ran through the schedule on one computer while ringing her up on the other. The phone beeped, reminding me I had someone on hold. I scrawled out an appointment card for Mrs. Klavandish and took her credit card receipt from her.

"Could you also make sure Courtney gets this?" she asked, handing me thirty dollars in cash. Jeepers, practically a fifty percent tip. Way to go, Courtney.

"I sure will. Thank you so much, Mrs. Klavandish. Stay warm out there!" With a wave and smile, she was out the door. "I'll be right with you, sir. I'm just going to finish up this phone call," I said, flashing him an apologetic smile.

"No problem. I'm actually waiting for someone anyway," he said, smiling back at me. He removed his heavy coat, showing off his pressed white shirt underneath with a bright red tie. Just coming from work possibly? Or maybe just a man that always dresses nice?

I turned my focus away from him and hastily pulled up Sunday's schedule. "Thank you so much for holding, ma'am. I have an opening tomorrow at three o'clock with Shawna. She specializes in deep tissue massage. Would that work for you?"

I typed in the woman's name, phone number and address into Shawna's three o'clock time, pressed save and ended the call. By the time I was putting the phone back in the cradle, a woman had joined Mr. Suit and Tie in the salon. She looked to be in her twenties, with platinum hair and big blue eyes. She took off her coat to reveal a slinky blue dress, patterned tights, and stiletto heels. Her boobs were way too big for her petite body— silicone I was sure—and her waist was practically non-existent. I didn't know what to think of the couple.

"I can help you now. Thank you for your patience," I said to them both, even though the man was really the only one waiting.

"We're checking in for a couple's massage. Marcus Baylor and Tamara Schmidt," the man said, putting his arm around Tamara's tiny waist. She smiled up at him, her eyes sparkling. So they weren't husband and wife. Maybe today was a special day, explaining the outfits. Maybe it started with a romantic brunch of strawberries and champagne, followed by a couple's massage, then a romantic dinner and a proposal tonight! I loved making stories up in my head about the clients that came to Blissful.

"Okay, I have you both checked in. If you can just fill out this form for me, I'll let Allie and Courtney know you are here." I handed them each a clipboard with a pen attached, and they took a seat in the corner and started writing, Tamara practically in Marcus's lap. An engagement was coming, I just knew it. How exciting for the two!

While they finished their paperwork, I hit the check-in button on the computer, alerting the therapists in the back that the clients were here. By the time Marcus and Tamara came back up with their clipboards, Allie and Courtney were approaching the front.

I was exhausted by the time Julia came in at two o'clock, and the Ibuprofen was beginning to wear off. My hangover was insistent on clawing its way back, making me feel sluggish and starving for a greasy cheeseburger. I tried to wait until Dani arrived before I went to get myself some lunch. I had told her not to rush when we were texting, but if she could be there around three that would be best. I felt bad making her change her plans, but I didn't think it was fair for me to destroy my day either. By 3:30, still no Dani. From her messages I thought she should be there shortly, but decided it was best to eat. I didn't want to wait any longer for fear I would a) throw up on the salon floor or b) not be hungry when I got to Bellini's.

"Hey, Julia, do you think you'll be okay for a few minutes?" I approached the desk with coat and hat on, purse in hand. "I haven't eaten yet today and really need to feed my stomach."

"I'll be fine. Don't worry!" she answered in her soft voice, pushing a blonde curl away from her face. I knew that Julia actually preferred to work alone, and the girl could upsell better than myself. I assured myself she would be fine, and I would be gone for no more than ten minutes.

"Okay, I'll be right back then. I have my cell phone on me if you need me. Do you want anything?" After she declined, I raced out the door and over to my Camry. I made it back to Blissful in seven minutes flat. Opening the salon door, I saw Dani at the desk with Julia. Finally! I could get home now.

"Hi, guys!" I said, feeling my spirits lift at both the thought of eating and being able to get home.

"Hi, Alex. How are you today, sweetie?" Dani said, giving me a warm smile.

"Good. It's been a busy day. We called Katie in about two hours ago to help clear us for walk-ins. I just went to grab myself some lunch," I said, feeling as though I needed to explain my absence. I held up the bag as proof.

"Terrific. Sales look great today. Thank you so much again for coming in. You were a real life-saver. You can head into the office to eat quick if you would like. Kevin's back there," Dani said, her eyes seeming to darken for a quick moment when she said her husband's name.

"Okay. I'll probably take off after that then. If that's okay, I mean," I tacked on. Dani was planning on staying until close, right? Please let her stay.

"Yes, that's fine. Kevin and I will be here the rest of the night. Thanks again for covering today. I really can't tell you how much I appreciate it."

"Sure. I just want to get home quick because I have that second date I was telling you about." I grinned at Dani, unable to hide my excitement about seeing Henry again.

"I totally forgot this was your date night! Oh, honey, please eat quick and get up out of here. Do you want anyone to do your hair or makeup here? Free of charge of course. I'll cover it for you."

"No, no, that's okay. But thank you. My friends are planning on helping me, so I should be good."

"Okay. Well, I hope you have a fabulous time with Henry. Henry, correct? I'm so excited for you. I'll want details!"

I grinned at my boss, feeling the stress of the day slowly melt away. I really did like Dani. So what there had been a mistake today? It wasn't her fault. It was her bastard husband's.

"Thanks, I'll make sure I tell you everything. Have a good rest of the night!" I headed back to the office clutching my bag of food. I was so ready to devour my burger and fries. I was starting to feel light-headed from the lack of food. Like Dani said, Kevin was at the desk, typing away at the keyboard. I smirked when I saw him typing, one finger at a time jabbing the keys. For such a smart businessman, you'd think he would learn the proper way to type.

"Alex. You're here," he said, turning to face me. I didn't like his tone of voice. Sarcastic maybe. Condescending even.

"Yep. Went to get myself some lunch," I said, once again holding the bag out as proof.

"I thought I went over this with you already. We want a manager here at all times."

Before I could stop it, my mouth dropped open. Was he kidding? "Um, I've been here all day. I literally was gone for seven minutes to get myself some lunch," I said, my hand beginning to shake.

Kevin shook his head, looking down at his phone. "Julia isn't trained enough to be left here by herself. What if something had happened and she couldn't fix it? The whole salon would have looked bad."

My anger was to a boiling point. I had come in on my day off, worked my ass off, filled in for *him,* who couldn't bother to call anyone including his wife to say he couldn't come in, and now I was getting reprimanded for getting myself *food?* For having lunch at four o'clock instead of a decent lunch hour? "Kevin, I'm sorry, but I haven't eaten yet today. I had to have some food or I would have literally fainted at the desk. I was called in this morning, on my day off, to fill in." I wanted to say *for your sorry ass,* but I wasn't feeling bold enough. "I'm not sure what I could have done differently in this situation. I rushed here this morning to try to open on time so I couldn't get breakfast or lunch to pick up. I had to eat at some point." I was surprised at how level my voice was coming out. I wanted to scream at him. How could I not be granted a lunch break?

"Next time, get something delivered. Or have one of the employees get it for you," Kevin snapped back at me. His phone started ringing at that moment. "I have to take this. This Kevin," he hollered into the phone, storming out of the office.

I stood there, stunned. So I couldn't take a lunch break. I wonder if that was noted anywhere in the employee handbook. Or if the other employees were aware that I could force them to go get me food. Like I would ever ask anyone to do that. I ate my lunch without really tasting it, wanting to cry. I was bone-tired, furious, and really needed to turn my mood around. I couldn't be snapping at Henry and taking my frustrations out on him. I needed to get out of this place. This soul-sucking, happiness-draining chamber called Blissful. What a joke.

I threw my fast food bag away and bundled myself up. Grabbing my purse, I opened the office door and started to walk down the hallway. As I passed the spa area, I could hear low voices coming from one of the rooms. I paused outside room number one, Allie's main room. I could definitely make out Kevin's low rumble and then Allie's high-pitched laugh. I wondered what they could be discussing. I hoped it wasn't me. Kevin wouldn't talk shit about his own manager to another employee though—would he? I hoped not. But after what I had seen today, I knew not to trust Kevin.

I was just getting ready to keep walking when I heard a different noise. It sounded like—no, it couldn't be. Kissing? Disbelief crawled through my skin. The soft smacking noise sure sounded like kissing to me. Before I could react, the door was pressed all the way closed. The click had me jumping out of my skin, and I practically ran the rest of the way into the salon area. Mandy caught my eye when I walked in, cocking her head in a silent question. I knew my smile was weak, but I forced it anyway and continued to rush to the front desk. Maybe it was Kevin and Dani in the room. Maybe they just needed a private moment. Maybe—

"Taking off then, Alex?" Dani asked me. Fuck. It wasn't her. What the hell was Allie doing in her massage room with Kevin?

And what the hell was Kevin doing with Allie just hours after he got done with Kamille? I felt dizzy.

"Yep, I'm off. I'll see you on Tuesday." My voice sounded shaky to my ears.

"Have fun tonight on your date. I can't wait to meet this Henry guy," Dani said, giving me a friendly wave. I waved back and said good-bye to Julia, then hurried out to my car.

What the hell was going on with Kevin Dohlman and the Blissful employees?

CHAPTER 13

"I will have the manicotti al forno with the salad, please," I said, pleased at my selection and that choosing was easier than I anticipated.

"For you, sir?" Our waiter, clad in a tuxedo and bowtie, turned to Henry.

"And I'll have the toasted ravioli with meatballs, please. Salad as well." Henry handed the waiter our menus and he was off. I breathed a sigh of relief that the ordering part was over. Bellini's had an extensive menu and luckily there were several items I was okay ordering. Even though the place was seriously fancy (I mean, the waiter was in a tux!) the menu was pretty self-explanatory.

"So I know you said you had a crazy day. What happened?" Henry asked, taking a sip of his soda. I liked the fact that he didn't order alcohol. I didn't want to feel like a dunce because I wasn't drinking, but I wasn't comfortable using my fake here—or anywhere really.

"Well, it was supposed to be my day off at Blissful, but I ended up getting called in. The regular girl called in sick and the owner was supposed to work but she had to shop and then. . ." I trailed off, realizing how heavy my body felt just talking about Blissful. And how disgusted I felt knowing about Kevin and his sleazy ways with the staff. "You know what? I don't even want to talk about work tonight. Some stressful things are going on there, and I just want to really enjoy myself. With you," I added, hoping that wasn't a blush I felt creeping into my cheeks. Henry looked good tonight, in pressed khakis and a white dress shirt with faint blue lines running vertically through the material. His dark hair was neatly combed and his blue eyes, well, were doing funny things to my stomach. I kept having to remind myself it was only the second date. I wasn't in love with this guy or anything.

"That's fine by me. Lila mentioned you might be a little stressed about it today."

"She did? When?"

"When you went back into your room to get your gloves. She just said you've been working extra hours and the no sleep is getting to you. And that I had to make sure you eat tonight." He chuckled, but I felt mortified. Was Lila implying to Henry that I was anorexic? He must have noticed my stricken face because he quickly added, "I don't think she meant anything bad by it. Just that you're so busy you rarely get any time for yourself anymore. That's all."

I relaxed into my seat. Of course that's what Lila meant. "Yeah. It's been a little crazy. And apparently I don't get a normal lunch break like everyone else."

"I'm sorry, what? You don't get a lunch break? Isn't that illegal?"

I shook my head, trying to get Blissful out of my thoughts. "Sorry, no, never mind. No Blissful talk. Just a weird situation that happened today."

But Henry didn't look convinced. "Alex, are you not allowed to take breaks when you're working? Because that is illegal. For every four hours you work you get a fifteen-minute break. Or something along those lines. I don't remember the exact numbers, but you can't work all day without one."

"No, today was just a weird situation with getting called in and all that. I'm sure it won't happen again." I wasn't so sure. "But really, let's just change the subject. Where do you work?"

"I work at the youth center downtown."

"Really? Doing what?"

Henry shrugged, but the look on his face was unmistakably proud. "This and that. I do a lot with the kids and sports. Ref the basketball games, coordinate all the schedules for the gyms, try to drum up interest in the sports program."

"The youth center. Isn't that where kids go when—well, when they. . ." I wasn't sure how to phrase my question.

"It's mainly used by kids whose parents don't have a lot of income. Many times the kids are told to go to the youth center to keep them off the streets. Their schools will make them go there."

I nod my head, impressed by Henry's obvious interest in helping these kids. "I guess I was going to say underprivileged, but didn't want that to come out the wrong way or anything."

"No, underprivileged is a good word to use. Most of these kids come from broken homes, or parents that are in jail. Some just don't have the money to be able to belong to the fancy gyms around here."

"Do you like what you do?"

"I love it. I like working with kids and teaching them sports. I've always loved sports, but everyone in my family was always too busy for me when I was growing up. My dad owns his own business and my brother was always into designing and building things, not really sports. I did a lot on my own and then with Peter and Max when we became friends."

"What's your favorite sport?"

"Probably baseball. I was the starting pitcher my junior and senior year. I got offered a scholarship to play at a college in Wisconsin, but didn't take it."

The waiter appeared then, dropping a basket of warm bread and an oil dipping sauce at our table. He made a big production of dropping some black seeds into the oil and mixing it around, then placing tiny bread plates in front of us. I reached for a piece of bread and dropped it on my plate, avoiding the oil.

"Why didn't you take the scholarship?" I asked, curious.

"My family preferred me to stick with business. Hopefully join my dad's company one day, take over the family business kind of thing. My brother only wants to do the design part, more of the architecture, than actually run the business."

"I see. And what kind of company does your dad run?"

"He deals a lot with properties. Like buying old homes, flipping them, and then selling them for a lot more."

"Flipping them?"

"Cleaning them up, making them look nicer, more sellable. Jacob is a big asset to him with his architecture work. I think Dad wants me to fall into either business."

"And you're not really interested in either?" I took a guess.

Henry shook his head, leaning back in his chair. "No. Not really. I don't care much about either. I interned at Jacob's company when I first came to Kaufman, and I can do it. I really can. I understand the blueprints and the designing aspects and all that. But I didn't feel anything when I was doing it. It was just. . .mundane. Boring. Tedious. And with Dad's line of work, I mean, it's cool. It's awesome to see the before and after of these houses. But all the work that goes into securing the house, then hiring the people to do the work, then putting the house on the market, blah, blah. It's boring to me."

Our meals came then, steaming plates that smelled like heaven in a meatball. My manicotti looked exquisite. I didn't think I had ever thought exquisite when it came to a meal prior to coming to Bellini's, but that is just what my dinner looked like. The salad even looked like a high-class salad, with lettuce that looked so crisp I just wanted to crack it, tomatoes and cucumbers piled high, tiny little croutons, and a mystery nut sprinkled throughout. I wasn't sure what the dressing was, but as Lila warned me, it surely wasn't ranch.

"This looks amazing. I'm almost afraid to eat it. It's like art," I whispered, then immediately felt a little silly. Henry had eaten here before, and from the way he spoke about his family, it sounded like they had money. I was just the poor starving girl who always forgot to eat.

To my relief, Henry grinned back at me, his smile flapping the wings of the butterflies taking up residence in my stomach. "I know, right? If I can tell you the truth, this place always scares me a bit. I feel like I can't make one mistake or I'll be kicked out. Heaven forbid I don't eat my salad with the correct fork or don't place my napkin in the proper place to signal I'm done."

"Where does the napkin go when you're done?"

"On the plate. Not on the table. I learned that lesson here."

"Really? I don't know any of those rules. I'm much more of a. . .well. . .Applebee's kind of girl." I was embarrassed to admit it, but so what? Henry came to Applebee's with me on the first date. He could have declined.

"Same here. I'm a messy eater, and I feel like I should have napkins covering my whole body when I eat. I like places where they give you wet naps because they just know things are going to get messy. Or bibs. I'm a big fan of bibs."

My laugh was loud, maybe a little too loud for Bellini's. Patrons at the other tables glanced our way as if I just stood on my chair and started performing the Macarena. "Whoops, my bad." I blushed, wanting to crawl under the table.

"Don't even worry about it. I've done much worse here."

As we tucked into our dinners, Henry regaled me with stories of embarrassing his parents at fancy restaurants, sometimes on accident, sometimes on purpose just to get a rise out of them. I hung on to his every word, laughing louder and louder at each story. The night passed fast, too fast in my opinion. Before I knew it, our waiter was removing our plates (after we placed our napkins on them) and bringing the check.

Henry settled the bill, then looked up at me. "Well, now what?"

"What do you mean?" I asked, confused.

"Do you want to just go back to Wacker? Or is there anything else you'd like to do tonight?"

"I—I'm not sure, I guess. Did you have anything in mind?"

"Well—and tell me if I'm being totally out of line here—but I don't really want this to end just yet. I'm having too much fun."

Fun? With me? I wanted to die from happiness. "I don't want it to end either," I said softly, my eyes piercing straight into Henry's. Damn, I was lucky.

"Do you have to work tomorrow?"

Instantly, my body grew tired. Just the mere mention of work and I felt exhausted and worried. "No, I don't have to work. Hopefully I won't get called in again either."

"Do you want to come back to my place? Maybe we can stop by and grab a movie to watch or something?"

Going back to his place? On our second date? My toes tingled. Did I want to do that? Um, hell yes!

"That sounds perfect. What are your roommates up to?"

"Peter might be home, but both Max and Kyle were going to some Irving party tonight." He named the other popular business college in the area. "And my guess is Peter is probably studying."

We stood up to leave, gathering out winter coats and slipping into them. "Hannah is probably doing the same thing back at our place. They are so meant for each other."

"Peter talks about her a lot. I think he really likes her." Henry held open the restaurant door for me, doing the same when we reached his car. Such a gentleman. And score for Hannah! I couldn't wait to tell her.

"Does he? She told me she is going back to Truvista with him over Thanksgiving. Quite the step for them," I said, turning on the button for my seat warmer. I really needed to get a car with that function.

"Yeah, Peter mentioned that too. Your family is in Seattle, right? What do you do for the holidays?" Was he asking me if I wanted to go home with him, or just curious?

"I always go to Seattle over Christmastime. My sister goes all out for the holiday. Usually for Thanksgiving I go to Okana with Lila. Her family is like a second family to me."

"Is that what you're doing this year?"

"That's what I plan on. Hopefully my work schedule will work in my favor."

"That's cool." Henry was silent for a while, and I wondered again if he was going to invite me home. Should I invite him to Seattle for Christmas? That seemed way too forward. A second date to traveling by air to visit my family for a week? And with my sister's five kids—any guy would go running for the hills.

Idle chitchat filled the car as we left Bellini's and headed back in the direction of Henry's house. We stopped at a Redbox on the way, picking out a Will Ferrell comedy that neither of us had seen. When we got back to his house, Peter was indeed at the table studying, textbooks and notebooks spread out on every available inch of surface. I could just picture Hannah beside him with her books and notes and highlighters, the two of them helping each other figure out problems they were stuck on and pausing between assignments for lingering kisses. It was so romantic! Nerdish, but still super romantic.

"Hey. How's the studying going, man?" Henry asked when we walked into the kitchen. I stood awkwardly between the kitchen and living room, not sure of my place.

"Fine, fine." Peter took off his glasses and rubbed his eyes with his fists. "About finished finally. Maybe I can actually watch football with you guys tomorrow for once. Hi, Alex. How are you?" he asked, bringing me into the conversation. I stepped into the kitchen with a bit more confidence.

"Hi, Peter. I'm fine. Thanks." I managed to spit out before clamming back up again.

"What are you crazy kids up to tonight?" Peter asked, looking from me to Henry.

"We just rented a movie. Going to watch it in the basement if you don't mind," Henry answered, opening the fridge. "Do you want a beer, Alex?"

"Sure!" Beer might not top my favorites list, but I could still swig one down. And maybe it would help take the edge off. I couldn't believe how nervous I was.

"Fine by me. I'll probably just finish up here and hit the sack," Peter said, slipping his glasses back on. "My eyes are beginning to lose focus."

I wanted to bring up Hannah somehow, but couldn't figure out a way to be casual about it so I just stayed silent. Henry grabbed us two beers, then opened up a cabinet drawer and pulled out some microwave popcorn, sticking it in the microwave after my enthusiastic nod. It was like a movie theater date, but at his house and with beer. Okay, so not really close to a movie theater date, but whatever.

After saying good night to Peter, we traipsed down the stairs and headed to where the TV was. The basement looked a lot better than the last time I saw it—the Halloween party—and I said so to Henry.

"That next day was hell to clean." He laughed. "Peter actually offered to hire a cleaning service to come in, but I would have hated doing that to a stranger. Max actually clipped his nose shut with a chip clip to avoid the smell."

"Yikes. Remind me never to have parties then!"

"Do you plan on moving off campus anytime soon?"

I thought about it. "Not really, I guess. We never discuss it anyway. I think the five of us like being around each other, but I'm not sure a house could handle all of us under the same roof. Maybe after this year we'll talk about it more. We'll all be twenty-one—finally might I add—so probably better to get off campus."

"When's your birthday?" Henry asked, flipping the television on and firing up the DVD player.

"January twenty-third. Less than two months away now. I can't wait to be able to go out with everyone. Hannah is the only other one that isn't twenty-one, and I know the other girls like a few bars around here. I have a fake, but I hate using it. But then I feel bad when they stay in just for me." I took a seat on the couch, after deliberating where to choose. The middle? Was that too forward? I finally sat on the right side, but closer to the middle than the edge.

"I remember how that felt. My birthday is in April, so I was one of the last ones to become legal. It sucked. I had a fake too, my brother's, and it was pretty decent. I still had to be careful though. Didn't want to screw over myself and my brother just to go to a bar."

The DVD started, and Henry walked away from the area without a word. The lights dimmed, and he appeared again with a thick blue quilt in his arms. "It can get chilly down here. I thought this might be good to have."

He sat down on the couch, right next to me. With his hip touching my hip and his arm on my arm, I felt like I could faint. He smelled delectable, manly with a hint of Italian restaurant lingering on his clothes. The white button-down he was wearing made his blue eyes stand out even more, and the way he unbuttoned a few of the top buttons made him look casual yet sexy. I wondered briefly if I was going to be spending the night. My black leggings would be fine to sleep in, but Lila's silky green top with pearl buttons might not be as comfortable. I would make that decision later.

Henry flipped the tops on the beers and handed me one. He placed the popcorn bowl to his left, where there was room. We settled in as the movie began, sitting side by side and just barely touching. I relaxed into the sofa, pulling the quilt over my legs and feeling blissfully happy. As soon as that thought reached my thoughts, I banished it. No Blissful anything tonight. Tonight, I was simply there to enjoy myself.

About twenty minutes and forty-seven laughs in, Henry shifted on the couch, leaning closer to me. His arm brushed mine, and then reached down and held my hand. Flutter butterflies, flutter. His fingers interlaced mine and gave them a squeeze. I dared to look over at him and when I did, he was staring back at me. "Is this okay?" he whispered, even though we were the only two down there.

I nodded my head and gave him a smile, squeezing his hand back. I tried not to look too giddy at the mere fact of hand holding. What was I—in sixth grade again? Our attention went back to the movie, with Henry's thumb stroking my hand ever so slightly. My toes were tingling.

About halfway through Henry let go of my hand, and the cold crept around my fingers that were used to his warm palm protecting them. It was crazy how that one gesture deflated me so much. "I have to go to the bathroom. Do you mind if I pause it?" he asked, remote in the hand that was just holding mine.

"Yeah, that's fine," I answered, and he got up and I could hear his footsteps on the stairs. I pulled my phone out of my purse which was beside the couch, and hastily thumbed a text to Lila. *Dinner=amazing. At Henry's watching movie. Might stay???*

Her immediate reply: *Holy shit girl. Stay stay!!! Naughty ;)*

We're not being naughty. Holding hands. Will text later. Don't wait up!

NAUGHTY! From all of us. Good luck!

Great, so she was with the girls. Who now probably all thought we were rounding third base. Hand holding did not equal naughty! And who would do that on a second date? Well, probably Carmen and Emma, but certainly not Hannah and probably not Lila. And not me. Definitely not me. . .but Henry was looking good. And was obviously sweet and charming and I thought he was into me. What would be the harm? Damn!

Could he really be weakening my resolve? No funny business on the second date. Really, not even the third. Maybe the fourth. I had to stay strong.

That resolve lasted until our first kiss. When Henry came back from the bathroom, we shifted positions on the couch. Instead of sitting up we laid down, Henry in back with one arm draped over me, hand once again holding mine. At some point during the movie, I felt the urge to turn my head and look at Henry. He was staring at me again, and then we were kissing. Who started it? I thought it was him, but I came to find out later that he swore it was me. It didn't matter. What mattered was his lips were on mine and I was melting into his body. I've had first kisses with guys before, but none like the experience with Henry. I didn't want to ever let up.

The first was slow and sensual, where my brain was still trying to catch up with my body. The second was less timid, more tongue, and I felt a small moan escape my mouth. Embarrassing or hot, it was a toss-up. The third was powerful, where I grabbed the back of Henry's head and brought him closer with urgency, and he grabbed my hips and pulled me into him. He was excited. And holy shit was I excited. And feeling naughty. All resolve of third and fourth dates went out the window. I wanted Henry Landon.

The movie was long forgotten as we finally pulled away and looked into each other's eyes, slightly out of breath. My bottom lip was sore from where he had bit down softly, which had only turned me on more. I struggled to sit up and Henry followed suit. I swung my legs around so I was straddling him and we were face to face. I grabbed his head again and pulled him towards me, lips on lips once again. He touched a palm to the top of my head, a gesture that cried out with intimacy and emotion. Goosebumps flew up around my arms, and the hair on the back of my neck prickled.

Adrenaline and lust went surging through my body, and I boldly started to undo the buttons on my shirt. To my surprise Henry stopped me, placing his hands over mine and halting my motion.

"What's wrong?" I asked, feeling stupid suddenly. He didn't want me. Why didn't he want me?

"Maybe we should get back to the movie," he said, pushing a lock of hair behind my ear.

I tore my body off his, once again sitting up on the couch next to him. My thoughts were buzzing. I was just rejected. One hundred percent rejected. Who does that? What male species in his right mind rejects a clearly willing girl? I remembered Hannah talking about the Halloween party, where a girl had tried the "passing out" trick in Henry's bed. He had turned her down. We all thought it was because of me, but now. . . .

"Do you want another beer?" Henry asked, breaking the awkward silence.

"Um, no. I probably shouldn't if I want to drive home," I said, then realized I didn't have my car with me. The only way home was through Henry. "Oh, shit. I guess that won't work either, huh? I can just have Lila come pick me up."

"I can drive you home if you would like. Or you're more than welcome to spend the night here," Henry offered, looking once again like his sweet self, not someone who just flat out denied me. Now he wanted me to spend the night? My brain hurt trying to figure this guy out.

"Ah, well, I'll leave that up to you, I guess. I can just sleep on the couch or something and have Lila get me tomorrow. Those girls are probably all drinking anyway." Except for Hannah, who I could have called, but I was curious about Henry even more now. How would the rest of our night go? Would we kiss again? Just be more awkward?

"That's fine. Unless you want me to drive you home, of course. I don't have a problem with that."

"Okay, well, let's just finish the movie for now. And I'll take that second beer." I smiled at him, trying to avoid the word "reject" that was flashing through my mind. I fished my phone out again and shot off a text to Lila the second Henry started up the stairs.

Just got denied. By a boy. What is wrong w me? Be on standby to pick me up tmrw.

WTF? I expect full details tmrw. *Text me when ready. Ur beautiful. Love you.*

Love you lil :(

Don't be sad! He's blind. Or maybe just a nice guy. I'll buy u breakfst in the am.

Okay. G2g talk tmrw.

Henry and I didn't talk much the rest of the movie. The awkward feeling was definitely there, and I didn't know how to break it. Once the movie was finished, Henry stood up and stretched his arms over his head. At some point, he changed out of his khakis and collared shirt into basketball shorts and T-shirt. He looked even sexier dressed down.

"Are you sure you want to sleep on the couch, Alex? I hate to make you stay down here," he said, collecting our beer cans and placing them on the pool table.

"I'll be fine," I said, not wanting to ask to sleep with him or have him stay with me. I might have given in earlier when we were kissing, but now I was just mad. And embarrassed. Denied. Rejected. How I so wanted my car so I could get the fuck out of his house.

"Well, if you're sure." He paused, giving me another chance to blurt out my thoughts. I refused and just smiled up at him, fake and phony. "Okay, well, you can come up and get me if you need. My bedroom is the first door on the right in the hallway off the kitchen. Wake me up when you want a ride home tomorrow, okay?"

"Got it. Thanks," I said, the icy tone impossible for him to ignore. Right?

"Well, goodnight, Alex," he said, turning away.

"Night," I replied, on the verge of tears. What had I done wrong?

Before I could think another thought, Henry was back in front of me, his lips on mine. My eyes widened in surprise before fluttering shut, happiness once again coursing through my veins.

When Henry finally pulled away, we were both breathless again. He leaned his forehead against mine, then found my mouth again. I could only keep kissing him back, no questions asked. "You have no idea how badly I want to invite you into my bed," he growled against my mouth, his words causing my body to react with excitement.

I just stared at him, my eyes asking why. He kissed me again, this time soft and sweet. "I like you, Alex. I like you a lot. Sleep well." And then he was gone. Grabbing the beer bottles off the pool table and disappearing up the stairs. I leaned back into the couch, mulling over his words. Maybe Lila was right. Maybe he was just a nice guy. Could he be gay? No. No gay guy would take me on two fantastic dates and kiss me like that. A player? Possibly. Involved with someone else? I hoped not. But maybe he had a girlfriend stashed away somewhere, like back in Truvista, and kissing didn't count as cheating but sex did.

I hunkered down on the couch, pulling the quilt to my chin. I needed Lila.

"So, wait, back up. He went to go upstairs, then came back down and kissed you again, and said he liked you?"

"All correct."

"But he made you sleep on the couch?"

"He didn't really force me, but he didn't invite me into his bedroom either."

"Very weird. What do you want to eat?"

"Just that sausage biscuit. And an orange juice." I leaned back in my seat and pulled my hat farther over my head. Lila's rearview mirror screamed that the outside temperature was a brisk twenty-two degrees. I wished she had seat warmers like Henry's car. My leggings were not protecting me against the cold leather.

Lila ordered our food and pulled her car towards the window. Fast food for breakfast was always the cure for a hangover, even though I wasn't really hungover. But I could tell Lila was, and she still came and picked me up from Henry's at six in the morning. A true trooper and friend.

I had felt like I was doing the walk of shame out of Henry's house that morning, especially since I believed Max had seen me sneaking out of the house. Right as I opened the front door to make my escape I heard someone say my name behind me, but I hurried out without looking back and ran to Lila's awaiting vehicle. I think the voice was Max's. I hoped it wasn't Henry's. Or Peter's. For some reason, Peter catching me walking out with smudged makeup and morning hair embarrassed me the most.

After we received our food and headed back towards campus, Lila started talking again. "So. What the hell. We need to figure this guy out. Maybe we could have Hannah ask Peter—"

"No! I do not want Peter to get involved. It would be too embarrassing if he starts asking Henry questions. Let's not go that route."

"Okay. No involving other guys. But, Alex, I'm confused. Why he turned you down," I winced when she said that, "why he didn't at least let you sleep in his bed, or why he said he liked you but then walked away. It's too weird for me."

"I know. Me too. Maybe Carmen and Emma will have some more ideas for us."

"He's gay."

"He's not gay, Carmen. I already thought it and ruled it out. He doesn't walk, talk, dress or act remotely gay. He took me on two amazing dates and kissed me like he actually liked it. And I felt *him* when I was sitting on top of him. Not gay." I shoved the sausage biscuit in my mouth, relishing in the grease. We rarely had fast food, especially with Lila's new diet, but sometimes you just had to cave.

"Maybe he's saving himself for marriage. Is he religious?" Emma wanted to know.

I paused, chewing thoughtfully. "You know, that could be it. Really. I know he has a somewhat religious family, and went to a Catholic school all the way until college. Do people really still do that? Save themselves for marriage?"

"Um, hello? Hannah," Carmen said.

"Oh, yeah. Hannah. I wonder if Peter is, too. Weird. What if all those guys are virgins?" I asked, the picture just not adding up in my mind. A house full of dude virgins? Practically unheard of. Minus the practically.

"No, I'm pretty sure Max is not a virgin. He's the partier of the group, the player. And I really don't think Kyle is either," Carmen said. "But Henry and Peter. . . .Peter definitely yes. Henry could go either way in my opinion."

"Hmm. Emma, you could be on to do something here. It's actually kind of hot if it's true," I said, sucking down some OJ.

"You find inexperienced guys hot now?" Lila wanted to know, crumbling her wrappers and depositing her garbage in the trash can.

"I don't know. No one to compare me to is kind of a nice thought."

"And you can train him. Teach him all your tricks," Emma said, her blue eyes sparkling with a devilish glint.

"Yeah, Emma, sweetie, I don't think I have quite as many tricks as you," I told her, causing Carmen to bark with laughter. "Or you, darling," I said, flashing my smile at Carmen. "I've only been with two guys before. I don't have the most experience in the world either. Oh, no. What if our sex is terrible? Two people just bumping uglies without a clue what they're doing!" I wailed, envisioning rotten, awkward sex with Henry.

"I'm sorry, what? Bumping uglies? Where the hell did you get that crass expression?" Lila asked, wrinkling her nose at me.

"I don't know. Probably a movie or something. But, guys, this is awful!" I shrieked.

"Calm down. For all we know, he is not a virgin and is really a man whore. Maybe he has herpes and had a flare-up and was doing the respectable thing by not passing them to you."

The three of us stared at Carmen. "What?" she said. "You never know these days."

I sighed. "Well, we've gone from he's gay to he's a virgin to he has herpes. I would say we're no closer to figure out his deal."

"Are you going to see him again?" Emma asked me.

"I don't know. We didn't plan anything last night. And I certainly don't want to make the first move. I guess I'll just wait and see if he texts me today," I said, my outlook feeling glum. "What if he doesn't? What if he's just done with me?"

Lila slung her arm around me. "Don't think that way. He's a nice guy, Alex. I have that vibe from him. You'll get this all figured out. Rome wasn't built in a day."

"Thanks. Thanks for waking up, too," I said to Carmen and Emma. They had both passed out in our room last night, and when Lila and I had woken them up this morning to discuss my issue, there were only minor complaints from them both.

"You're very welcome. Now, I'm going to go back to sleep in my own comfy bed. Alex, do you plan on getting called into work again today?" Carmen asked, standing and helping Emma to her feet.

"I fucking hope not," I said, then saw the startled expression on my friends' faces. "Sorry. Violence unnecessary. No. I hope not to get called in. I want to try to catch a few more hours of sleep, go to late mass, and I have so much homework to get caught up on. I can't afford to miss some of these assignments."

"Well, maybe we could all do lunch together somewhere. Get Hannah to come along as well. We'll go once you guys get back from church. Just have a nice girls date. We haven't had one in a while," Emma said, and we all agreed to the plan. I considered briefly turning my cell phones off so Blissful couldn't reach me with any problems, but I knew I would just get into more trouble that way. Better to leave them on and just hope and pray that there were no emergencies.

I said good-bye to the girls then made my weekly Sunday phone call to my sister, and was able to talk to all three of my nieces as well. The one time where I was hoping for a super quick phone call with only Alicia had to be the time all the girls wanted to chat. But I knew it was terrible to complain about being able to talk to them, so I forced a smile and kept my eyelids open while hearing about their school, friends, and all the new books Candace wanted to check out from the library. After almost an hour of phone time, I was finally able to hang up and think about sleep.

After wiping off my makeup and changing into suitable pajamas I crawled into my bed, carefully setting both my Blissful phone and personal phone on my nightstand. I wanted to be available if Henry called. Not so much if Blissful summoned.

CHAPTER 14

"Lila Medlin, here for my facial."

"Hello, ma'am. Have you been to Blissful before?"

"Nope. And I hear it's awful!"

Lila and I cracked up as I checked in her on the computer system. "Gee, thanks. Keep boosting my already fragile ego, why don't you?" I said, trying to make light of my situation.

"Still no word from Henry?"

"Nada. It's been three days. Do you think it's over?"

Lila drummed her fingertips on the glass counter. I noticed she needed a manicure as well and made a mental note to schedule her for one. "I don't know, Alex. I really thought he was into you. We all did. It's just so bizarre."

"Bizarre. Good word." I pushed a clipboard her way. "Fill out the form please, so Allie will have all your info when she's ready for you."

Lila continued to stand at the counter while she answered the questions. "Is my skin dry, oily, or a combination? Um, I don't know. Alex, expert opinion?"

I peered at my friend's face, thinking back to all the times I helped her with her makeup. "I would say more dry. Especially this time of year with the cold weather. She could do a moisturizing mask on you that I'm sure you'll love."

"Okay." Lila continued writing. "What are the reasons for my appointment today? Can I say to support my roommate?"

"Just say that you want better skin and for some relaxation. You get an awesome shoulder, head, and foot massage."

"Really? I don't think I knew that. What does that have to do with a facial?"

"I didn't tell you about the massages? My bad. They're my favorite part. But yeah, when the masks are settling in the estheticians have to do something with their time."

"Good point. Awesome." After a few minutes, Lila handed her completed form back to me. "I can't believe I spaced on Thanksgiving. Are you sure you're not mad that you have to stay in town?"

"Nah. I just found out this morning that I couldn't get it off anyway. We're closed on Thursday, but I have to work Friday. Most of the employees asked for it off, and Dani does the Black Friday shopping. It sounds like I'll be working the whole day actually."

Lila's meeting with Mary Strubaker was the Friday following Thanksgiving, so instead of going back to Okana to visit her family like we usually did, we would both be staying in town for the holiday. Lila and I were just going to celebrate the day together by doing nothing, being couch potatoes, and possibly ordering a pizza. Neither of us wanted to attempt a turkey.

"Oh. Sorry to hear that. I told Frank that I would work the weekend, but he only scheduled me for Saturday and Sunday. I have all of Friday off, which is good since I'm not sure how long the meeting will last."

Allie entered the front then, her black hair set in a high bun and very little makeup on. Her permanent tan always made her look like she was glowing, so she didn't need the help. "Hi, ladies!" she greeted us, enthusiastic as usual. I tried to make sure my smile looked as normal as possible, though I was still a tad shaky around Allie. Could she really be with Kevin on the side? There was just no way—I hoped. "You must be Lila. I've heard so much about you!" Lila and Allie shook hands, then Allie swiped Lila's intake form off the counter. "I know Alex says you have a pretty special occasion going on next week. Let's go and get started right away then, yeah?"

"Sounds good to me. Alex just informed me that massages are included!"

"That's right! Is this your first facial?"

"Yep. First time for any sort of spa treatment actually." Lila waved bye and she and Allie disappeared into the salon. I shook my head, grinning at how excited my friend was. I hoped she would enjoy herself.

A few minutes after they were gone, the bell tinkled when the door was opened, and in walked a familiar looking man with two young children in tow. I couldn't place how I knew him, but his face was familiar. "What do you say, kids? Does Mommy deserve a massage for her birthday?" he asked the two children.

"Yeah, yeah!" the kids shouted, jumping up and down. They looked adorable in poufy jackets and oversized hats. I had to smile at their enthusiasm for their mommy's birthday.

The man approached the counter. "Hello. Do you offer gift cards?" he asked.

"We do! You can place any amount you would like on one," I answered, smiling at him and his kids. The little girl gave me a big grin back, her mouth full of tiny baby teeth. I giggled. She giggled.

"Okay then. I'm thinking a massage will be great. Maybe the ninety-minute massage. Yeah, that will be good."

"All right. Would you like to add a gratuity on there?" I asked, pulling out a gift card from the drawer and clicking 'gift card sale' on the computer screen.

"What do you mean by that?"

"You can add a gratuity onto the gift card so that way the person receiving it doesn't have to worry about leaving a tip after the appointment. It's all taken care of for them," I explained.

"Oh, I see. Yes, great idea. Let's add on twenty percent."

I went through my screens then scanned the barcode on the card. I rescanned the card just to make sure everything was loaded properly. Looked good. "Do you want me to write out the to and from for you on the gift card holder?"

"That would be great. My handwriting is terrible, and I can't quite trust these kiddos with that duty yet," the man said, glancing at his children.

I laughed. "I can see your reasoning. Are they twins?"

"They are. Only three minutes apart. Luke is the older one, and sure likes to let Erin know that. He's the big bully but protective big brother all rolled in one."

I glanced at the children again, who now sat on the floor with each other playing with a red truck that appeared out of nowhere. I assumed one of them was holding onto it when they walked in, because they surely wouldn't have found it in the salon. They looked to be around three or four I guessed with my inexperienced eye. I took the client's credit card and ran it through the machine, pausing when I saw the name. Marcus Baylor. Marcus Baylor? It was him! He was Mr. Suit and Tie from Saturday. I would have never guessed the woman with him that day was his wife. They had acted too, well, giddy and lovey dovey for a husband and wife. I remembered thinking they were going to get engaged that day. But they already had two kids? I was way off.

"Here's your card back, Mr. Baylor," I said, handing it to him. "What was your wife's name?" I thought it had started with a T, but couldn't be sure.

"Lisa. Lisa Baylor. If you can just say from Dad, Luke, and Erin, that would be perfect."

I scrunched my nose as I wrote in my best calligraphy skills. I could have sworn it was a T name. Lisa rang no bells. I finished writing, slid the gift card into a Blissful envelope, and handed it to Mr. Baylor. "There you go. And here's the receipt for you. Thanks for coming in! I hope she enjoys her gift," I said, itching to pull up the schedule from Saturday.

"Thank you so much. Ready, kids?" He scooped up Erin in his arms and pressed Luke into his side and with the tinkling of the bell, they were off. I clicked out of the sale screen and found Saturday's schedule. Sure enough, a twelve-thirty couple's massage for Marcus Baylor and Tamara Schmidt.

I leaned forward on the counter, thoughts in overdrive. Clearly, Marcus had been cheating on his wife with Tamara. They were all over each other on Saturday. I couldn't even begin to pretend it was his sister or just a friend. Scumbag. And he seemed like such a nice guy! I was a little surprised he didn't recognize me and feel bad that I had just checked him and his mistress in for a couple's massage three days prior. And the kids? They were so cute and unknowing their dad was a two-timer.

The icky thoughts stayed with me until Lila and Allie reached the front again. Lila had her makeup reapplied, but her face glowed with difference from the effects of the facial. "How did everything go?" I asked.

"Great! It was really good, Alex. Thanks for making me try that," Lila said. Her words sounded sincere, but her voice seemed a little off. And why was she staring at me so weird? I smoothed down my hair, wondering if something was out of place. Was there lipstick on my teeth?

"Glad you liked it, hon. You'll have to come back in for another one after you get signed with Mary." Allie grinned at Lila, who smiled faintly back. Something strange was definitely going on with her.

"I sure will. And I hope so. That I get signed, I mean," Lila tripped over her words. "Oh, let me get you some money." She fumbled around to open her wallet, but I pushed it away.

"No, no. This is my gift to you. I'll take care of it."

"What? No way, Alex. I can't have you doing that," she protested.

"I want to. Trust me. My treat. A good luck present."

Lila tried arguing a few more times, but I stood firm. "I insist. I have all this extra money that I can't find time to do anything with. I might as well treat my best friend who somehow doesn't think I'm a lunatic to a facial."

"Why would she think you're a lunatic?" Allie asked.

"Just because I've turned into a crazy workaholic that runs around the house screaming about schedules and advertising and conference calls."

"And who I have to watch and make sure she eats, like I'm a freakin' anorexic guidance counselor or something," Lila chimed in.

"Hey! In my defense, it's not like I'm trying to be anorexic. I literally just forget sometimes that I need food to survive." I tried to stand up for myself. I hated feeling like people thought I wasn't eating on purpose. That was truthfully not the, well, truth.

"I know, I know. And I'm happy to watch over you." Lila patted my hand. "Well, I have to run. Meeting Joel tonight for a late dinner."

"You are?" I had barely heard Lila speak a word about Joel. We all knew that he was furious over her impending appointment with Mary.

"Yep. I could come home tonight a single lady," she confessed.

"Seriously? You really think you might break up?" I was shocked, at least a little bit. The other girls and I had been anticipating that it would happen, but I really wasn't sure Lila would ever pull the trigger.

"We'll see. He'll probably try to keep talking me out of going to meet with Mary and just piss me off. Whatever. I can't deal with the drama. I have bigger things to focus on. Like my own life."

"Good for you, Lila. We need more strong women like you in the world," Allie chimed in, earning a strange look from Lila. Almost. . .tepid? What had happened during that facial?

"Thanks. Alex. . .I'll just see you at home, okay?"Lila was giving me some sort of look with her eyes, but I didn't know how to interpret it.

"Um, yeah. Okay. See you at home. Good luck with Joel." And she was gone. This was turning into a strange evening.

"Hey, Allie, can I ask you a question?"

"Sure, hon." Allie was scrolling through tomorrow's schedule on the second computer, taking a look at her clients.

"Do you remember doing a couple's massage for a Marcus and Tamara on Saturday? In the afternoon, with Courtney? Both were pretty dressy. Girl had Dolly Parton boobs and no waist."

"Yeah, I remember them. Nice couple. What about them?"

"Did they ever say what they were? Boyfriend/girlfriend? Friends? Mere acquaintances? "

Allie pursed her lips together, cocking her head to one side. "I think they were just dating. She was actually his secretary or something, I think. Yeah, that was it. He's a lawyer at a firm downtown and that's how they met. Why do you ask?"

"No reason. Just curious." Ah, the classic lawyer banging the secretary on the side. Scumbag, scumbag, douchebag. Poor Lisa. She gives birth to twins and her husband screws around on her.

"I'm going to go clean up my treatment room. Have you cut any of the stylists?"

"I let Katie go about an hour or so ago. Jewel and Carolyn are still on the floor. You can let one of them go if you want, as long as most of the cleaning is done." It was nearing eight o'clock, closing time. Carolyn was finishing up a haircut so I couldn't close down the register yet. I got out the cleaning supplies and set to work on dusting and polishing the desk, stopping only to check out the client. I quickly swept the floors, switched the Open sign to Closed, locked the front doors and counted out the drawer. I filed the receipts, checked the next day's schedules, and closed down the computers. Walking back to the office with the cash and receipts, I waved goodnight to Carolyn as she headed out.

Allie was in the office putting her coat on when I came in. "Big plans for the rest of the night?" she asked me.

"Nope. Just some homework. I have to make sure I stay on top of my classes. I've let myself slip the last few weeks of the semester."

"Well, do you think you could come out to lunch with me and Dani tomorrow? Sort of an informal meeting to talk about the Christmas schedule."

"What time were you thinking?"

"Probably around twelve or twelve-thirty. What time is your last class out?"

"Not 'till one. But I can just skip it. I have some ideas for the schedule that I wanted to discuss with Dani anyway."

"Are you sure about skipping? Maybe we can push it back."

"Nah, it'll be fine. One of my friends is in the class too, so I'll just get her notes."

"If you're sure. Or else I can let Dani know what your ideas are?" I looked at Allie's face, always so bright and open. She wouldn't screw me over like Kamille had, would she? Any other day I would have answered an emphatic no. But after the weird moment with her and possibly Kevin in the treatment room, plus Lila's behavior after the facial. . . .my instincts were telling me to hold off.

"Um, that's okay. I need to put them all together tonight anyway so they make sense." There went my homework idea. "But I'll be sure to be here tomorrow for the meeting. Should I just meet you both here?"

"Yep. See you tomorrow! Drive safe, hon."

"Thanks." My shoulders drooped and a walloping headache came at me full force. I just wanted to sleep.

Just as I was opening the front door to Wacker, my cell phone began to ring. It was my personal cell, and I reminded myself yet again to see about merging the two. I stopped inside the doorway and dug it out, eyes widening in surprise when I saw Henry's name on the caller ID. "Hello?" I said, trying not to sound too hopeful.

"Alex? Hi, it's Henry."

"Hey, Henry. What's up?" I struggled to keep my voice casual as I started climbing the stairs.

"Not much. Just hanging out at home. What are you doing?"

"Just getting home from work. Literally. I'm just walking in the door." Lila was on the couch with a textbook on her lap and a glass of wine in one hand. I waved and mouthed 'Henry' at her, pointing to the phone. She placed her wine glass on the floor and clapped her hands together quietly.

"How was work tonight?"

"It was fine. Lila came in and got her first facial." I debated about telling the story about Marcus Baylor and his two-timing ways, but I was more curious as to why Henry was calling. I hadn't heard from him since he left me on his couch Saturday night. Alone.

"Did she like it?"

"I think so. How was your night?"

"Good. A lot of studying. I have two big tests before Thanksgiving break. Then two more before Christmas break."

"Ah, gotcha." An awkward pause descended over our conversation. *The point, Henry, the point!* I wanted to scream.

"So. I just wanted to ask if you had plans for the weekend. Peter and Hannah are going mini-golfing at that indoor place downtown, and I thought you might like it too."

A double date? He was asking me on another date, right? "Sure! I mean, yeah, that could be a good time. Though I can't really see Hannah mini-golfing," I said honestly. Lila gave me a quizzical look from her perch on the couch.

"Truthfully, I don't see Peter that much into putt-putt either. Maybe we can be on teams. I have a feeling we would dominate."

I laughed, feeling all the emotional stress and wondering about Henry fade away. He did still like me. We were going on a third date. "I bet we will. We'll have to think of a good bet to place."

We chatted for a while longer, while I tried to get out of my work clothes and into some sweats. Henry told me he would finalize the plans with Peter and make sure to work around my Blissful schedule, then we hung up. I finished pulling the T-shirt over my head and ran back into the living room.

"We're going on a date. We're going on a date! A third date, Lil. Third!" I squealed, hopping on the couch and jumping up and down like a kid when they find out school was canceled.

"Yay! I'm so happy for you. But what was with the three-day silent treatment? Did he mention anything about your last date?" she asked, bringing me down from the clouds.

I took a seat next to her, then hopped right back up. I was too excited to sit still. "No, not really. I'll ask him when we're on our date though. Maybe Hannah will even have some info on him. Maybe Peter discussed it with her. But, hello. What are you doing here? I thought you were meeting Joel for dinner? Unless. . .?" I trailed off, wondering if they had broken up that quickly.

"I canceled on him. I just didn't feel like going through with it tonight. Maybe I should just wait until after my meeting. I mean, what if Mary hates me and I decide just to stay in Des Moines and become a housewife? Why risk breaking up with Joel over nothing?"

I sat again, this time with more resolution. "Lila. You can't stay with Joel out of convenience. What you just said made it sound like you were settling. Joel's good enough for right here, right now. But I think you know that's not what you really want."

Lila was quiet for a moment, reaching over to pick up her wine glass and taking a gulp. "I don't know. I'm so confused. I don't want to make any hasty decisions without being sure. I just need some more time to think."

I sat in silence with her for a few minutes, trying to show my support. I guessed that she did know what she wanted, she just couldn't admit it to herself yet. I think all the girls knew it, really. But we would wait, let her come to the conclusion herself.

"Another reason though—I canceled because I wanted to talk to you," she continued, glancing up at me.

"Okay. What's up?" I asked, leaning back into the cushions and closing my eyes. Ah, relaxation.

"How do you feel about Allie?"

My eyes snapped open. "What? Allie? Why?"

Lila shrugged. "I'm just curious. I know you've said you really like her and you think she's a great friend and all, but. . . .I don't know."

"You don't know what? Did she say something about me?" I couldn't believe that Allie was talking behind my back, especially to my best friend. That just didn't add up.

"No, no. She didn't say anything about you. Bad, anyway. She did say that she thought you were a great manager and all those other glowing things, but. . . .I don't know."

"That's the second time you've said that. Clearly something is on your mind. Spill. What the hell happened?" I was on the brink, ready to explode if Lila didn't tell me what was going on. Maybe my weird feeling about Allie was about to be proven correct.

Lila's blue eyes met mine. "I just got a weird feeling about her. Something didn't add up."

"By that you mean. . .?" I prompted. Could Lila get the feeling about her and Kevin? I always knew she had some heightened intuition, but this could be huge. I would never doubt her again.

"I just didn't think she was being entirely truthful. She asked me if I had a boyfriend and I started to tell her a little bit about Joel. Then she talked about her fiancé and how they're getting married next year. And I got the feeling that she isn't excited about it. I don't think she loves this guy."

I frowned, thinking about what she said. "I don't know. We've talked about it before too, and she said that she is marrying for love and that he would make a great father and all this stuff. She sounded pretty happy to me." My thoughts flashed back on possibly hearing Kevin and Allie in her treatment room. I hadn't proved it was Allie, but something was telling me it was her. I knew her laugh, but I didn't want to admit it to myself.

"I just think that something else is going on in that relationship. My guess is that there is someone else, either on her side or his. Maybe he is cheating and she knows about it but doesn't know what to do? I don't know, just something was off."

"Lila, I'm going to tell you something, but please keep it to yourself. Don't tell the other girls. I didn't want to tell anyone because I didn't know what to think. And it might not even be true. So just keep quiet about it, okay?"

Lila's eyes were wide as she looked back at me. "Promise," she said, voice solemn.

"Okay. It happened last week when I was leaving the salon. The day I got called in." I launched into my story about possibly hearing Kevin and Allie in the treatment room together. I explained the sounds, how I thought I heard Allie's laugh and Kevin's voice and the door closing. When I finished, Lila's eyes were even bigger than when I started. I felt relieved to get that story off my chest. I didn't realize how much it was killing me to keep it inside.

"So you think that possibly Kevin and Allie are hooking up? That is just fucked up," Lila bluntly stated.

"I know, right? And the sickest part—Dani was in the salon at the time. She was right at the front desk! If something weird is going on, it's so shitty that they're doing it with Dani just a few feet from them. Can you imagine?" I cringed, not understanding how people could be so horrible and shady. And poor Dani! Not only her husband, but her employee and friend? I was devastated for her.

"Wow. That's just awful. I can't believe—"

"There's more."

Lila looked at me, incredulous. "More? What the hell do you mean more? What kind of more?"

I reached into my purse for my cell phone, scrolling to the pictures of Kevin and Kamille kissing. I handed Lila my phone.

"This is Kamille, right? Bitchy front desk girl?"

I nodded. "I caught them in the back alley the same day I heard Kevin and Allie in the treatment room."

Lila studied the pictures some more. "Well, this is solid proof, Al. Show these to Kevin. Or Kamille. They can't keep doing this to Dani."

"But—what if I get fired? It sounds terrible, but besides all this crap, I really love my job. And I'm good at it. And it's

giving me the knowledge and possibly future references to go
on to bigger and better things. I don't want to go back to being
a Tastie's girl—no offense."

"None taken. But, okay. So you stay quiet for now. What
happens when Dani catches them? Or another staff member or
a client? Or—what if Kevin starts making moves on you?"

I stayed silent for a minute. "I don't know," I answered
quietly. "Honestly. I don't know. I'm so confused. And I'm sad. I
really thought Allie was a good person. And even though I may
have had doubts about Kevin and Kamille, I never wanted it to
turn out this way."

Lila and I talked for another hour about Blissful and the
closed-door happenings. We didn't get much farther, only to
discuss how disgusted we were with cheating men and women
who agree to be "the other woman." I still didn't know how to
handle my newfound knowledge about my boss and employees.
Stay quiet and keep at my job? Spill what I knew and possibly
lose it?

I went to bed that night uneasy about my professional
situation. Could I really keep working for philandering Kevin?
Would I crack and spill the secrets to Dani? Dani was my friend.
She didn't deserve to be kept in the dark. Lila agreed that if I
knew Joel was cheating on her she would want to know. I said the
same thing. It would be humiliating for everyone to know your
boyfriend or husband had a wandering eye. Kamille seemed like
she could be a bitch, but what about Allie? My thoughts about
her were completely screwed up. How could I look her in the
eye tomorrow and watch her smile and chat with Dani like she

wasn't screwing her husband on the side? What had I gotten myself into?

The next day, I asked Emma to take notes for me in Music Appreciation and skipped the class so I could head out to Blissful. Dani and Allie were both at the salon and ready to go by the time I got there just after noon, and the three of us piled into Kevin's BMW and headed towards the mall. We were having lunch at The Bowl, a restaurant attached to the mall that specialized in salads and other healthy dishes.

We were seated promptly, and got a table by a big picture window. The view of the outside was desolate: gray skies, bare trees, and people bundled up in winter gear to protect them from the chilly temps. We placed our orders for various salads and drinks and Dani started the conversation.

"I wanted to get together to talk about the holiday schedules. Thanksgiving seems to be all worked out and that wasn't an issue, but we need to figure out Christmas."

"What is the store schedule like for then? Are we closed Christmas Eve and Christmas?" I asked, taking a sip of my Sprite.

"Well, we need to discuss that too. Christmas Eve is still a pretty popular shopping day, and the stores stay open longer. I think we should be open on that day, at least in the morning. Maybe nine to one or something? What do you think?"

"I think it's important to know that we can be staffed before we decide on store hours," Allie said. "Alex, what did the leave requests look like for the desk?"

I took a folder out of my briefcase, where I had been keeping track of the requests. "Kamille has requested the twenty-third through the twenty-eighth off. Sounds like she will be out of state visiting family. Julia requested Christmas Eve and Christmas off, and Tiffany can work Christmas Eve but on a limited schedule."

"Okay, so I'm assuming no Christmas, right? No one will be thinking massage on Christmas," Allie said, glancing at Dani.

Dani paused for a moment before answering. "Right. We'll be closed on Christmas. What day is Christmas?"

"Sunday." Allie and I answered together.

"Yeah, no problem being closed then. But I still think we should have a few hours on Christmas Eve. Alex, why don't you call around to a few other salons today, see what their hours are? Let's try to be comparable in the area. If everyone else is opened all day, we should be too."

"But do we have the staff? Tiffany can only work a short time and I usually take Christmas to fly out and be with my family in Seattle," I said, my heart starting to beat faster. I was already giving up Thanksgiving. I couldn't believe they wanted me to miss Christmas too.

"You need time off over Christmas?" Dani asked, looking at me with confusion. "Kevin told me you would be working it."

"What? No! I never said that. I told Kevin when you asked me to work over Thanksgiving that I would want Christmas off then to go to Seattle. I need to go see my family at some point. I haven't seen them since last Christmas." I could feel tears threatening and knew it was the exhaustion settling in that was making me fragile. I couldn't miss Christmas. Not for this place. And why was Kevin making up stories about me?

"Oh. Well, okay, that might change a few things then. Maybe I misunderstood Kevin. But I could have sworn he said you would be here. Is your family coming here by chance? Maybe that's what he meant."

"No, and I can't see that happening. My brother-in-law works around the clock and my sister has five kids under the age of nine. I don't think traveling by plane on the holiday is on their list of fun activities." Kevin had lied about my schedule, for whatever selfish reason.

"Hmm. I'll talk to him. We'll be in town this year, but we're hosting Christmas at our house. I'm not sure when we'll be able to watch the store."

"So maybe we should be closed Christmas Eve and Christmas then? I'm sure a lot of businesses do it. I don't think those are particularly busy spa days," Allie said, and I shot her a grateful smile for sticking up for me. Or was she only sticking up for me because she had a grudge against Dani and wanted Kevin all to herself? My migraine pulsed.

"I don't know. Kevin really wants to be open Christmas Eve." Was it my imagination, or did Dani give Allie the evil eye when she said that? "Alex, just make sure you get those calls done today to the surrounding spas. Allie, do we have stylists that can work that day?"

"Morgan can work esthetics, Shawna's the only massage therapist, and Sophia and Lindsey can work the floor. I can probably be there a little bit on Christmas Eve, but we're traveling to Winlap that night," she said, naming a city about forty minutes from Des Moines.

"That might be good enough. We'll make a final decision after Alex makes the calls." We all nodded, and I scratched notes for myself.

We paused when our food arrived, and I eagerly tucked into my trusty chicken ceaser salad. The hunks of chicken were smothered with finely shredded cheese and creamy dressing, and I struggled to recall the last time I had eaten a full meal. I had become accustomed to granola bars and bags of chips to keep my energy up.

"I had a question about scheduling," I said, when I had eaten about half of my salad and felt a stomachache coming on from all the food I had quickly consumed. "Do we have any kind of system in place that tracks when employees request off and who gets time off—such as around the holidays?"

"I don't think so. What exactly do you mean?" Allie asked, picking through her salad and finding a piece of roast beef.

"I was just thinking, maybe we should have a system to track when employees ask off around the holiday time. That can be Thanksgiving, Christmas, New Years', Fourth of July, et cetera. And then we can show who actually got the time off, so the same people don't keep getting the holidays off. Just try to make it as fair as we can. For example, say Sophia and Jewel both ask for Christmas Eve off. We give it to Sophia. Then next year or even just the next holiday, New Years', they both ask off again. That time we give it to Jewel. Does that make sense?"

"Actually, yeah, it does. I'm surprised we haven't thought of that before. That's a great idea, Alex," Dani praised, giving me a warm smile. I smiled back, feeling better after her remarks about my wanting time off. I just needed to keep coming up with ideas to prove my worth—and show that I deserved some time off too.

"It really is. Even though salon turnover can be high, mostly with the front desk as opposed to stylists, it will still be a handy tool. Good thought, Alex," Allie said.

"Thanks. I'll get working on that when we get back," I said, biting into a warm roll.

The rest of our lunch passed smoothly, even though I was constantly on the lookout for tension between my two lunch partners. Everything seemed to be fine though, and soon we were packing up and heading back out to the car.

I flirted with the thought of straight out asking Allie if there was something going on between her and Kevin, but quickly dismissed it. She wouldn't tell me the truth. I didn't need Lila's intuition to tell me that. I would just have to try to figure out Blissful's mystery another way.

CHAPTER 15

"Alex! Come on, the guys are here," Lila yelled for me. I stood in my bedroom on New Year's Eve night, dressed for a party in a shimmering black and white dress, black lace booties, and patterned tights. My hair was pulled out of my face and sat on the top of my head in a thick bun, and my makeup was flawless thanks to the help of my friends. I was ready to party. I wasn't ready to confront the text message on my phone from Kevin Dohlman.

"Alex! Don't make us leave without you. Get out here, girl!" Carmen hollered.

I snapped my phone shut, trying to erase his words from my mind. I didn't want to be a Blissful employee tonight, or Kevin's prawn, or anyone's manager and confidant. I just wanted to relax, be with my friends, and welcome in the New Year. Without breaking down.

"Coming, I'm coming," I said, grabbing my phone and hurrying out into the living room. My four friends stood by the door, all wearing glittery frocks as well. Hannah and I stuck with simple black and white, but Lila, Carmen, and Emma were donning purple, green, and pink respectively.

"Finally. Everyone got everything? Phones? Extra shoes?" Emma asked, and we all held up our phones and a pair of much more comfortable shoes for the end of the night.

"I have our overnight bag," Hannah said, holding up the tote that contained five sets of T-shirts and shorts and various face washes. We planned on spending the night at Peter and Henry's house, since they were driving to the party. We were going to get a cab at the end of the night though, just to be on the safe side.

"All right, let's go. They're already here." Lila shooed us out and we tromped down the steps, laughing and giggling like we were in a commercial featuring college kids ready to party hardy.

We reached Henry's vehicle and piled in. I sat in the back on Lila's lap, and Emma sprawled vertical on our laps, her face in Max's crotch. Neither seemed to mind. Nine people in a vehicle that fit five, maybe six, seemed like a good idea when the plans were being made, but now. . .not so much. A cab would definitely be necessary later. No reason to give out free passes for cops to pull us over.

We drove towards the party house, some friends of the guys, and chatter ensued the whole ride there. I tried to distract myself from my work issues by meeting Henry's eye in the rearview mirror. My body tingled when he winked at me. I couldn't wait for the ball to drop so I could kiss him. Though technically, I would probably kiss him sooner.

Henry and I were teetering on the edge of the official boyfriend/girlfriend status. Since our awkward Saturday night date that left me sleeping alone and confused over Henry's status, a lot had changed. Our double date with Hannah and Peter had been amazing and insightful. We kicked their asses at mini-golf, which led to them having to buy the movie theater snacks on our next double date, but Hannah and I also found out why Henry left me alone on the couch. Emma had been right. Religion. Turns out, Peter was indeed saving himself for marriage, which thrilled Hannah. Henry was not, as he had already lost his virginity at the beginning of college to the girl that he thought he would marry one day. They had dated in high school, and she attended college at a Des Moines nursing school. She cheated on him, he found her cheating on him, and he swore off sex until he was actually going to be married. Both were firm Catholics, and I had to appreciate and respect Henry's decision. That cleared up a lot of confusion, and put me more at ease around him. Our dates continued from there, mingled with long phone conversations and even spending some nights with one another—stopping before rounding all the bases, of course.

I was able to go to Seattle for Christmas, but only spent three days there instead of the usual seven or eight that I typically took. That was the compromise between me and Kevin and Dani. My sister was beside herself when I told her all about Henry and the fact that he came from a strong family with religious beliefs. Though our mom and dad raised us Catholic, after Mom's passing we drifted away from the church. After having her children Alicia found her faith once again, baptized all five kids, and went as many Sundays as they could. I tried to follow suit and Lila and I often went to services ourselves, she coming from a religious family. Hannah attended every week.

Learning that we had our faith in common, Henry quite a bit more serious than I, had helped our relationship tenfold. The awkward moments weren't there, and we respected the boundaries.

We pulled up to the house, vehicles already cramming the street. Our clown car exploded as we all jumped out, us girls pulling our dresses down and patting our carefully coiffed hair. No precipitation was in the forecast tonight but the air was damp and cold, the promise of snow looming on the horizon. Our group trundled to the house, Peter and Hannah hand in hand, Carmen and Emma chatting animatedly with Max and Lila, and Kyle falling into line. Henry swung his arm around me and pulled me close, planting a kiss on my forehead.

"Well, hello there. You look beautiful tonight," Henry said, causing my smile to widen.

"Thank you. You've all cleaned up quite nicely," I responded, giving his hand a squeeze. "Are the guys all cool with a house party instead of the bars?"

"Oh, yeah. We actually prefer it this way. New Years' Eve is just like St. Patty's Day—amateur hour," Henry said as we reached the doorstep. Kyle opened the door without knocking, and a blast of music hit our ears. The party was already in full swing.

"Amateur hour? What does that mean?" I asked, following my date into the kitchen. He whipped out a ten dollar bill and paid the pimply guy in a flannel shirt that held the cups, then offered to pour me a beer from the keg. I nodded my answer.

"Amateur hour. Where everyone thinks they can drink and drink and drink and then get beyond belligerent. Fights, puke, passed out people on pool tables—that's what those holidays are all about. People that don't normally party all of sudden get it in their head that they can do eighteen shots in one hour and still function. The bars are a mess. House parties are the way to go."

I nodded in agreement, taking my red cup from Henry and waiting for the foam to disappear before I took a sip. Cold and delicious. Kind of. For a beer. But I wasn't going to complain. "That makes sense. We just have to make sure we call a cab tonight. No one needs to get a DUI."

"Of course. How comfortable was the ride over here?" Henry asked with a laugh.

"Ugh. Not so comfortable," I replied. We weaved our way through the crowd in the kitchen, finding the stairwell that would take us into the basement. Loud music thumped from speakers in the area, and a guy stood in the corner scrolling through an iPod.

"That's one of our friends who lives here. Come on, I'll introduce you." Henry took my hand and led me to the guy, who was tall and lanky, with closely cropped brown hair and shiny brown eyes. He also looked bombed.

"Hey, Lance, how you doing, buddy?" Henry and Lance did a slap hands/half hug sort of move, where Lance was a little too enthusiastic and ended up pouring beer down Henry's back.

"Aw, dude, I'm so sowry!" Lance slurred, trying to wipe the beer off Henry's shirt but really just soaking it in further. I didn't know how to help so I just stood back and watched, cringing.

My first impression of Lance was that he was a hot mess. More accurately—a drunk mess.

"That's okay, man, that's okay. Don't worry about it." Henry tried to get Lance to stop touching his shirt, and finally just took a step away from him. "Anyway, thanks for having us tonight. I wanted you to meet someone. This is my girlfriend, Alex."

Girlfriend? I looked at Henry with raised eyebrows. We hadn't called ourselves boyfriend and girlfriend yet. Henry just grinned back at me, winking.

"Well, hello, Alex," Lance said to me, holding out one hand. I stuck mine out thinking we were going to shake, but instead he brought my hand to his lips and kissed my knuckles. Sweet yet creepy. "The pleasure is all mine."

"Nice to meet you, Lance," I said, trying not to laugh.

"You take care of this fella here. He's a good fish," Lance continued, looking at me through squinted eyes. Was this guy going to make it till midnight? Something was telling me no.

"I'll do my best. Thanks for having us, and it was nice to meet you," I said, biting down on my lower lip so I wouldn't laugh in his face.

Henry put his arm around my waist and led me away from Lance, who went back to his iPod and sang along with the music. "Sorry about that. Lance is our soak."

"Soak?" I asked.

"Alcoholic. Lush. Drunk. Soak." We were about halfway across the room, heading in the direction of two tables that were being used for a massive flippy cup game. I stopped Henry before we could reach the group and join in.

"Gotcha. But bigger question. Girlfriend?" I asked, staring into his blue eyes.

"Beautiful. Special. Alex. Girlfriend," Henry answered, before finding my mouth and placing the most romantic kiss on my lips. I positively melted into him, feeling euphoric. Henry was officially my boyfriend.

The rest of the party passed quickly, too quickly for my liking. We played multiple games of flippy cup, beer pong, darts, and pool. I danced with my girlfriends to the tunes Lance cranked out. I did jello shots, drank too much beer and snacked on chips, chips and more chips the owners had been thoughtful enough to provide. I didn't think about Blissful or Kevin or the text message on my phone. I just partied like the twenty-year old college student I was, surrounded by my best friends and new boyfriend.

"It's starting!" A girl wearing hot pants, fishnets, and a hot pink jersey shirt called for everyone's attention at exactly 11:59. She turned up the volume on the TV, and we saw a shot of New York City and Times Square, overflowing with people as they watched the ball drop.

Henry slipped behind me and placed both hands on my waist and I leaned into him. Lila was to my right, and I wondered if she was going to kiss anyone. She and Joel had finally called it quits a few weeks ago. Hannah was on my left, holding onto Peter's hand. I could see Carmen and Emma across the room, and raised my cup in salute to them. They raised their cups back and continued to chat with Max.

"Thirty, twenty-nine, twenty-eight!" More people in the room started to chant, watching the TV screen and pairing up. I glanced again at Lila, wondering if she was okay. She seemed to take her breakup with Joel fine, but New Years' Eve could bring up some sour feelings. She caught me looking at her and winked at me.

"I'm happy, Alex," she told me, without me even asking her. I winked back, relieved.

"Nineteen, eighteen, seventeen!"

"Quick! What was your favorite part of this year?" Henry asked me.

I turned to face him, already knowing my answer. "Meeting you," I said, smiling up at my boyfriend.

"You stole my answer," he smiled back.

"Ten, nine, eight!" the crowd roared, eagerly anticipating the final seconds.

"Happy New Year, Alex," Henry whispered, his face coming close to mine.

"Happy New Year, Henry," I said.

"Three, two, one. Happy New Year!" everyone shouted as someone threw confetti, poppers popped, and people cheered. The pandemonium was silenced by the kiss I shared with Henry.

"I feel like it's cruel and unusual punishment to clean the apartment the day after New Year's Eve. Why are we doing this again?" Lila asked as she listlessly squirted some blue ammonia onto the glass.

"Because our place looks like a train wreck, I have to work all week, and you're going to be flying on a jet plane in three days to meet with an agency in Los Angeles. Or have you forgotten about that already?" I asked my friend, a smile on my face.

"I know! I still can't believe it. I wake up every morning and ask myself if it's true." Lila shook her head in amazement, the forgotten Windex streaking down the glass. "I'm so nervous, but that has been the best diet. I'm seriously throwing up everything I try to consume."

"Lila! That is disgusting. Please don't turn into some crazy bulimic once you get out there. Please, please," I begged my friend, running my eyes over her body. She did such a good job working out and watching what she ate the weeks before she met with Mary Strubaker. I would hate to see all her efforts be thrown away because she started to vomit everything back up.

"Trust me, that won't happen. And I don't throw up after every meal. Just when my nerves get the better of me. I have real casting calls that I have to do. I have to speak lines and make faces and pretend to report news and put my voice infliction lessons to the test and," Lila started to turn red in the face, "I think I'm going to be sick."

I rushed over to my friend. "No! No, you are not. Just breathe, okay? Big yoga breath in. Do it with me." We breathed in together and exhaled. Breathe and exhale. Breathe and exhale. "Feeling any better?" I asked, concerned.

"Much." Lila finally turned and wiped the bathroom mirror, and I turned my attention back to the toilet, squeezing the bottle of cleaner and watching blue liquid fill the bowl. I hated being on toilet duty.

Lila and I chatted a bit more about her upcoming week, where she would be flying to LA with Mary Strubaker and two other girls from Mary's agency. Mary had lined up casting calls and meetings with "important people" out in sunny California, and it would definitely be a make it or break it moment for Lila. Who knew if she would ever have this chance again? Lila tried saying if she didn't get any offers in LA then at least she would still have Iowa and Mary's agency. But appearing in a farming ad versus having a shot as an entertainment reporter paled in comparison. And I mean really paled. Vampire pale. I was nervous but thrilled for Lila. Not so thrilled that if she got offered a contract or job that she would be moving away from me. Life without Lila. . .I sniffed a bit, feeling the tears start to threaten.

"Oh, Al, you're not crying again, are you?" Lila asked, looking at me with her big blue eyes. I'd been known to break down over the last few weeks every time I thought about her moving away.

"No," I lied, as one tear spilt over and ran down my cheek. Traitor.

"Who knows what will even happen when I'm out there? I could totally bomb and have to stay in good ole Iowa the rest of my life."

"Don't talk like that!" I threw an unused rag at Lila. "I want you to succeed. I want you to get contracts and offers and be on TV with a spray tan and eight pounds of makeup. I really do. I just don't want you to leave me."

"You could always come with me." Lila had mentioned me going with her many times. And why not? I would actually be closer to my family in Seattle, and it wasn't like I had much going on in Des Moines anyway. One more year of school that I could finish online. My job? I hated Blissful and all the baggage and secrets I had to carry around. Henry? I didn't want to leave my new boyfriend. Plus, I did have more friends here than just Lila. And I was comfortable here. I liked my life in Iowa. I couldn't begin to picture myself in California and rubbing elbows with famous people. It just wasn't my scene.

"I know, I know." I sighed. "And I've thought about it, I really have. I just. . .can't. I have so much going on here. And I wouldn't have anything lined up out there, no job or anything. It just wouldn't be smart. And I don't think I would fit in with the LA crowd anyway. I don't have the celebrity knowledge like you do."

"That's the truth." We declared the bathroom clean and headed towards the kitchen. "I don't know what will happen, but if for some crazy reason someone likes me out there, you have to at least promise to come visit me. Someone has to keep my ego in check if I become a star." Lila struck a ridiculous pose with one hand on her hip and the other in the air like she was waving at adoring fans.

I laughed, but still felt the tightness in my chest over possibly losing my friend to the world of Hollywood. "I will. I have to make sure you won't forget all us little people when you're schmoozing it up with Brad Pitt and Jennifer Aniston."

"Seriously, Alex? Brad and Jen split years ago. He's with Angelina Jolie now."

"Really? How did I miss that?"

"I have no idea. Angie stole Brad from right under Jen's nose when they were filming together. They even posed on a magazine cover together with all these kids like they were a family. It was so distasteful." Lila turned her nose up and started to load the dishwasher.

I opened the fridge and started chucking expired food in the garbage. "Wow, how rude. But speaking of couples, how did you really take last night? Was it weird not having Joel around?"

"Yeah, it was. But you know what I felt when we broke up?" I shook my head, even though she had already told me three times. I knew she needed to keep reminding herself that she did the right thing, and I was happy to listen."I felt relief. I felt light and free and ready to do anything. I didn't realize that I was letting myself suffocate all these years. I was letting myself settle when my dreams were so much bigger. And if he can't support them, he's not supporting me. I don't know if I can ever be just a dutiful housewife who loves nothing more than waiting on her man and popping out kids. I need more. I need to live, I need the excitement. I at least need to try, or I'll constantly be wondering what if. I'm just glad I finally realized it before I was super old—like twenty-five or something."

"Excuse me? Twenty-five? When did that become the new eighty? And you'll hit that age in four years, need I remind you." I laughed.

"No, don't remind me! It's just harder to get jobs out there when you're past twenty-five. Thirty is practically deceased."

"That whole town makes no sense. But back to the original topic—I'm glad you're okay with the breakup. And that last night wasn't too weird for you. I half expected you to find someone to kiss."

"Nah. I thought about trying, but the last thing I want to do is find my Mr. Right before I leave. I don't want any baggage here in Iowa."

"Besides me," I reminded her.

"Besides you, of course," she reassured me.

We worked side by side for most of the afternoon until our apartment sparkled and shined. We gave ourselves a much needed break and went to dinner with Carmen and Emma. Hannah was on yet another date with Peter. After dinner we rented two movies, a scary one and a chick-flick, and headed back to Wacker to have an enjoyable evening with friends, movies, popcorn, and vodka. I limited myself to two drinks since it was back to Blissful for me tomorrow. I didn't want to face Kevin. I wasn't sure how I could face Allie.

Alex, let's talk when you get in on Tuesday and keep the incident to yourself. I feel a bonus coming your way! Happy New Year, Kevin.

I re-read the text from Kevin on my drive to Blissful. Wonderful. Another bonus to keep my mouth shut. When had my job turned from manager of a spa to secret-keeper, spineless, but much richer Alex? I stopped at a red light and looked at the text again. As well as an older text from Kevin, dated right before Christmas.

Dani shouldn't know about this. Think about our family, Alex. A check will be in your mailbox tomorrow.

A check indeed had been waiting for me in my employee mailbox. A one thousand dollar check. That payoff was for the first time I had caught Kevin—actually caught him and he knew I did, not just spying at him from my car or outside a treatment room. I didn't even know the woman he was with, the woman he was screwing on one of the massage beds. Why did I have to stay late to run year-end reports that night? Why couldn't I have done the work from home?

I knew it didn't really matter. I had caught Kevin with other women three more times at the salon. All were different, and once with Allie. Yes, Allie, my friend and spa confidant. The one who told me she loved her fiancé and couldn't wait to marry him. The woman who spilled "gossip" to me when I first started at Blissful about how Kevin could be a little overbearing but Dani was the biggest sweetheart. But there she was, riding Kevin like there was no tomorrow in her treatment room on the Friday before New Years'.

Kamille had officially resigned from Blissful around the holidays. After she stole another idea of mine—this time for a holiday gift basket prize for a lucky client who rebooked an appointment—I had reached a breaking point. I suspected she was snooping through my computer files and I was tired of coming up with new ideas, doing the research and getting everything prepared, just to have it stolen under my nose and passed off as someone else's genius. I printed off the photos from my phone and stuck them in Kamille's employee mailbox in a large envelope. I typed up a cryptic note that read: YOU'RE CAUGHT. LEAVE NOW OR DANI KNOWS.

Kamille put in her two weeks' the very next day. I didn't know if she had figured out it was me who caught her, and I didn't care. She was gone, my ideas were safe, and that was one less employee I had to worry about Kevin screwing. I didn't let Kevin know what I had done, or that I knew about him and Kamille. I still wanted to keep my job intact, at least for the time being. Once I found a new job and got my reference, I would be out.

I shook my head and kept driving. I hadn't told anyone about the new twist at Blissful, the checks that were coming in or how I had forced Kamille to quit. Not Lila or the girls, Henry, my sister. I felt sick to my stomach every time I thought about what was going on behind closed doors. And how I was going along with it. I had even been physically sick when I thought about Dani and her three daughters. Did she have any idea her husband was having multiple affairs? Allie had told me once that Dani had her suspicions, but stayed with him for the money. But how could I possibly trust Allie and anything she said? She was sleeping with Kevin—a married man, her boss!

I barreled into Blissful just before two o'clock. Tiffany was behind the desk, wiping down the counters with a dust rag. I gave her a wave and continued towards the office. The floor was pretty slow, with only Lindsey cutting a woman's hair and Carolyn sitting on her chair reading a magazine. She straightened when she saw me and put the glossy down, attempting to appear busy cleaning her area. I didn't even bother to reprimand her. I requested that stylists go in the break room when they didn't have clients. I thought it was tacky for them to be lounging in their chairs where everyone could see them. Carolyn was lucky I had bigger issues to deal with.

I made it to the back office and swung open the heavy door. Kevin and Dani were both there, Dani sitting in the computer chair and Kevin hovering over the printer. Documents were spitting out, and he had his cell phone pressed against his ear.

"These numbers are not acceptable, Tony. We need to open three more stores in the next nine months. Three stores, nine months. That's what we want. You need to figure out how to help us achieve that."

He hung up and turned to face me, a big smile on his face. I wanted to puke all over his shiny black shoes. "Alex, hello! Did you have a good New Year's?" he asked, his bushy brows pulling together like he was actually concerned about my holiday.

"I did, Kevin, thank you," I managed between clenched teeth. "And yours?" I tried to sound as polite as possible.

"Oh, we had a terrific time," Dani piped in, swiveling her chair away from the computer. "We stayed in and had family time with movies and Wii games, and then on Monday we took the kids to Blair's Mountain to go snow sledding and tubing. Well, baby Cam just watched of course, but the other girls had so much fun."

The sick feeling in my stomach churned some more. Happy family time. Right. I forced a smile. "That sounds wonderful. Oh, Dani, you might be happy to hear that Henry officially asked me out. I am off the market," I informed her. At least that was a happy thought.

Dani stood and hugged me, her giant boobs pressing into me. I wanted to cry. I really liked her. I hated Kevin. I hated Blissful. I was so confused. "Good for you, honey! Are you going to invite him to your birthday party?"

My birthday party. I had almost forgotten. Dani had offered to throw me a party at Tango, one of the hottest restaurant/bars in town. The bottom floor was a fancy restaurant and the top was a happening dance club. The two would seem to clash, but it actually worked. The reservation book was full for months, but Kevin knew somebody who knew somebody who knew the owner and had reserved the twenty-third, a Saturday, for my twenty-first birthday blowout bash.

"Yep, I'll be sure to invite him. He'll probably bring some friends too, if you don't mind. His friend Peter is dating my friend Hannah. And he lives with two other guys."

"Bring them all! The more the merrier for your special day. I remember my twenty-first birthday." Dani's eyes turned wistful as she thought back a whole seven years.

"Really? Most people don't remember their twenty-firsts," I joked, thinking about how hungover Lila was the day after hers.

"Oh, I was pregnant with Brianna when I was twenty-one. No alcohol for me on that birthday. I was about seven months along and in full-on nesting mode already. Kevin and I ordered, what was it, four large pizzas and boxes of breadsticks and after all that, I still made him drive to the store to buy me a gallon of ice cream. I was a walking cliché of pregnancy." Dani laughed and squeezed Kevin's hand. Tears poked behind my eyes. I hated Kevin. "Anyway, I need to get going. I have to pick up Bri from school in a half-hour." She kissed Kevin good-bye and gathered her things, floating out the office door.

Kevin and I stood alone in the office, the first time we were face-to-face since I caught him with Allie. I was speechless. And really wanted to be anywhere but in a small office with him.

"Well, Alex, let me start off by saying that I am so sorry you witnessed what happened between me and Allie. I don't know

what came over us, but I can assure you it won't happen again."
His words sounded fake, phony, scripted.

"That was the first time you'd ever been with her?" I didn't
believe that for a minute.

"It was. And the last. I had come here from drinking with
some of my buddies and I guess I had my guard down. I had
been holding off Allie's advances for some time now, but that
night she just proved too much for me. I'm devastated about
it." He hung his head, but I still didn't believe a word he said. A
man that was smacking another woman's ass while she rode him
didn't seem like he had tried too hard to hold off her "advances."
But was it Allie that did come onto him? Or was it mutual? My
head was spinning.

"What happens next?" I wanted to know. Did I have to fire
Allie? Would he tell Dani and she would fire Allie?

"I'm going to keep this little discretion from Dani. She's
not in the right state of mind to deal with something like this.
You see, we're trying for another baby, and she might even be
pregnant right now. The timing just doesn't work."

I sucked in a breath, horrified. Dani might be pregnant with
her fourth baby with this cheating, slimy bastard. "And Allie?"

"I spoke with Allie already and let her know that she is to
never try something like that again. She apologized immensely
and agreed that she was in the wrong. I agreed to let her keep her
job for now. But one more slipup and she will be terminated."

I wanted to laugh. And throw up. None of this made any
sense. Dani wasn't to find out, Allie got to keep her job. And
what about me? I was just going to have to live with this secret?
It was eating away at me.

"As for you, Alex, you've been doing a tremendous job as manager. Morale is up, our numbers are better from last year, and you've shown that you can successfully handle all the challenges being a manager has thrown your way." *Like seeing my boss bone one of my top employees.* "I spoke with Dani, and we wanted to give you a little bonus for it."

"But you just gave me a Christmas bonus," I said. A five thousand dollar check with *Merry Christmas—you're a star!* written in the memo.

"That was just a Christmas present to you. We give bonuses to all the employees," Kevin said with a wave of his hand. "This is an employee-deserved bonus. You've done a great job."

Kevin handed me an envelope and walked out of the office. I stood still for a moment, dreading opening it. This wasn't an *I'm doing so great my bosses want to thank me* check. It was a cover-up. A buyout. Hush money. I opened the envelope and took the check out. A ten thousand dollar hush check.

CHAPTER 16

The following Saturday was date night between me and Henry. Peter was out dining Hannah and Max and Kyle were both out of town. With Lila in LA and Emma and Carmen both at parties, I was off to Henry's so he could cook me a fantastic dinner of spaghetti and meatballs—his specialty.

I showed up just before six, dressed in black leggings and an oversized white men's dress shirt. I wore only ballet flats that made navigating through the melting snow a bit difficult, bright red lips, and my hair in waves. I had to dress, apply makeup, and style my hair all on my own with the girls being so busy. I wasn't sure how I felt about my abilities to achieve greatness with my looks.

The door was open so I stepped right into the house, slipping my flats off at the door. "Hello? Henry!" I shouted, walking through the living room and into the kitchen. My boyfriend was standing at the stove, a pot of bubbling water on one burner and thawing meat on another. Henry had a spatula in one hand and was dressed in dark jeans and a navy sweater. His hair looked a little damp and when I went to hug him, the fresh scent of body soap enveloped me. Delightful.

"Hey, babe. You look gorgeous." Henry greeted me with a kiss on the lips, instantly putting my fear of not looking good to rest. "I hope you're hungry because I am making a boat load of food."

"Smells delicious. And I am starving. I played catch-up on homework all day and barely ate a thing."

"Did you get slammed with assignments too after winter break? I thought it was just my instructors that did that."

"Nope, same here. It's awful. And with term ending in February, all our finals are coming up and I am stressing out over it." I sighed. "But let's not talk about school. Can I help with anything?"

"You can help by keeping me company while I finish up and drinking that glass of wine I poured for you minutes ago. It should still be cold." Henry pointed to the kitchen table, where a wine glass was waiting.

I smiled at him and kissed his cheek. "You're spectacular. Anyone ever tell you that?"

"Only the women I pour wine for." He smiled back, stirring the noodles without taking his gaze off me.

I scampered over to the kitchen table and took a seat, drawing my legs up on the stool. The wine was delicious—fruity and bubbly and cold. "Are you a wine drinker, Henry?" I asked.

"Not so much. I can try a glass every now and again, but I much prefer beer. Though beer doesn't really go with pasta, so I might try a glass of the wine."

"It sounds weird, but I love to drink milk when I eat pasta. But I don't like milk any other time, except in my cereal of course. Is that weird?" I took another sip and savored the taste.

"Um, yeah, that's a little weird. But everyone has those odd preferences."

"What are some of your odd preferences?" I wanted to know.

"Well, speaking of cereal, I won't eat any cereal that turns my milk a different color. You know, like those chocolate cereals when you have chocolate milk by the time you're done. That freaks me out."

I laughed. "That's a good one. Thanks for sharing."

We continued to talk about odd preferences, then morphed into favorite foods and then favorite movies. Twenty minutes later, Henry declared dinner complete and we feasted on spaghetti and meatballs, cheesy garlic bread, and yummy caesar salad.

"You are an amazing cook," I said, my mouth full of lettuce.

Henry laughed. "None of this stuff was too difficult to whip up. It's mostly just time consuming."

I nodded, taking a sip of wine. I wasn't a wine connoisseur, but the fruity taste seemed to pair well enough with my meal. "Well, I think it's great. Lila and I don't eat the best at home. We barely ever cook."

"When will she be back?"

"She'll get in tomorrow night. I can't wait to hear how everything went."

"What if she tells you she's moving to LA permanently?"

I looked down at my plate. My best friend moving away from me? "Um, I haven't really thought that far ahead yet. It's just too. . .bizarre. I can't imagine not having Lila here."

Henry gazed at me, and I forced myself to meet his stare. "It's okay to be sad about it, Alex. I can't imagine Lila leaving either. But on a different hand, I can."

"And which hand is that?" I questioned, pulling another piece of garlic bread away from the rest.

"The hand that sees Lila is bored. I've only hung out with her a few times, but she's fairly easy to read. She's always talking about what the celebrities are wearing or doing or filming or screwing. She talks like she knows them already. I think she would probably fit in really well out there."

Henry had realized all of that from just talking to Lila a few times? Why hadn't I picked up on that? Oh, right—I didn't want to. I didn't want Lila to leave.

"I don't want Lila to leave," I blurted out.

"Of course you don't," Henry said, matter of fact. "She's your best friend."

"But I want my best friend to be happy," I said slowly.

"Of course you do."

"So I'm just going to be happy for her either way. If she gets the opportunity, then great. If she doesn't, I'll just push for her to keep trying." I looked at Henry for confirmation.

"That's right. That's what you'll do, because you're a good friend."

I chewed silently for a moment. "My boss is sleeping with another employee."

Henry froze with his fork halfway to his mouth. "I'm sorry?"

"My boss. Kevin. He's cheating on his wife. With a lot of different people." Why was I spilling these secrets to Henry now? Not even Lila knew what was going on at Blissful—to the full extent anyway.

"Okay. Um, I think you might have to give me the full story here, Alex. Start from the beginning."

So I told Henry. I went through all the sordid details of Kevin and how he treated the employees and how I had caught him with several other women. About Kamille and my note to make her quit. And the money I was making on the side to cover it up. By the time I was finished, my wine glass was empty and dinner was gone.

"Wow. That's a pretty rough situation. What are you going to do?" Henry looked stunned by all my bombshells. Poor guy. He thought he was just getting a nice date with a normal girl tonight.

"I have no idea. I haven't cashed my latest check. How the hell do I explain a $10,000 check? My sister has access to my bank accounts; what if she looks one day and questions me? How I am supposed to explain myself, my ethics, my morals? I'm helping a married man carry on with his affairs. All for what? To keep my job? I hate my job! I hate Kevin! I don't get the respect from him that I deserve. I'm treated like some lowly assistant rather than a manager. The employees are great, except for Kamille and her backstabbing ways, but now she's gone and I love running the place. But the no time off is killing me and my grades and my social life and the whole place just makes me feel. . .icky. I feel icky, Henry, every time I walk in that place."

"Icky isn't good. Your job—or really, your career—shouldn't make you feel this way. Do you consider Blissful and being a manager your career? Is that where you want to stay, or at least do with your life?"

I stood and helped Henry carry our dishes over to the sink. He started rinsing them and loading the dishwasher while I thought over his question. "I really love what I do at Blissful. I've always been interested in the spa business, and running the place makes me happy and I feel important. It's so empowering to make decisions on when to run sales and how to advertise and think of good marketing deals for the holidays. I would love to open my own spa one day and really run it the way I envision it."

"Have you ever looked into what it takes to open one?"

"Not really. I don't have the time. I know that sounds like a poor excuse, but I really don't. I barely have time to eat a full meal anymore."

We moved into the living room, where we sat side by side on the couch. Henry wrapped his arm around me and I snuggled into his shoulder. I was flattered that he was talking this out with me. It made me feel that he was invested in me, that he really cared about my thoughts and feelings.

"Maybe you need to make that time. We could do it tonight if you want to," he offered.

"Tonight? But we have movie night planned out," I protested, not wanting to ruin our date.

"I think this might be more important. I won't lie to you, Alex—after what you said about Kevin, I'm pretty uncomfortable with you working at Blissful. This man seems shady, and I'm wondering when he's going to make a move on you."

"On me?" I scoffed. "Kevin hasn't tried to pull anything on me. I don't think I have to worry about that."

"You never know. It's just a concern I have. I would hate for something to happen between you two when you're alone at the spa some night. What if he really tries to hurt you? I think it's best if you start looking for other jobs right away, but still do some research on opening up your own."

"But I'm only twenty. Twenty-one in a few days sure, but still. What bank is going to give me a loan for that? I have six months of managing a salon under my belt. Big whoop. That's nothing."

"You should talk to my sister. She opened her own boutique all on her own, with barely any experience. And she opened her store right out of college. I bet she could give you some pointers and advice."

I had yet to meet Henry's sister, Kate, who lived in Milwaukee. He talked about her quite a bit and she sounded like a smart woman who had her act together. Maybe she would be able to help me.

"I don't know. It's a big risk, opening a business. What if it fails?"

"Honestly, it probably will." I glared at Henry, who immediately put his hands up in defense. "Hear me out. Most small businesses fail. You've taken the courses. I'm sure you know that a lot of small businesses go under in the first year.

That's why you can't rush this process. Start looking around for other jobs first. Spa jobs, maybe a managing position if you can get lucky. But I don't think you can keep getting your soul sucked at Blissful. You're not happy, Alex."

I absorbed Henry's words. How the hell did I find such a smart guy? "I'm not happy. I'm not. I'm sad and disgusted and horrified and mad. I feel angry whenever I just think about Blissful. I hate how corporate Kevin is and how he only cares about money and women. It's gross and disturbing and I can't work for someone like that. The hours kill me. My schoolwork is slipping. I do see the benefits—the experience I'm getting—but I can't make that one positive outweigh all the negatives. You're right. I need a new job."

Henry and I sat in silence for a while, me thinking about what the hell I was going to do next. Would I really get a second chance at managing a spa? Would I really be able to pull together a business plan and open my own company? It seemed too daunting to even take seriously.

Henry and I were able to watch the movie we rented, only after I promised three times I would start a new job hunt tomorrow on my day off. In between kisses, I took a moment to reflect on how happy I was with Henry. What a frickin catch I had made.

The next night, Sunday, Lila strolled into the apartment around four o'clock. I had offered to pick her up from the airport, but she told me during one of our phone conversations that Mary had arranged a car service to take her home. A car service. Lucky duck. I was lounging on the couch, making final notes on the Valentine's Day specials we would be running at Blissful when the door opened.

"Honey, I'm home!" Lila shouted, throwing her suitcase aside and stretching out her arms.

I squealed, jumping to my feet to embrace her. "You're home! And you're so tan. I'm extremely jealous. Did you work at all or just lay on the beach? Did you get signed? Did you meet Brad Pitt?"

Lila laughed, letting me go and taking a seat on the couch. I joined her. "So many questions! Okay—no I didn't get to go to the beach. We were constantly moving around and meeting with people, but Mary did have me do a spray tan once I got there, so that's all this is." She gestured towards her bronzed arms.

"A spray tan?"

"Yeah, I had to get naked in front of some lady and she basically painted a tan on me with a nozzle. It was bizarre, cold and a little uncomfortable, but look how tan I am! And no UV rays or any chance of skin cancer."

Lila did look good. I made a mental note to think about adding a spray tan to Blissful. That could be a popular option for those who avoided tanning beds.

"Besides, it was a little chilly out there. Definitely not like here, but I'd say in the fifties and sixties. It rained almost every day, so the beach wasn't really an option, even if we did have the time."

She paused, and I stared at her expectedly. "So? The biggest question—were you signed? Did you find someone to represent you and make you into a star?" *Are you moving away from me?* I bit my tongue from asking that last question.

Lila took a deep breath, and I saw my answer in her sparkling eyes before she spoke. "Yes. Yes! Can you believe it, Alex? Mary helped me get signed with Ross Ricchio, who runs Ricchio Talent Management, or RTM. I actually had a few offers, but Mary steered me towards Ross and I signed on the dotted line and—and I'm doing it. I'm really doing it." Lila suddenly burst into tears, which threw me off balance.

"Hey, hey, what's the matter? Aren't you thrilled? This is your dream come true. You're getting a shot with a real agent and agency and someone who can find you great jobs." I wrapped my friend in a hug and tried to soothe her. "What's with the crying? You have to be so excited."

"I am. I am excited. But I'm terrified, Al. What if I mess it all up? What if I'm no good? What if I can't make any friends out there and I'm alone and have to start buying cats? What if I turn into a spoiled celebrity and get triple D boobs and injections that make my lips look like fish and dye my hair platinum blonde?"

"Did you make a detour at that bunny house you're always talking about?" I asked, only half joking.

Lila laughed, pulling back and wiping her face with her fingertip. "The Playboy mansion. No, we didn't get to stop there, unfortunately. But I saw a ton of girls who looked like plastic versions of the same person. It was creepy. I don't want to turn into that."

"You have to make sure you stay grounded. Call me a lot. Call your family a lot. I'm sure you'll be able to find one other person out there who hasn't turned into a Barbie zombie. It might take a little bit, but you'll find that person. And then you two have to rely on each other to keep your cool and not get a ton of plastic surgery—which by the way—would totally freak me out. You better not look plastic when I come out to visit you."

"How am I going to leave you?" Lila burst into a fresh set of tears. "And my family, my sisters? You and Hannie and Carmen and Emma? I'm scared to start over. Everyone I know and love is here. Iowa is comfortable."

"But you're bored here, Lila. You'd continue to be bored here if you don't go. You at least have to try. Maybe once you get to LA and get in the groove of things you'll realize it's not for you. And that would be okay too. I would not complain if you moved back. But at least you'll know you tried. You chased your dream." I knew that Lila wasn't really doubting her move to LA. It had been all she talked about for years. But it was normal to be scared, and I could recognize her fear above all else.

"I guess it will be nice to get away from these shitty winters," Lila admitted, giving a little sniffle.

"Um, are you kidding me? I think I got frostbite the other day when I went to scrape off my car. I'm definitely making sure to plan my trips to see you in the January time frame."

Lila's blue eyes started to sparkle again. "I can wear my cute dresses every day and open-toed shoes."

"And get more spray tans when you can't go to the beach."

"And rub elbows with celebrities. You'll never guess who I saw eating lunch at the same place Mary and I were eating."

"Who?"

"Alyssa Milano!"

Blank stare. "Who?"

"Seriously, Alex. Alyssa Milano. *Who's the Boss?*" Blank. "*Charmed.*" Blanker. "I'll Google her picture. You'll know her when you see her."

"Okay. I guess I'll have to be much more up to date on celebrities so we still have things to talk about when you call me. You will still call me, right?" My own fear kicked in. I was just realizing that my best friend was going to be moving miles and miles away from me. Everything was about to change.

Lila must have noticed the terror in my own eyes. She smiled and squeezed my hand. "Of course I'll call, Alex. And email. Even Skype. You're my best friend."

I nodded, holding the tears back with all my might. I was happy for Lila. She deserved to get her big chance. I really wasn't even jealous—at least not for the fact that she was moving and her life was about to become a million times more exciting than my own. That was her destiny, not mine. But I was jealous that she had figured it out, and I was just stuck at Blissful watching Kevin cheat on his wife.

"When are you going to tell the girls? I was thinking we should all do a big dinner tonight to celebrate. Get dressed up and go out and have a few drinks. I'm thinking Mexican, that way Hannah and I don't get carded." We never got ID'd at our favorite Mexican restaurant, La Bamba, and they had killer margaritas. "Then you could tell everyone your news together."

"Sounds like a plan. I'll send them a text." We were quiet for a few moments while Lila texted and I gathered up my advertising plans and stuck them in a folder.

"Everyone's in. They'll meet us here around six-ish," Lila said, tossing her phone back in her purse. "I'm going to try to unpack a little bit. Want to help me?"

"Yes." I answered immediately, and we smiled at each other. I think we both felt the same way—we just wanted to be by each other. Our days as roommates were numbered. Which reminded me—"Hey, when are you actually moving? And what about classes?"

"They want me out there as soon as possible, so I'll be leaving after this term. Mary is helping me with the paperwork that Kaufman will require and setting me up with online classes once I'm out there. I don't want to go through three years of school and have nothing to show for it. I want to get my degree. There's no guarantee this will work out, so I would like to have a backup plan. "

I followed Lila into her room, finding a seat on her bed amidst all the clothes, shoes, and makeup items scattered about. "That's smart. I think that's a good decision. So terms ends February second. About two more weeks then?"

"Yep." Lila paused, then unzipped her suitcase. "Gosh, that doesn't seem far away. Holy shit. I'm moving to LA."

"Holy shit," I echoed. I worried she might get emotional again, so I quickly asked, "Tell me about your agent! Ross? Do you like him or is he creepy?"

Lila chatted away about Ross, who seemed like a fairly normal guy (by LA standards) while she unpacked the rest of her suitcase. I asked her about her living situation (Mary and Ross would help hook her up with an apartment and roommate) when she thought she would start jobs (hopefully within three months) and what she thought of the LA guys (very tan, very white teeth, very metro). By the time she finished talking and unpacking it was nearing five-thirty and we had to get ready for our dinner.

After changing our outfits—me in dark skinny jeans and a lace long-sleeved top, Lila in a dark blue sweater dress and knee-high boots—we crammed into the bathroom to do our makeup. It felt strange knowing that our time squeezing ourselves into this miniscule bathroom was now limited. Afraid if she or I brought it up and we would start crying, I decided to fill her in about Blissful and see if she could help me make a decision about staying.

Somewhere between the primer and fake eyelashes, Lila stopped with the makeup application and just stared at me as I spoke. "So your weird feeling about Allie was correct. I still can't believe she would fool around with Kevin. I cashed the five thousand dollar check because it was doubling as my Christmas bonus. But ten thousand? What the hell am I supposed to do with that?"

"Holy shit, Alex. That's a lot of money you're talking about. I can't believe he can just throw that many Benjamin's around. Sheesh."

"Yeah, they have a shit ton of money. Which doesn't make me feel so bad that he's giving so much to me, but isn't Dani noticing these checks?"

"Do you think Dani knows about Kevin's ways?" Lila asked, turning back to the mirror and running a blush brush over her cheeks.

"Like, does she know about the affairs? And that he can just pay people off?"

"I don't know, just wondering. You would have to think that with so many women and so much money being spent she would have to know. Or at least have an idea."

"Look at that golfer—Tiger Woods. He was with how many porn stars and his wife said she had no idea."

Lila blinked at me. "How the hell do *you* know about Tiger Woods?"

I shrugged, slicking some pink gloss over my lips. "I do know some things about Hollywood, Lila. And when a pro golfer who seems like such a wholesome dude has this creepy sex life with porn stars while his hot wife sits at home with their kids, that tends to stick with me."

"Alrighty then. You remember the strangest things. Anyway, maybe Dani knows, maybe she doesn't. Maybe she just doesn't care."

"I guess. And with the money—well, I was kind of hoping to maybe one day start my own spa. And this money, though tainted, could really help me start saving up towards that goal. Or do you think that's lame?"

"No, I think it's a great idea! I'm sure you need, like, capital and all the crap to put up, and you might as well use that money for your own business. Make something good come from it."

"Henry was really supportive of it too," I said, catching Lila's expression in the mirror. "Lila?"

"You already talked to Henry about all of this?" she asked, looking crestfallen.

"Well, yeah. I told him about it last night. I just couldn't hold it in any longer and it all just came tumbling out." I paused. "Are you upset?"

Lila shook her head, her blonde hair bouncing off the lights. "No, no. I'm sorry. I don't have any right to get upset. It's just—usually you would talk to me first about all this. Not some guy. But I understand because I was gone and pretty soon I will be *really* gone. I can't expect you to wait for me to tell me this stuff. It's just—different." Lila's voice broke on that word.

I reached over to give her another hug. "Lils, you will always be my best friend. It doesn't matter that we have to be separated for a while. You get to go be awesome in LA and get spray tans every day while I sit freezing in Iowa and work for a pervert. I'm still going to come to you with my problems. Just maybe not as much. But I can guarantee I'll come to you when I'm having issues with Henry, because let's face it—I can't really go to him!"

That got Lila to crack a smile. "Sorry I'm being such a drama queen. It's just been a lot to take in and I don't think I've really got my head all wrapped around it. It just might take me some more time to get used to the situation is all. Then I promise I'll stop crying all the time."

"No worries." We smiled at each other, then went back to putting the finishing touches on our makeup. The girls would be arriving any moment. "Back to this Kevin and money debacle––I have to say that in a weird way, I'm excited. To know that I'm saving to open my business, to be a real business owner. That's pretty sweet. I almost feel like Kevin's handing me the golden ticket or something."

"More like the green ticket. Get it? Green, money." Lila laughed at her own joke, and I chuckled along with her. It was the truth. "But I'm proud of you, Alex. And if you decide you really can't stick it out any longer at Blissful, I know you'll find something great to replace it with. Even if it takes a while. You know Big Frank would take you back to Tastie's in a heartbeat."

"Ugh, I don't know if I can go back to flashing my bra every night after all this Blissful shit," I said. "When are you going to put in your notice?"

"I think tomorrow. I have the day off, but I might as well go in and get it over with," Lila said as a knock on the door sounded.

"Hello? Bitches? We're here and we're starving!" Carmen's voice rang through the apartment.

"In the bathroom!" Lila shouted. "Thanks for listening to me, Alex. I love you, girl."

"I love you, Lils. You are going to be a star, and I'll get to say I knew you when you had to flash your bra as a waitress. Now let's eat!"

"So you're moving away? Officially?" Emma asked, staring at Lila after my best friend broke her big news.

"Yes. I'll be finishing out this term and then. . .I'll be gone. Man, that seems so weird to say," Lila said, taking a gulp of her margarita.

"Wow. Well, obviously, congrats. That's a huge fricking deal and you should be thrilled. Like, take your pants off kind of thrilled," Carmen said, causing the rest of us to glance at each other. I hoped nobody would be taking their pants off in the middle of the restaurant. "Of course we'll all be sad to see you go, but you have to do it. It's your dream. And it's huge. Not everyone gets a chance like this."

"I know. I am so lucky. I'm lucky I made a great connection with Mary who knows all the right people in LA. And I'm lucky Ross wanted to take me on. Now I just have to fake my confidence out there until I really feel some."

"I don't mean to cut in on your parade, Lil, but what about you?" Hannah turned to me, where I was idly chewing on my straw, thinking about Lila and her spray tanned body going surfing and meeting celebrities. I was actually trying to slot myself into that daydream, but I just couldn't do it. LA was not for me.

"What about me?" I asked.

"What about your living situation? Won't you have to pay double rent if you don't have another roommate by next term?"

"Oh, shit." During our entire conversation about Lila leaving Iowa, I had never thought about what that would do for me. "I guess I didn't think about it. You're right though. I have to find someone or else pay the full amount. Shit." I started to panic, until I remembered all the checks from Kevin. I wasn't going to have to cry to my sister to try to help me out financially anymore. I could back myself up. But I really wanted that money to go toward opening my own spa. Damn.

"Oh, no! I'm so sorry, Alex. I didn't even think about the rent. Maybe I could talk to housing and get it extended or something. It's not your fault I'm leaving; you shouldn't have to deal with the consequences."

"It's all right, I'll figure it out. I'm sure I have some extra money lying around that I could use." I tried to send her a signal with my eyes, reminding her about the thousands of dollars I had thanks to Kevin's affairs. A light dawned in her eyes and I saw her shoulders relax for a second, then tighten back up. I was sure she was thinking about what I originally wanted to use the money for. I gave a quick shake of my head, trying to indicate we would discuss it later. I didn't want all the girls to know yet since I was still unsure of what my next step would be, and communicating telepathically with Lila was getting exhausting.

"Well, I have an idea. I'm not sure if you'd be up for it, but it's an offer," Hannah said, right as the waiter came and set our steaming plates in front of us. We paused while we opened our napkins and shuffled our silverware out, tucking in for our first delicious bites. The white cheese sauce in my quesadilla oozed as I cut in daintily with my fork and knife, then gave up and picked it up with my hands, shoving the triangle piece into my mouth. Heaven.

"All right, what's your idea?" I asked Hannah after a few bites.

"Why don't you move in with me? I have a second bedroom that isn't being used and plenty of space. It wouldn't be too difficult to move your stuff up a few flights of stairs."

"Really? You would really give up your huge-ass apartment and quiet quarters for me? Hannah, are you sure?" Hannah lived on the fifteenth floor of Wacker, or the 'penthouse' as us commoners liked to call it. Her apartment was a spacious two-bedroom unit, with a large bathroom and even a dishwasher. The fifteenth floor was definitely for the rich kids. Hannah used the second bedroom as her "study room" and we all knew that she loved her peace and quiet for when she was working on homework. I was a little surprised at her generosity, but then again, not really. That was just Hannah.

"Of course. I get lonely by myself sometimes and if it will help you out, then I'm more than happy to give up my study room."

Carmen let out a giggle. "Study room. Gets me every time."

Hannah shook her head but was smiling. "Anyway, what do you think? You don't have to answer now, you can think about it for a while. Just know the offer is open."

"I don't have to think about it. Of course I would love to be your roommate! Thank you so much, Hannah. This will really help me out." I leaned across my seat to give her a half hug. "I'm moving to the fifteenth floor. The penthouse! Everyone will be so jealous of me. Wait—Hannah, how much is rent there after we split the cost?" Would the move actually hurt me more financially?

Hannah waved away my concerns. "I'll talk to my dad about it, but I'm sure he won't mind you living there. He pays my rent now. I don't think adding a roommate will make a difference."

"Hannah, no. I can't ask you to give up your space and then just be a freeloader. Please let me pay my part."

"You didn't ask, I offered." Hannah took a sip of her water, trying to signal our conversation was over.

"What if I paid what I pay now? I'm sure that's barely a fourth of your rent, but it would really make me feel better. Please, Hannah. Or else I'll just feel like I constantly have to be quiet and do all the dishes and make you dinner every night. I'll feel like a house guest instead of a roommate."

Hannah considered my proposal. "All right. You can pay what you pay in rent now. If that will really make you feel better."

I nodded, satisfied. "It will. Whew, what a relief."

"Wow, things are really changing around here," Emma said. "Lila moving to LA, Alex and Hannah going to be roommates, Hannah has a serious boyfriend, and Carmen and I. . ."

"Carmen and you what? Do you have news too?" Lila asked.

"Nah. We're just Carmen and Emma. The unexciting gals with no cool news," Carmen finished up. "Maybe we should get working on that, Em. Be more exciting. Move, get a cool job, a boyfriend. Anything! We used to be the exciting ones in the group."

"Truth. We'll just have to work harder. Hey, that new bar downtown is hiring girls to go around and dance and hand out shots. I think they call them shot girls. We could apply for that."

"Sign me up! I love dancing and I love shots."

We all laughed and started discussing what we thought the job duties of a shot girl would entail. Our dinner passed smoothly, full of laughs, fruity drinks, and way too much chips and queso. I thought back over our dinner when I was in bed that night, in awe of how much things were about to change.

CHAPTER 17

"Hi, Alex. How are you today? It's almost your big day!"

I swallowed the lump of shame in my throat, forcing myself to greet Dani like I didn't know her husband had knocked boots with the employee giving a facial in treatment room one. Or that treatment room one was where they preferred to do the boot knocking. "Hey, Dani. I'm doing good. Looking forward to Saturday!"

"Same here! I think almost everyone here accepted their invite. And all of your friends are coming, right?"

"Right. Are you sure Hannah will be able to get in okay since she's not twenty-one yet? I would hate for her to get in trouble just because of me."

Dani brushed off my concern, taking a seat next to me behind the front desk. I had been trying to go through Wednesday's schedule to make sure everything looked okay, but found myself

271

distracted. I hated being at Blissful and I hated having to pretend like I didn't know what was going on here even more. "Oh, yes, don't worry about her. Kevin knows the owner, even did some business with him in years past. He's aware of the situation and knows that we won't cause a scene or anything. Anyone else that isn't twenty-one yet will be just fine. They just need to say your name at the door."

I did feel kind of important once she said that. Like Saturday night I was really going to *be* somebody. I just wished I could feel better about it since it was Kevin that was doing me the favor.

"Are you doing anything for dinner today?" Dani asked me, just as the phone rang. "Ooh, I'll answer it!"

I smiled and shook my head. Dani was always enthusiastic to talk on the phone. I had to hand it to her—she really loved her business, and talking to the clients was always a highlight of her day. I wished she were around more. Maybe I would like Blissful more if she was actually here with me, instead of it usually being Kevin just bossing people around or fucking the staff.

"Thanks, Mrs. Tillman. We'll see you at three o'clock tomorrow. Have a wonderful day!" Dani placed the phone back in its cradle and clicked the mouse a few times. "Shoot, I put the wrong appointment in. She just wants a perm and I put in a highlight. I don't think Mrs. Tillman's gray hair needs highlighting. Alex, do you know how to fix this?"

"Yep." I got up from my chair and stood behind Dani. "If you just click appointment detail it will let you into the appointment. And then click manage. Okay, then click where the highlight is and just hit remove. That will take it out. Then click perm and hit add. Yep. Done!"

"Thanks, honey. Want to do an early dinner? Allie and I are just going to pop into the café across the street if you want to come along. I have to take off right after to go to Bailey's parent/teacher conference, so it'll just be a short one."

I glanced at the clock. It was only four-thirty, a little early to be thinking about dinner. And to suffer through the meal with Allie and Dani, knowing what I knew about our head esthetician? I could think of a lot of other places where I wanted to be instead. Such as the dentist or gynecologist.

"Um, thanks, but I'll probably pass. I had a big lunch." Lie. I had half a turkey sandwich on my drive between Wacker and here. I stayed late in my last class to beg the professor to give me an extension on my final term paper. The extension was granted, and I was seriously hoping I could finish it on time. My grades were really starting to fall.

"Oh, just come with us then and grab something to go. You can eat it here later tonight when you get hungry. Did you bring anything for dinner?"

Before I could lie again, I shook my head. Damn. I really did love the chef salads at that café. I could just have them give me the dressing on the side and bring it back for later. "Okay, okay. I give in. I'll come with."

"Excellent! Allie should be done in about thirty minutes and then we'll head right over. I'm supposed to be to Bailey's school no later than 6:15. What time is your interview with Kamille's replacement?"

"Not until eight. I scheduled it later when hopefully it won't be too busy."

"Plenty of time then. I hope you like this one. We really need to get her shifts covered. Shame she left us. She always had such a fabulous ideas!"

I bit my lip to keep from screaming out the truth.

Thirty-five minutes later, I found myself face to face with Kevin's wife and Kevin's. . .mistress? Girlfriend? Did they really only hook up one time or was Kevin lying to me? How many more times had they been together? No way was Kevin telling the truth of it being a one-time thing. Was it a full-blown affair? Could Dani and Allie read the expression on my face, the one that screamed *your husband's cheating on you with the filthy whore you pay health benefits for!*

"Alex, are you getting excited for Saturday?" Allie asked me. Her expression looked normal enough, but I could see it in her eyes. She knew that I knew. Bitch. I couldn't believe she had lied to me about loving her fiancé. I felt like a fool.

"Yeah, it should be a great time. I'm excited to be with all my friends. And thank you, Dani, for planning such a great party. You've really done a lot for me, and I just want you to know how thankful I am for everything." I raised my eyebrows just an inch in Allie's direction. Suck it. She looked down at her hands.

"Well, of course. You're welcome, sweetie. I just hope everything runs as smoothly as I planned it in my head! And your new boyfriend is coming too, right?"

"Right! Henry will be there my friend Hannah's boyfriend, too. And they have two other roommates that will come as well."

"Jewel can't make it, and of course Julia isn't coming. I didn't think we could swing a high school girl into the club. Maybe,

274

but I don't want to risk it. Mandy said she could drop by but not stay long. She's in the uncomfortable pregnant stage where she finally looks pregnant and going to bars is awkward for her. But I think most everyone else will be there," Dani said, as our number was called at the counter. We stood and gathered our food, mine already packaged up in a Styrofoam box.

We sat back at the table, Allie and Dani digging into their salads. I took a sip of my lemonade and tried to pretend like I was having a good time.

Between getting Blissful ready for Valentine's Day—a huge spa holiday—and trying to keep up with schoolwork, see Henry and squeeze in as much time with Lila as I could, Saturday approached at warp speed. Though it was never spoken aloud, the five girls gathered in our apartment, one of the last times we would be getting ready for a night out in Wacker 12.

Carmen was working on my hair, rolling strands of red in between hot rollers while Emma fussed with Hannah's. Lila, who had been on the receiving end of yet another spray tan in Des Moines courtesy of Mary, was struggling to apply lip liner just right to her already full lips.

"Since when have you started using lip liner, Lila? I thought that was just reserved for my home girls," Carmen said, indicating her pouty lips complete with liner.

"Mary said that I should emulate how I want to look in LA while I'm here. And each time I got my makeup done, lip liner was used. So I bought myself this pencil, but I think I look too weird with it on. What do you guys think?" Lila gave us a sexy pout.

"Yeah, I think it looks weird," I said bluntly. "Like you have clown lips or something. Did the makeup people give you any hints or tricks?"

Lila turned back to the mirror, frowning at her appearance. "No. It's not like I'll have to apply my own makeup on the jobs anyway. I just want to try to learn a few new skills for when I go out at night or something. If I can ever find anyone to go out with me, that is."

My poor roommate's face looked so forlorn that I wanted to start crying for her. I knew Lila was extremely nervous about making friends in California. I didn't think she would have to worry, but I was a little scared about what her new friends would be like. Blonde, bimboed, plastic? What if they changed Lila into a completely different person? What if she didn't want to be my friend anymore?

"Did I tell you girls I invited a guy to meet us at Tango tonight?" Emma broke the awkward silence with her somewhat surprising news.

"You did? Who? Where did you meet him?" we all peppered her with questions. I hadn't known that Emma was seeing anyone, and she rarely did the inviting. She preferred men to chase her.

She gave a coy shrug, blasting Hannah's hair with hairspray. "His name is Corey. I met him a few months back when we did the pancake and beer thing," she said, nodding towards Carmen. "He goes to Des Moines University, is a senior, tall, blonde hair and blue eyes, super fit, majoring in psych work or something like that. We've met up at a few more bars here and there, and I just thought it might be fun if he comes out tonight. That's all."

"Have you two ever hung out anywhere else besides a bar? Have you done dinner or anything?" Lila asked, sliding her eyes to meet mine. I could count the number of times Emma invited a guy somewhere—twice. And to invite him to a party where all her girlfriends would be? That was Emma's version of having the guy meet her parents.

"Nope. Just bars. Would you guys stop looking at me like that? It's no big deal. Seriously." Emma turned back and fluffed Hannah's hair once more. "You're golden. Peter will fall all over you tonight."

"Am I going to be the only one without a date?" Carmen asked, taking a sip of her margarita. "Damn it, I knew I would be the last single one in the group!"

"I don't have a date," Lila reminded her.

"Yeah, but you're. . ." Carmen let her voice trail off, but we all knew what she was about to say. *Leaving.* Would Lila be considered part of the group anymore? Surely she would find her own group in LA to be a part of.

"Look at the time!" my voice was high pitched as I spoke, frantically gesturing to my watch. "We better get dressed. The limo will be here shortly." We actually had plenty of time to get dressed. I just didn't want to keep thinking about my best friend moving away from me.

The five of us shuffled out of the bathroom and into Lila's room, where our outfits were all laid out on her bed. I squeezed Lila's hand as we walked and she shot me a grateful smile, but her eyes were shining with tears.

Carmen started the conversation again, talking about how perhaps she would hit on Max at the party just to feel like she had a date too. We all laughed at that, but I secretly wondered if my exotic friend hadn't fallen for the blonde Max. What babies they would make. I shook myself out of that daydream, knowing how much Carmen would scold me if she could hear my thoughts, and focused on the clothes again. It was still bitterly cold in Iowa, but since we were going to a dance club and apt to get sweaty, our outfits reflected on our destination, not our journey.

Lila slipped into a light green mini-dress, which she paired with a chunky silver bracelet and necklace, dangly silver earrings with diamond crosses, and thigh-high tan boots. Those were a purchase she made in LA, and I knew it would make her stand out amongst us.

Hannah dressed more demure, and while she had insisted on just wearing skinny jeans, Emma somehow persuaded her to at least bump it up to leggings. Her black leggings and red shirt— borrowed from Emma that was backless—made Hannah look like a completely different person. Peter wasn't going to know what hit him.

Emma and Carmen had on similar sequined dresses, but Emma's was a dark gray with silver sequins and Carmen's was more beige with black sequins. Sky-high stilettos and lots of jewelry completed their looks.

I had chosen a tulip miniskirt for the night, light pink in color, and found a funky white top that was splashed with different colors along the fabric. It was loose and dipped down to show off some cleavage, and I borrowed a pair of Lila's heels and kept my jewelry minimal for the night. My hair was set in bombshell curls, and I was feeling pretty confident about my party. Especially since we were to arrive in a limo. Dani had really gone all out for me, renting us the limo to pick us up at Wacker and deposit us back at the end of the night. I felt like a celebrity.

After dousing ourselves in perfume, rechecking our hair and makeup one last time and making sure we had everything we could need crammed into our tiny clutches, we declared ourselves ready and headed out the door. As we stepped outside, the wind hit us and we all linked arms and tried to huddle together, walking as fast as we could in our heels to our awaiting limo. The driver got out and opened the door for us, and we hurriedly ducked inside to get away from the wind.

"Holy shit, this is a nice limo," Carmen declared once we were all inside. "And what is this? Yes! Anyone up for a bit of bubbly?" She waved the champagne bottle in the air like she had just scored a personal victory.

"I can open that for you, miss," our limo driver said, producing a corkscrew from a small tray next to where champagne glasses stood at attention. He popped the bottle and some champagne sprayed out, making me understand why he wanted to do it instead of us getting his limo drenched.

We eagerly held out our glasses as he poured champagne in each cup. "Thank you so much! What is your name, good sir?" Emma asked, taking a sip and licking her lips. "This is amazing."

"My name is Tony. If you need anything else, just let me know and I'll be glad to accommodate you." With a tip of his cap, Tony disappeared around the front and back behind the wheel.

"Dang, I could get used to this," Carmen said, settling back in the plush seat and knocking back another drink. "They're really going all out for you, Alex. Lucky bitch."

I snuck a glance at Lila, who was looking at me. Yeah, so lucky. This was probably just another "don't-talk" tactic employed by Kevin. Butter me up, make me feel special, put me in the spotlight in front of my friends. Anyone from the outside looking in would be totally confused if I quit my job. I had it made at Blissful.

"Emma, I just have to know more about this guy. Please, more details!" Hannah said, causing the rest of us to laugh. "What? What's so funny?" she asked, confusion on her innocent little face.

"It's just so fun to see how you've changed since becoming a girlfriend. Before Peter, you rarely wanted to know about our men. Barely asked about them. But now, you ask questions and you seem into what we have to say about them. It's weird. But in an awesome way." Lila filled in the blanks for Hannah.

"Yeah. You were all about school and studying and that was about it. Peter has definitely relaxed you. It's a good look for you, Hannie." I smiled at my friend, my soon-to-be new roommate. "It's nice to see you like this."

"Geez, was I just awful before? You guys make it sound like I never had any fun before Peter!" Hannah took a small sip of her champagne, looking around at us.

"Well, lovely, you never wanted to come out with us, barely took a drink of anything because you always had more studying to do, rarely participated in our shopping events or movie nights. We love you either way, but this Hannah is definitely more. . .approachable," Emma said.

"And we've been able to call you Hardcore Hannah more in the last few months than we have in years!" Carmen pitched in.

"Huh. Well, I guess that's a good thing then. To me!" Hannah held up her champagne glass, and we clinked our glasses before dissolving into a fit of giggles. We spent the rest of the limo ride to the party chatting about boys—the good boys, the bad boys, the ones in between. The boys Lila might meet in LA and the ones she would bring home for us to meet.

It wasn't long before we were pulling up to Tango. Tony came around to the side and helped us out, one by one. I was last—emphatically told so by Lila—and reached for Tony's hand once it was my turn. I carefully slid out of the limo and placed my heels on the cement, popping up and out without flashing any of my business.

"Happy Birthday!" I heard a shout before confetti rained down on me, blinding my vision.

"What the hell?" I shouted through a smile. Once the confetti cleared, I could see almost all of the Blissful staff standing outside Tango, including Allie, Kevin, and Dani. I saw Henry, Peter, Max, and Kyle standing there as well, holding confetti in their hands. Henry was also balancing a digital camera, and the flash kept going off as he got pictures of my shocked face. My girlfriends were also now holding confetti, tossing it in the air with glee. Other patrons were stopping to stare, some even taking their own pictures. Was I a celebrity? Maybe they thought so—how cool! I might not have been interested in a life in LA, but the attention was good for my ego, I had to admit. I smiled and waved at everyone, shaking my head and seeing the confetti fall to the ground.

"Did you know about this?" I asked Lila, grabbing her arm as we walked towards the group.

"Maybe," she answered with a sly smile. "Come on! You have a lot of people to greet." She hauled me up to the entrance where my fans awaited. Okay, friends and co-workers. Jeesh. When I did visit Lila, she was going to have to keep me penned up inside. It was like a wedding receiving line, with Lila only giving me a few minutes to chat with each person. I thanked everyone from Blissful for coming—even Allie, though it was done through a forced smile and Lila tightly holding onto my hand—friends from Kaufman that Lila and the girls had invited, and finally Kevin and Dani.

"Happy Birthday, Alex!" Dani squealed when I got to her, wrapping me in hug. "Were you surprised? Are you having fun? How was the limo?" Her face radiated happiness, but instead of being able to bask in it with her, all I could feel was a tug in my heart and guilt from knowing the truth. I pasted the smile anyway.

"I was surprised, thank you! Thank you so much for setting this all up. I can't believe you went through all this trouble. I'm blown away. Truly. Thank you." To my horror, my eyes started to well up. I didn't know if it was the fact that my birthday party was so extravagant and unlike anything I had ever had, or the fact that images of Kevin and Allie were swirling in my mind. Probably both.

"Come here, you." Kevin pulled me into a hug, my feet leaving the ground. I could feel my entire body stiffen, and I was sure he could too. That didn't deter him from keeping the broad smile on his face. "Happy Birthday, Alex. I hope you have a fantastic night. One to remember—or hopefully forget! You're twenty-one, bitch!"

I looked at Kevin closely. It was clear he already had a few cocktails in his system. I hoped he would pass out early and leave me the hell alone. And not make a move on any of my friends. Or anyone here, for that matter. Not with Dani in the vicinity.

"Thanks. Thanks again, both of you. This is much more than I imagined. Shall we go inside?" I was itching to get over to Henry, but I didn't want to be rude to my party planners, the people that were footing the entire bill.

"Let's go! And please, introduce me to your boyfriend. I've been dying to meet him!" Dani said, linking her arm through mine.

We breezed through the door, the bouncer just nodding at us all. I watched Hannah walk in with confidence on the arm of Peter. And then I saw Henry making his way towards us. He looked delectable in black slacks and a cobalt blue dress shirt with the sleeves rolled up. He even had a bit of gel in his hair, the first time I had seen that look. His blue eyes sparkled when he finally got to us.

"Hi, babe. You look absolutely stunning," he greeted me, handing me over a bouquet of deep red roses.

"Henry! Thank you so much, these are beautiful. Dani, do we have a place to put these?"

"I'm sure we can rustle something up. I'll go check it out in a sec."

"Oh, I'm sorry. Dani, this is my boyfriend, Henry Landon. Henry, this is Dani Dohlman, co-owner of Blissful."

My boss and boyfriend shook hands, then Dani wrapped him in a hug as well. "Oh, it's so good to meet you, Henry! We've heard so much about you. I'm thrilled you could make it tonight. And these are just gorgeous! Let me just run quick and see if I can get some water for them." She scuttled into the throes of the restaurant as Henry and I continued walking towards the stairs, heading to the upstairs level that had been reserved for the party.

"Well, she seems friendly," Henry observed, watching Dani scurry through the crowd and get swallowed up by the partygoers.

"I'll be curious to see your reaction to Kevin. Come on, let's go upstairs." I linked my arm through his and we continued to the staircase. Tango had an upper and lower level, the lower level being a fancy restaurant that featured menu items like filet mignon and a wine list a mile long. The upper level was the dance club, with a massive tiled dance floor and cozy booths sprinkled around it. The DJ booth stretched along the east wall, enclosed behind a barricade of glass. There were three tall blocks in front of the booth and girls were already on the blocks dancing their little hearts out. The lights were low and strobe lights flickered throughout. Music videos were showcased on the walls which I thought was neat since no TV station played them anymore.

I squinted in the darkness, wondering where the group was. I didn't have to wonder long. Almost the entire room was filled with people there for my party. A row of booths were adorned with pink and black balloons, streamers, and a big banner proclaiming, "Happy 21st Alex!" There was also a large picture of me, Lila, Hannah, Carmen, and Emma in a frame that was resting on an easel in the corner. I recognized the photo from the New Year's party we attended. Little bowls of snacks sat at each of the booths, along with more confetti and napkins that also wished me happy birthday. Overwhelmed couldn't even describe what I was feeling.

"Holy shit. I feel like this is my sweet sixteen party or something. Are there TV cameras here?" I joked to Henry, but my eyes flitted about the room. I wasn't going to put anything past Dani and her party-planning skills again.

"I wasn't aware of that detail, so I think you're okay. Come on, you have to see your cake."

In a daze, I let Henry take my hand and pull me gently to the booth where my girlfriends and Dani were sitting. I noticed that Dani had indeed found a vase, wrapped a pink ribbon around it, and placed my bouquet of roses at the head table. My party was beautiful.

"Do you love it?" Lila shouted to me, giving my hand a squeeze.

"I can't believe you guys did all this work for me. And kept it a surprise! You sneaky bitches." I tried to glare at my friends, but it turned into a huge smile. "I don't deserve you ladies."

"You bet your ass you do! Here, the bartender has a special drink for you," Carmen cut in, handing me a champagne glass filled with pink liquid.

"What is this?" I sniffed the drink before taking a little sip, followed by a much larger one. It was an explosion of fruit and bubbles in my mouth.

"It's called the Alex-osa. I named it myself. It's like a mimosa, but with liqueur instead of orange juice. It's a lethal concoction. Drink slowly if you want to remember this night," Carmen warned, taking a generous swig of her Alex-osa.

"Wow. I've never had a drink named after me before. And where is this cake that I have to see?"

"Ta-da!" Emma flung her arms out in flourish, walking alongside Dani and helping her roll out a cart with a four-tier cake settled on it. My cake was out of this world beautiful. I'd seen less fancy cakes at weddings. The bottom tier had pink and brown stripes, the third tier had pink frosting with silver squiggles, the second tier had brown frosting and pink dots covering it, and the tiniest tier was all pink with an exquisite stiletto perched on top. Upon closer inspection, I could tell the shoe wasn't actually *on* the cake, it was on a little stand with four prongs going into the top layer. I also saw that it was no ordinary shoe. The red sole gave it away—it was a Christian Louboutin. Only *the* most coveted shoes in the world. I didn't have to be a celebrity follower to know that design, and know that women everywhere would do anything for a pair of these outrageously expensive shoes. And one was my cake topper.

"Holy fuck!" My manners went out the window. "How the hell did you guys get a Louboutin shoe as a cake topper? Is it real? Can I touch it?"

"You can touch it, Alex. Actually, it belongs to you. And yes, it's real. As is this one." From underneath the cart, Dani produced a tan box with the squiggle of a signature on it. *Christian Louboutin.*

"What? What? I don't understand." I was near hyperventilating when I opened the box and found the matching shoe. A black lace, peep toe, red-soled beauty of a shoe. That were apparently mine.

"This is a gift from me and your friends," Dani said, smiling at me.

"Put them on, put them on!" Lila urged me, already leading me over to a booth. I followed in a daze, still unsure what was happening. The limo, the entrance, the people, the decor, the cake, the shoes! I didn't know what I did to deserve all of this, and I was overwhelmed in gratitude. And already planning my thank-you cards.

I took off Lila's shoes and carefully slipped on the Louboutins. They fit like a glove. I was Cinderalla. That was it. This was my fairy tale night.

CHAPTER 18

How could a fairy tale go so wrong? That night was my night. It was finally my time to have some fun. To not worry about schedules and ads and employees and the stress that Blissful caused me every day. To not have to worry about my homework assignments and if I would pass my classes. It was my night to just have some fun.

As the night went on, I really started to believe. Believe that my birthday party would go off without a hitch. I had all my girlfriends around me; I had Henry. Henry was looking at me like I was the only girl in the room—the only girl in the universe! My friends were having a great time—Hannah cutting loose on the dance floor, twirling in Peter's arms. Carmen grinding against Max. Emma trying her hardest to hide that glow when Corey grabbed her hand and led her to the dance floor, pulling her close. And Lila holding court at a booth, regaling some of our classmates and the Blissful staff about her upcoming trip and new life that she would be starting in LA. I even caught some girls asking for her autograph! Lila, blushing furiously, obliged with a smile on her face.

Everyone was content. Everyone was happy. As the clock neared 12:30, I realized that I wasn't actually that drunk, considering it was my twenty-first birthday and I probably should have been passed out in a pool of my own vomit by then. But I had done so much talking, taken so many pictures, showed off my new shoes so many times, that I really hadn't overindulged on too many drinks. The Alex-osa's were bomb, and I think I had two. . .maybe three. I knew I did a shot with Lila at the beginning of the night, a jolly rancher that tasted just like, well, a jolly rancher. It felt a little weird drinking in front of so many people that called me their boss, so I was being conscientious of that fact. But I was still enjoying myself, don't get me wrong. My birthday party was exceeding anything that I could have thought of. Until it happened.

Kevin, who was piss-ass drunk before I even showed up at Tango, was in prime condition. I was keeping an eye on him, as were both Henry and Lila, but he seemed to be doing all right. Sure, he was loud at times. And yes, he made some off-color remarks to my party guests—including both Allie and Carmen. Allie's fiancé—who was a perfect gentleman and who I thought was quite handsome in the looks department—just took Allie's hand and led her to the dance floor after Kevin told her she should have worn a shorter dress because she rocked "legs that that bitch Cameron Diaz would pay for—after she bought herself a pair of real tits." And Carmen simply flipped him the bird and flounced away after he announced to her that, "Mexico wants its hot tamale back, hot damn, baby!"

But my party literally screeched to a halt just minutes after I checked the time at 12:30 and was congratulating myself on a night to remember. I wandered over to the booth were Lila was sitting, and Henry was soon by my side. He gave me a light kiss on the forehead, snaking his arm around my waist and pulling me close. "I think it's just about closing time," he whispered in my ear—loudly, since the music was so loud.

I nuzzled into his shoulder. "You're staying at my place still, right?"

"Nowhere else I would want to be," he responded, causing goosebumps to spread up my arms. A half-naked Henry in my bed sounded like just where I wanted to be at that moment. I was thinking about herding my girlfriends together when I heard Kevin shout my name behind me.

"Alex! Alex, you owe me a dance, you dirty slut. Come on! Come dance with me." I turned around to find Kevin on the edge of the dance floor, his shirt all the way unbuttoned and half off. I watched in horror as he took it off and stuck it between his legs, thrusting back and forth while whooping and hollering. Everyone was starting to stare.

"Oh, Jesus. Where the hell is Dani?" I looked around Tango, trying to spot Kevin's wife and the only one who could calm him down. She was nowhere to be found.

"He is out of control, Alex. I can't believe you have to work with him every day," Lila said, staring at Kevin. "Kudos to you for still being there. I probably would have snapped by now."

Kevin started coming closer to us, gesturing wildly and throwing his hands in the air. "Alex! I said now!" he hollered, finally reaching the table. His eyes were bloodshot, he was sweating profusely, and he reeked like someone had dumped bottles of liquor on him. It was disgusting. He grabbed my hand and started pulling me to the dance floor. "Dance, little girl! Come on, show me your moves. I know you got them buried under that prissy exterior!"

My mouth dropped open. How dare my boss say those words to me? "Kevin, I don't think that's very appropriate to say to one your employees. Especially your manager," I retorted, my hands going to my hips. Fuck no! I was not going to dance with this douchebag.

"I don't think *this* is appropriate either, but I want to see them!" I stared confused at Kevin when he said that, having no idea what he was talking about. Before I could think or react, he reached up and put a hand on either side of my v-neck top. . .and ripped. Ripped my shirt off in the middle of the dance floor of one of the busiest night clubs in Des Moines. Completely ripped my brand-new birthday shirt in half, leaving me exposed and in a lacy bra that was meant for Henry's eyes only. In front of my friends. Classmates. And employees.

"Yeah, baby! We gotta get you a deal for Gropers! Someone! Anyone! Grab me my phone. Call Chris—she needs a photo shoot!"

The club seemed to go silent. I swear, I thought the DJ did that halt the records thing that sounded like a zipper, but I knew the music was still playing. I saw black and could hear my heartbeat in my ears. I couldn't move, couldn't cover myself up, couldn't do anything. Shock. I was in shock. Kevin had officially humiliated me on my birthday.

"Alex! Oh my God, here!" Lila had run over to me, throwing someone's jacket over my exposed body. I could see Carmen running towards me from the bar on the other side of the dance floor, fire in her eyes. I could see Emma and Corey coming my direction. I saw Hannah gripping Peter's hand as she rushed my way. And I saw Henry push Kevin backwards. It wasn't that he pushed him hard, but Kevin was already so off-balance that he tumbled to the ground, landing in a heap at Henry's feet. I blinked, still not understanding what had just happened. Did Kevin really say he wanted to see my boobs before ripping my shirt off me? That couldn't have happened. There was just no way.

"Where the fuck is Dani? Someone find Dani. Now!" Carmen screamed as she finally made it to me, wrapping both arms around me. "Are you okay, Alex? Are you okay? We're going to find Dani. We're going to figure this out. Alex? You okay?"

I finally snapped out of my daze, focusing on Carmen's dark eyes. "What. The. Fuck?" I finally managed to get out, pulling the coat around me tighter. I didn't even know who it belonged to, but that was the least of my worries. I glanced around, seeing Allie and her fiancé staring at me. One of the front desk gals, Tiffany, was standing in a circle with two stylists, Sophia and Lindsey, the three of them just staring at me in shock. Morgan and Shawna, an esthetician and massage therapist, gaped at me. How the hell was I supposed to act normal around my employees now? They had seen me in my bra! Shirt ripped off by the guy that signed their paychecks. What happened next?

Kevin was still on the ground, struggling to his feet. I noticed security making their way over to us. Lila and Carmen started to lead me to the stairs. Hannah and Peter were gathering our things at the booth—our clutches and the gifts I had been given. My Louboutins, which had been so comfortable all night, suddenly felt like they were cutting off my circulation.

"Sir. We're going to have to ask you to leave." Security had made their way to Kevin, and they were now helping him off the ground.

"I'm not leaving! This is my party! Do you know who I am? Where's Rick? Someone get Rick up here! He'll tell you who I am. I probably paid both of your wages tonight!" Kevin was screaming in their faces, his own face red and eyes bulging. I cringed, just wanting to get far, far away from the whole scene. I wondered if I could ever show my face again at Tango. Probably not.

"Sir. We saw what you did, which is grounds for needing to leave. Right now," the second security guard, who had even bigger biceps than his partner, didn't even flinch at Kevin's words. I was sure they heard it at all being bouncers at bars.

"To Alex? Oh, come on, she knows me. Alex! Alex, sweetheart! Tell these nice men that it's no big deal. We know each other!" Kevin started shouting to me. I paused and looked at him. He was sweating and it looked like he laid in a spilt drink when he took his Henry-assisted tumble. He did not look like a businessman, a husband, or anyone with class or an ounce of respect. I felt for him—for a just a second. I wondered if he realized how badly he fucked up this time, and how publicly.

Without a word, I turned around and kept walking towards the stairs. I was determined to hold the tears in, at least till we got to the limo. Carmen and Lila flanked me, and I could see Henry, Max, and Kyle quickly following behind us. Hannah and Peter came after them. Right when we got to the top of the stairs, Dani appeared.

"Hey, guys! Where are you going? What happened? Alex, what's wrong?" She took one look at my face and knew a disaster had taken place. A disaster named Kevin Dohlman.

I didn't say anything, just looked at Dani and slowly opened the coat I was wearing. Showing her that my outfit now consisted of a mini-skirt and white lace bra.

"What in the hell? Who did this to you?" Dani searched my face, and I saw her expression darken. "I'm so sorry, Alex. I thought. . .I didn't think he would. . .I apologize for him. I can't believe he would pull this tonight. In front of everyone. Oh, God, did everyone see?" Her eyes welled with tears, and I felt terrible for her. Her husband clearly had a lot of issues, and it was always Dani's job to pick up the pieces after the hurricane and put everything back together.

I nodded, still unable to speak. Lila took over for me. "We're going to get going. Kevin is in the process of being thrown out by security. You might want to help him."

Dani stared at me for another second, her pain cutting right into me. "I'm really sorry about this, Alex. I. . .I'll call you tomorrow." And she rushed to the dance floor, where we could now see that Kevin was being physically removed by the bouncers, screaming his head off about lawyers and lawsuits.

We made it unscathed to the lower level and out into the night. Our limo was just around the corner, and Tony helped us all in. As I sat down and laid my head on Henry's shoulder, I realized how exhausted I felt. How exhausted I felt every time I did a Blissful function. Whether it was working, meetings, phone calls, whatever—Blissful always left this feeling with me.

"I don't know whose coat this is," I said meekly, wrapping it tighter around me. "I just stole someone's coat."

"Don't worry about it. We'll figure out who it belongs to and make sure they get it back. I'm sure they won't mind you borrowing it," Lila said, sitting to the right of me.

I nodded my head. I thought the tears would come once I made it to the limo, but they hadn't showed yet. My body just felt numb. I had to quit my job. There was no way I could continue on after that night. How could I have an ounce of respect for myself if I did? "I have to quit, don't I?" I asked my friends. They were all in the limo—Lila and Henry on my sides, Hannah holding hands with Peter, Carmen sitting in between Max and Kyle, and Emma sitting beside Corey. My own little support group.

"Could you stay?" Emma asked me. "Could you stay after this incident?"

I shook my head. "There's no way. No way. How would I act around Kevin? The employees? What kind of example would I be setting for them if I just brushed this under the rug? That they all need to lie back and take whatever shit Kevin throws their way? I can't do that. I just can't. I'm better than that."

"You are better than that, Alex. Just keep remembering that. You're better than what just happened in there." Henry squeezed my hand and kissed my temple.

The limo first dropped Max and Kyle off at their place. Peter was staying at Hannah's and Henry was staying with me. "I'm going to hop out here, too, if that's okay with you, Alex. Unless you want to stay up and chat at all. I'll come back to Wacker," Carmen said. Even in my current condition, I could see she was finally closing the gap of "friendship" between her and Max.

"No, please. Don't worry about me. I'm exhausted and just want to sleep. I don't want to think anymore until the morning. Have a good night." I managed a wink at her, and she winked back before grabbing her clutch and exiting the limo.

The rest of our group rode back in near silence. Tony helped us all out of the limo and tipped his hat to us as we filed silently inside Wacker. Everyone gave me a hug as we parted, even Corey. I remembered thinking I liked him as he grabbed Emma's hand and led her down the hallway. Lila unlocked our door and we stepped inside the apartment.

"Well. Great night, everybody. Let's try that again next year, shall we?" I said bitterly, throwing my clutch on the kitchen table. I ripped the stupid Louboutins off my feet, wanting to throw them as well but realizing that carelessly treating shoes that could very well cost thousands of dollars wouldn't be my smartest move. "What a fucking joke."

"It is a fucking joke, Alex. I mean, what the hell are you going to do tomorrow? What do you even say to him? To the employees? Dani? What the hell is Dani going to do?" Lila fired off questions that she knew I couldn't answer. Henry sank onto the couch, shaking his head.

"I really don't even know if I can think about this anymore tonight. My head feels like it could explode. But there is no way in hell I am going back to work for him. No freaking way."

"Can you sue? Could you have any sort a case of sexual harassment against him or something?" Henry asked.

I shrugged my shoulders. "Honestly, I doubt it. He has so much money anyway he could hire much better lawyers than I ever could. I know he's won lawsuits before when he definitely should have lost. Money buys everything in his world."

"But Henry's right. You're quitting because of what he did. You'll be out of job because of his actions. And what about the money that he's given you? You could show how he's tried paying you off."

"But that's going to make me look bad. I accepted it. I helped keep his secrets because he kept handing me checks. What does that say about me, about my character? I look like any cheap hooker would, choosing money over my morals. Why didn't I just get out of it right away?" Tears leaked through my eyes. I should have known better. I should have gotten out. I should have told. Should have, should have, should have.

"Alex, you can't blame yourself." Henry grabbed my hand and led me gently to the couch. "It's not your fault what Kevin does. And remember what we talked about a few weeks ago? You were going to use that money to help start your own business. It's not like you were taking the money and going on shopping sprees and buying cars. Or worse—it's not like you started sleeping with Kevin, too."

I thought of Allie once Henry said that. Was she being paid by Kevin? Was she getting "bonuses" on the side? I wondered if her fiancé knew. I wondered if Dani knew. I wondered if Allie was sleeping with him when we had our heart to hearts when I had first started Blissful. "I just have too many questions right now. I want to sit down with Dani and get this figured out. I like her. Maybe she knows about Kevin's infidelities, maybe she just doesn't want to believe them. But I don't want to believe Allie. She told me she thinks Dani knows and sticks around because Kevin has money. But what if that was just a lie? Allie's been lying to me since I came on board. I wouldn't be surprised if she was making Dani out to be this terrible person. She's the one cheating on her fiancé. Sleeping with her boss. Sleeping with her friend's husband. I cannot believe what a mess this is. My dream job. What a joke."

We went to sleep shortly after that. I decided I would call Dani tomorrow and ask her to meet me somewhere where we could talk, really talk about what the hell was going down at her business. And I needed to turn in my resignation—effective immediately. I had to start looking for new jobs. I had to call Alicia and explain what the hell happened. That was going to be a terrific phone call. My sister was going to be livid. Maybe another trip to Seattle was in my future; just to get away for a second and breathe and try to forget these past six months.

I fell asleep cuddled in Henry's arms, dreading the next day.

"Okay. I'll see you in an hour. Bye." I hung up the phone with Dani after making plans to meet at the deli by Blissful. Dani apologized about eight times in our ten-minute phone conversation, and said she really wanted to meet with me as well. I had woken up early that Sunday, made it to church with Henry, Hannah and Peter, then came back to Wacker to shower, change, and prepare myself for lunch with Dani. Henry and Peter had gone back to their house, but Henry left me with a kiss and plenty of words of encouragement. The girls all gathered in apartment 12, watching me get ready.

"I just wonder what she's going to say. Will she make excuses for Kevin? Make you feel like you were in the wrong? Or will she be totally against him and want a divorce?" Emma wondered, watching me pull my hair back in a ponytail.

"If she doesn't at least separate from Kevin for a while, I will be fucking flabbergasted. I know marriage is tough and all that bullshit, but this man clearly doesn't know how to stay faithful. I'm dying to know if Dani has knowledge of the other affairs. Or of Allie! Shit could get very real at that spa." Carmen added her thoughts to the situation.

"I think it's so sad. Kevin really could have a lot going for him. Money, business, wife, kids. It's sad he wants to throw all that away just to have sex with other women. What is wrong with men?" Hannah wondered.

"They're all pigs. Selfish, usually lazy, pigs. Text us throughout lunch, Alex. Seriously. We're going to be on pins and needles over here," Lila said.

"Don't worry. You'll get all the details soon enough. How do I look?" I was aiming for business casual with a crisp white shirt tucked into wide-legged khaki pants and nude pumps.

"You look good. Here's your binder." Lila handed my bulging black binder that was always filled with Blissful documents. This morning, it also contained copies of my letter of resignation.

"All right. I'm going to head out. I'll text you and let you know how it's going." I was out the door with a chorus of "Good luck!" ringing in my ears. I climbed in my Camry and directed it on the familiar path to Blissful. I was sad that I wouldn't be making the drive anymore. I was sad that I lost a job that I truly enjoyed, one I thought I was good at. I was disappointed in myself that I hadn't spoken up sooner. Maybe if I had, it wouldn't have come to what happened at my birthday party. Maybe Dani would have left Kevin months ago. Maybe, maybe, maybe.

I pulled into the deli parking lot with time to spare. Dani was notorious for being late, so I gave myself a few extra breaths to pull myself together. Not one for confrontation, I knew this lunch was going to put me eons away from my comfort zone.

I grabbed my binder and exited my car and, to my surprise, found Dani seated at a booth already. "Hi, Alex," she greeted me, getting to her feet and giving me an awkward hug. "Thanks for meeting with me today."

"Thanks for meeting with me," I said, dropping into my seat. Dani looked like hell, the first time I could remember ever seeing my boss not looking polished and put together. Her face was free of make-up, making her look more like she was twenty-one instead of twenty-eight. Her hair was pulled back into a haphazard ponytail, with strands falling all around her face. The dark circles under her eyes made me wince and I could see puffiness there as well. I knew it wasn't directly my fault, but I still felt like I was causing her pain in some way.

"Well, I guess we should just dive right in, huh?" She let out a nervous giggle and I followed suit. This was so freaking uncomfortable. "Alex, I want to apologize for Kevin's actions last night. He was completely out of line, inappropriate, and I know his behavior cannot be excused. He clearly drank too much and forgot that he was in an official work capacity, not just partying with his buddies."

I nodded, thinking it sounded like Dani was just making excuses for her douchebag husband. Great. So she wasn't going to do anything more than apologize on his behalf. The selfish prick couldn't even do it himself.

"Kevin wanted me to ask you not to press charges against him. He offered to get help in exchange for your silence."

"Excuse me?" That was it. "You're here not to say sorry and mean it, not to make sure I'm okay, but to make sure I won't press charges? Are you kidding me?" The anger flew out of my mouth. I couldn't believe the audacity of Dani. And to think I once thought of her as my friend. I flipped my cell phone open under the table and shot off a text to Lila's phone: *she wants to b sure i don't press charges. WTF!*

With that, Dani's face crumbed. "I am sorry, Alex. You don't know how sorry I am. I hate this. I hate apologizing for him. I hate sticking by him and trying to make sure everything's okay, always. I hated seeing your face last night and knowing what you must think of me. I am sorry."

My resolve weakened. Dani looked like a lost little girl. "Dani. Please talk to me. Talk to me like a friend, not someone you have to put a show on for."

Dani's floodgates really opened at that. "It's horrible, Alex. I don't know how to get out. I hate just standing around and watching him go so downhill. He's my husband. I love him. He's the father of my children. I think he needs help, professional help. But he won't listen to me. What do I do? Do I just leave? Break apart a family? Start over on my own? How can I? What do I do?"

I got up and sat next to Dani, putting my arm around her shoulders. "Dani. Listen to me. Kevin does not treat you right. He does not treat you fairly. I've been watching him for months and I can't stand it. I'm here today to talk to you, but also to put in my letter of resignation, to begin immediately. I can't stand being around him for more than six months. You've been married to him for, what, eight years? That's quite the feat in itself. But you need to get out of it. What he's doing to you and the stress you have to be under and the influence he might have on your daughters—you just have to get out."

Dani stared at me with saucer eyes. "What kind of influence do you think he has on the girls?"

"Think about it. If they can see or sense friction in the house, that will wear on them. If they see their daddy yell at their mom, that will leave a mark with them. If they grow up in a home that isn't happy, that will influence them. It's not fair to keep a marriage together just for the children's sake."

"So you don't want to work at Blissful anymore?" Dani sniffled, changing the topic.

"I just can't. I don't think anyone would respect me if I came back and pretended like everything was okay. I don't think I could respect myself."

"Do you know about Kevin's affairs?" The way she changed from topic to topic was making my head spin, but this was the one I dreaded most of all.

"Affairs?" I tried to keep my face blank, but she saw right through me.

"I know you know something about the other women. I've seen the checks that are written out to you. Kevin's paying for your silence."

So she knew. She knew about all of that. I wasn't sure how I felt. Relieved that she knew and I wouldn't be dropping a bomb? Disgusted that she knew and didn't do anything about it?

"I know what you must be thinking. You can't have much respect for me. Maybe you think I stay with him just for the money. How could I stick by when my husband has all these affairs right under my nose?" *Did that mean she knew about Allie?* "But it's not because of the money. I simply love my husband. I said those vows eight years ago and meant them. I thought Kevin was my soul mate. I want to watch our daughters grow up together and grow old together and *be* together." Dani started crying again, weeping really, and I knew what the real issue was. She had a broken heart. She loved Kevin with everything she had, but he didn't love her back.

I held her in my arms as she cried, not having a clue what to do next. I glanced around the deli, and saw a few strange looks being shot in our direction. "Dani? Did you want to go anywhere else to discuss this more? I'm afraid we might be calling some attention to ourselves," I ventured, still looking around.

"No, I'm okay. I'm okay, really. I think I just needed that real quick. I'll be fine." She straightened her shoulders and brushed the tears from her face with a napkin. "Sorry. I'll be fine though, really. Why don't you go put your order in?"

"Did you already order?"

"Yes, mine's in. You go order quick and I'll just run to the bathroom and try not to scare myself too much when I look in the mirror." She gave me a squeeze and a smile, though I could tell both took effort on her part. I let her out of the booth and made my way to the counter, where I ordered a chicken tender salad with ranch dressing and a lemonade. I was going to need some serious fuel to make it through the day. I sat back at our booth and fired another text to Lila: *It's a broken heart. She's just devastated. Knows about the affairs.*

I clicked my phone off without reading any of the seven texts that came from my friends after I sent the first one to Lila about the lawsuit. I could just imagine my girlfriends sitting around the living room discussing the Dohlmans and what a messed-up situation I was in. I was sure Carmen was supplying everyone with margaritas.

Dani came back to the table a few minutes later looking more put together. "I'm so sorry to be dumping all of this on you, Alex. I'm sure you've been through enough with Kevin and myself. I can't imagine why you would want to stay at Blissful. And I'm sure you can't image why I would want to stay with Kevin."

"Are you going to? Stay with Kevin, I mean."

Dani sat in silence for a few moments, playing with the straw in her lemon water. "I don't know. I don't know how I can. I really don't. He's—he's humiliated me. Time and time again. Everyone around town knows of his ways. So many people at the spa know. I keep trying to put this mask on every day and tell myself that it's me he comes home to, me he has a family with, me who goes on vacations with him but. . .I don't know if I can do it anymore. I can't pretend anymore."

"Dani, I want to ask you some questions, and I want you to be really honest with me. Please."

"It's the least I can do after the way you've been treated."

"Do you know about all the affairs Kevin has?"

Dani started shredding her napkin. "I think so. I've figured out most of them."

"Do you know—do you know about anyone from Blissful being included in them?" I had to know if she knew about Allie. I had to.

Dani's head shot up. "From Blissful? An employee?" I nodded my head. Uh-oh. "Who? I figured Blissful was where he took his women to, but I never thought it was with a staff member. Who? Who is it?"

I shrank back in my seat, afraid of the anger pouring out of Dani's tiny body. I'd never seen her so upset. Did I tell her about Kamille and Allie? Should I leave out Kamille since she was no longer there? I made a split second decision. "Um. Allie. It's Allie."

"That little bitch!" Dani bellowed and shot to her feet. I quickly got to mine and hurried after Dani as she sprinted towards the door.

"Dani! Dani! Where are you going?" I struggled to keep up with her as she approached her BMW. Kevin's BMW, technically.

"She's on the schedule today, right? Alex! Is Allie on the schedule today?" She threw open the car door and I did the same, quickly sliding in. I remembered my chicken tender salad with longing but brushed the thought of food aside. Dani looked like she could seriously turn into one of those women that ran over their husband eight times and got off on account of a "crime of passion."

"Yes. She should be there."

Dani started the car and zoomed out of the parking lot, tires squealing and everything. "Dani! Slow down. Think about what you're doing. What are you going to do? You can't just storm in your place of business and stab her in front of everyone. Or even just yell at her in front of everyone. That's going to make you look like the bad guy. Dani!" I screamed as she revved the engine and gunned it through a red light, just narrowly missing a black SUV that was barreling our way. "Seriously, Dani, think about this. Think about your girls and your business and your future. You can't do anything right now in your state of mind. Please, please, think about what you're doing."

We soon rolled into Blissful's parking lot, and Dani maneuvered the tiny car into the back lot and threw the gear in park. Her enormous chest heaved and her eyes had a panicked look in them. Before I could react, she opened her door and threw up on the pavement. I cringed, but started rubbing small circles on her back. "It'll be okay, Dani. It'll be okay. You'll get through this. I'll help you. Don't go in there. Don't go in there right now. Let's just think clearly about this, okay? We'll get you through this."

We finally drove out of the lot after an hour had passed. I knew that Dani had changed in that amount of time. No longer would she be the woman Kevin could step out on. No longer would she be humiliated by friends who slept with her husband.

I had changed too. I had seen a woman who looked so put together from the outside, who seemingly had this perfect life—husband, children, wealth, success, power. And I saw how one person's greed could rip that perfect life to shreds. I may have had to choose between morals and money, but Dani was struggling with morals versus love, and the life she thought at one time was complete. I did not want to trade places with her for a second.

EPILOGUE

NINE MONTHS LATER

"Thank you for calling Blissful Salon and Spa. This is Alex, how may I help you?"

"Hi, Alex. This is Mrs. Lombardi. I would like to schedule a massage for next week."

"No problem. How are you, Mrs. Lombardi?"

"Doing well, can't wait for my massage. I skipped last month's and my back is making me pay for it."

"Well, let me see when I can get you in then."

"Will Allie be available?"

"I'm sorry, Mrs. Lombardi. Allie no longer works for Blissful."

"She doesn't? Do you know where she went?"

"I'm afraid I don't have any forwarding information on her. But I can get you in next Thursday at your usual time of 1:30

with Vicki. You've had her a few times before. Would that be okay?"

"Sounds good to me. Slot me in. See you next week."

"Have a good day."

I hung up the phone with a smile on my face. It was a Saturday night, approaching closing time of six o'clock. Tiffany was mopping the front lobby, and I knew Dani was hovering in the back office pulling the closing reports. I had cut everyone except for Mandy, who was finishing up with her last hair appointment. I was thrilled she had stayed on part-time after she had her baby boy. She continued to be one of Blissful's top stylists. I stretched my arms above my head and tilted my head from side to side, hearing two satisfying pops that would make Hannah squirm with discomfort.

Speaking of Hannah, I felt my phone buzz in my pants pocket and knew it would be my roommate. Sure enough: *We're outside. No rush!*

I smiled as I thumbed back my reply, then stood and made my way to the back. Dani was in the office pulling the nightly reports off the printer when I entered. "How'd we do?" I asked, sinking in the office chair.

"Another great night. The Halloween ads you came up with are spectacular. They're really moving the products. Which is good because we'll have a new shipment come in probably within three weeks. The more we can get off the shelves, the better."

"Great. Henry is waiting for me outside. Mandy's just getting finished and Tiffany was almost done with the cleaning. Mind if I take off or do you need any more help here?"

"No, no. You go. I might even just take the reports home with me so I can get a better idea of the week we've had."

I gathered my purse and binder and slipped my light jacket on. It still felt weird to leave Blissful at a normal time, and not have to be afraid I was going to be reprimanded. "Brunch tomorrow?" I asked Dani.

"I'll be there at eleven. Have a good night, sweetie."

I waved goodbye and headed out, slipping into Henry's car once I was outside. "Hey, guys." Henry leaned over from the driver's seat to give me a kiss. Hannah and Peter were in the back seat, and we were on our way to Tango to celebrate Emma's engagement to Corey. I don't think any of the Wacker girls would have guessed Emma to be the first to walk down the aisle—including Emma. When Corey popped the question to her over summer at the lake—with a stunning princess cut sparkler—Emma said she about fell in the water she was so surprised. I was thrilled for my friend. Corey somehow tamed the wild child in Emma, and Emma had fallen head over heels for her prince charming.

"Did everything go smoothly today with Lila's flight? Carmen make it on time to pick her up?" I asked, running a comb through my hair. Heading straight to a party from an eight-hour workday wasn't ideal, but that was a sacrifice I was willing to make now that I actually enjoyed my job at Blissful.

"Yep, everything was fine. They're both already there," Hannah said. "Does it weird you out going back to the scene of the crime?" She was of course referring to the incident with Kevin at my birthday party.

"Eh, kind of. It'll probably just bring back gross memories. But I'm glad to go there on a much happier occasion."

"How was Dani today?" Henry asked me, merging right to get on the interstate.

"She was good. I know since her mom moved in with her it's been a lot better. Her stress levels have gone down now that she has help with the girls."

"What does she hear from Kevin?" Peter asked.

I shrugged my shoulders. "Really not much. They mostly speak through their lawyers, which I think is so sad. Dani said he only wants to get the girls one weekend a month. Can you believe that? One weekend a month is all he wants with his children. He's so disgusting."

"That's just sad. I can't believe you had to put up with him for so long. I can't believe Dani put up with him for years. I'm glad that you both can put all this behind you. Soon enough the divorce will be final and Dani can finally have some closure."

"She needs it." I looked out the window and thought of my boss, my friend. Dani had been in her own personal hell since the day I told her about Kevin and Allie. A lot had happened in the past nine months, and I was so proud of the way Dani handled herself. Her marriage had crumbled, her heart was broken, and her trust in friends was shattered. She had a lot of pieces to pick up, and I knew it couldn't have been easy for her. But she was surviving. She put on a brave face, she stayed strong in front of her daughters, and she refused to lie down and play dead. The one thing she wanted to make sure she had from the divorce settlement was Blissful. She put her heart and soul into her business, and I was thrilled when Kevin agreed to give her all the rights. Dani begged me to stay on as a manager, giving me a significant raise and more lenient hours. I had to say yes. There was a point in time where I loved Blissful, and I knew I was good at my job. Dani and I were in the talks to open a second salon in the downtown area of Des Moines and build a franchise. Together, as partners.

"I'd say this is rock star parking," Henry said as he pulled into a spot right outside of Tango. "It's like they knew we were coming." The four of us hopped out and headed towards the door. Henry put his arm around my waist and pulled me close to him. I snuggled into his embrace. "I love you, Alex," he whispered in my hair.

"Love you, Henry." He gave me a quick kiss before we headed inside, and then up the stairs to meet our friends. We were approaching one year of seeing each other, and I couldn't be happier with my relationship. He had accompanied me on a trip to Seattle in June to meet my family, and I had met his entire clan as well. I was madly in love with Henry Landon and excited about what our future would look like.

Lila was the first person I spotted once I got to the top of the stairs. "Lila!" I shrieked, running over to my best friend and practically jumping into her arms. She was spray-tanned to perfection, her teeth sparkling white and her white-blonde hair bouncing with curls. She looked like the same gorgeous Lila I had always known, just with a few subtle enhancements. I'm talking about her teeth and tan. She thankfully decided to forgo any plastic surgery.

"Alex! I've missed you so much! Seriously—you're coming out to visit me next month, right? Please tell me you're still coming out!" she said, her arms still wrapped around me.

"Yes! All us girls are coming out. You better be ready!" We finally pulled away, and Lila grabbed my hand and led me towards the direction of Emma and Corey. "I cannot believe Emma is engaged. If you would have asked me last year if I thought Emma would have a ring on her finger, I would have peed my pants from laughing."

"If you would have asked me a year ago if Emma would have a boyfriend, I would have peed my pants from laughing," I said, speaking the truth. It was crazy to look back over the year and think about how much had changed. Lila was on the rise in LA, just booking her first big-time reporting gig that would hopefully catch the attention of the producers of *Buzzworthy*. Emma was getting married next fall to a great guy. Hannah was in love with Peter, I was in love with Henry, and Carmen—well, Carmen was still Carmen. She had been dating Max on and off, but there wasn't anything too serious between them. I think they liked to hook up when the rest of us were coupled up, but Carmen seemed perfectly content with her situation. All my friends were happy.

"Everyone's here!" Emma squealed when we got to her table. I gave my friend a hug, noting how beautiful she looked in her deep teal dress with her blonde hair all in curls. We had thrown her one engagement party already, the weekend after she said yes, but we wanted another one so we could celebrate with Lila.

"We have to get a picture! Peter, will you take one for us?" Hannah asked, handing her digital camera over to her boyfriend.

"Oh, Henry, will you get one of us too? Here's my camera." I shoved my camera into his hands and went to take my place next to Lila.

"Corey! Grab mine too, please. I want to get a shot of this," Emma said, and Corey obliged by going through her purse and pulling out her camera.

"You girls know you can just tag each other on Facebook, right?" Corey asked, making us laugh. We'd heard that line a million times before, but it never stopped us from each getting a picture on our own cameras.

The five of us huddled close together, arms around each other and smiles shining. The flashes went off and we examined the pictures, declaring them perfect. Corey popped the cork on a champagne bottle and filled our flutes, and we toasted to the new life him and Emma would be starting. The night passed in a blur of drinks and dancing. With Lila gone and Emma about to move out and into a new house with Corey, we weren't technically the Wacker Girls anymore. But I knew that no matter what our futures held, our time together at Kaufman would always be looked back on fondly.

I learned a lot that year, and while some of the lessons I learned were painful, I was still proud of the outcome. I knew better than to let someone intimidate me, and I knew money would never fix a problem. I grew up. I'm sure a lot more obstacles would be thrown my way in the future, but I know now that I have a voice and how to use it. Isn't our world just a big game of money versus morals? I wasn't the only one who walked the thin and complicated line between the two. Heck, I'd probably face the same situation once or twice more in my life— maybe even more. It might have taken me some time to figure it out, but I know that in the end, I made the right decision. Morals trumps money, and the green ticket isn't worth the trouble.

ACKNOWLEDGEMENTS

Once again, I have a massive amount of people to thank and not enough space to include everyone. My family, who stands by whatever I decide and will always cheer me along. To my fiancé, for his continual support even when I run around screaming about formatting and other publishing woes. To my future in-laws, who will be accepting my craziness into their family soon and for their constant support. To my best girlfriends, Melissa and Holly, who let me talk their ear off in publishing slang and can still smile and raise their glass in a toast. To my lovely assistant Sara who has been so much help to me these past few months. To Cat, I loved having you cheer me on along the way. To my lovely proofreader Kira, your help is tremendous. To the Honor Girls from college—Melissa, Kira, Lindsey and Brittney—you helped make college a blast. To all the Chick Lit Plus supporters—I can't say thanks enough for the encouragement as I continue on this journey. And finally to my Grandma—I can only hope you are reading my books up there.

Miss you.

ABOUT THE AUTHOR

S amantha March fell in love with books at a young age. Thanks to her mother and grandmother, both avid readers, Samantha followed in their footsteps. Field trips to the library highlighted her week, and she went on to do volunteer work at her local library while in middle school. Her early works closely resembled characters from The Baby-Sitters Club and Mary-Kate and Ashley Olsen movies. In high school, Samantha excelled in writing courses and even the mundane tasks of writing history papers.

A slew of real work wake-up calls caused Samantha to shelve her dream of becoming an author. She took what she considered the practical route and enrolled in a business college in Des Moines, Iowa, where she graduated with honors in 2009. But her thoughts of writing never dissolved. In October of 2009, Samantha started the book blog ChickLitPlus.com. From her small blog, Samantha meant fellow readers and writers who pushed her to continue her goal of becoming published.

Destined to Fail is the debut novel from Samantha March, and was published by Marching Ink in October 2011. Samantha currently lives in West Des Moines, IA with her fiance and jumbled cast of friends who help inspire her writing. Besides reading, writing, and ChickLitPlus responsibilities, Samantha enjoys sports- especially the Green Bay Packers and Chicago Cubs- and will never refuse ice cream.

Visit her website at www.samanthamarch.com

Made in the USA
Columbia, SC
21 February 2020